ARRIVAL

MORETON SCIENTIFIC INVESTIGATION SERIES - BOOK 2

ROB NESBITT

Nessy Design Publications

BEFORE YOU DIVE INTO THE ADVENTURE...

Rob Nesbitt

Writer, Cartoonist, Designer

If you would like to read my other books, receive free short stories and other goodies please sign up to my author mailing list here at https://rnesbitt.com

Written in American English

PROLOGUE

Earth, an interesting prospect, turned out to be the jewel in the crown, with diverse, bountiful resources, an oxygen-rich atmosphere, and plentiful energy. The commander looked forward to reporting the findings to the next collective meeting, sure that no other commander in the search for new resources could better his amazing discovery. After exploring six galaxies and identifying twenty-two planets that met the minimum criteria, Earth, so high in value, made the others appear worthless.

During the last orbit of the planet, the commander faced a problem, which wasn't surprising. High command awarded the build and maintenance program for the new fleet to the Kreeg, a long-standing race of shipbuilders, well known for underperforming. Ships disappeared, exploded, or just died in deep in space, costing immeasurable time, money, and too many lives. Yet, against all logic, the Kreeg continued to be the fleet's shipbuilder of choice and the commander wondered who, in high command, benefited from awarding the contract for such incompetence.

With the final survey of the polar ice cap completed, the craft flew due south, passing the east coast of Iceland when the chief engineer reported a loss of power, while the commander's flight console indicated normal status.

By the time engineering identified the true reading, very little fuel remained, because of a simultaneous malfunction in the fuel calibration monitors. Failure, on two different propulsion systems, appeared impossible to all except the commander. The Kreeg's lackluster quality surfaced again as engineering reported a clash between the main and backup systems. Twenty thousand feet above Mid Wales, the commander concluded they might not get down in one piece.

The option for an oceanic landing disappeared after the malfunction shut down the fuel reactor. The ship, now unable to resist gravity, hurtled downward, with the coastline unreachable.

Auxiliary thrusters slowed the approach, but even at reduced velocity, impact on dry land would be fatal and even though three small fresh water landing sites lay ahead, could they reach them? The commander engaged the cloaking device to minimize attention from the surface, which automatically disengaged, seconds before impact, as the need for fuel outweighed stealth.

Alarms sounded throughout the ship as the surface came up to meet them.

The commander knew it would be a miracle if they survived.

ONE

Pools of rippling gold glistened from rising brown and rainbow trout; the only movement on a vast expanse of liquid mirror. Evergreens reflected on the water's surface, upturned and framed by the majestic peaks of the Brecon Beacons.

The lack of fish didn't bother him. Soothing, tattered nerves, was enough, washing away the stress of a fast-tracked, race-paced commuter life, traveling two and a half hours each way to the Banking Square Mile in London.

Five-star holidays, a large detached house and a top-of-the-range Mercedes, were always out of reach until the call from the head-hunter at Fosse Credit Banking changed everything.

For every cloud, there is a silver lining with a black shadow lurking when anything looks too good to be true. Silver, the huge pay rise that allowed luxury to flow without guilt, and the dark pallor around his eyes of unrelenting pressure, stress, and commitment provided the black shadow. How long could he manage the daily high-octane grind, forcing him to make sure the pressure relief valve opened enough times to keep sane? His predecessor, a thirty-something high-flying hot-shot, lasted six months, thinking it would be a breeze. She cracked in just four months, without a five-hour commute to contend with, taking another two months of sick leave before being edged out, paid off, and never to cross the marble threshold of Fosse Credit Banking again.

He contemplated a move to London, but the extra expense would cancel out a lot of the financial benefit and commuting from South Wales wasn't the problem in any case. Transaction after high-stakes transaction accompanied by sheer nerve-crackling energy emptied the tank in record time every day. By mid-afternoon, exhaustion set in. Drained, the train ride home allowed ten minutes to unwind, followed by two hours of fitful sleep and another twenty minutes of recovery, leaving him more tired than before he slept. By the time he reached Cardiff Central station, he was fit for an old folks' home.

He hugged himself as the lack of light sent shivers up his arms, wishing he could freeze this moment for another hour and relax without a care in the world. But, another week of hell awaited, and the sinking dread talked unwelcome common sense. It was time to pack up and head home.

The bubble float, static for two hours, was still visible, a dim orange blob almost lost in a sea of blackness. He stared harder. Was it moving? Must be the lack of light playing some serious shit with him. He squinted but with both eyes almost shut, the orange float blurred out of focus. He wiped his eyes and stared to the right with the float in his peripheral vision. It tilted and quivered and to double check it wasn't his imagination, he looked to the left. A surge of tingling excitement. Definitely bobbing up and down on the surface with a fresh bite. He dropped his right hand, feeling for the rod grip, stroking one finger down the cork handle before encircling his hand, closing it tight. The float twitched, stopped, then moved a few inches to the left before stopping again. A hungry fish probing the bait six feet below the surface, on the lookout for a late supper. What size would it be? Bigger than the others he'd caught earlier? Every time the float moved, he imagined a rainbow trout exceeding thirty pounds.

The unbearable suspense, waiting for the fish to take the bait, stretched on and on, but the leviathan-sized fish lost interest and life in the float vanished. He swallowed, took a deep breath and cursed, but enough adrenaline flowed to keep him at the water's edge a little longer, something he experienced long ago when his father taught him to fish on the Grand Union Canal and the sight of a float moving on calm water still gave him shivers of delight.

With an executive decision made, he sat for another quarter of an hour, which wouldn't hurt, even though a five am start and an angry wife beckoned. The fingers of darkness crept like black lava flowing from the mountain tops, creeping minute by minute, down the slopes of the imposing backdrop, dimming the water's surface, playing tricks on his eyes. The float had gone. Or had it? Was it moving again? He couldn't tell. Should he let it run? What if he missed his last chance? In one swift movement, he stood and struck hard. The fluorescent orange float skimmed across the surface without resistance. A hook without a fish. Disappointed, and admitting defeat, he reeled in for the last time, took the rod down, packed the bait and tackle into the seat box and gulped down a mouthful of stewed, lukewarm tea, throwing the dregs into reed grass, surrounding the shoreline.

With the seat box over his shoulder, he took a last look across the polished surface. The sun, almost gone for the day, left an orange halo above the distant peak and the panoramic view sank into blackness apart from a faint white glow of a distant light heading south, reflected on the north end of the reservoir. A plane or helicopter traveling fast? He looked up at the sky. One second, it seemed an insignificant blur, miles away. The next it dropped out of the sky toward him, increasing to a vivid intensity and with an ear-splitting crack that whip lashed across the valley it split and an orb of brilliant white light shot upward while two halves of the main body parted in opposite directions, twirling, glowing red hot. One half crashed into the slope of the mountain opposite, spraying rocks, shale, sparks, and a plume of thick gray dust into the sky. The other half screamed above his head, ripping into the forestry behind, shearing the tips of huge pines off like matchwood as it tore through, shattering the silence. A multitude of terrified birds, just settled down to roost for the night, burst out of the forestry in all directions in blind panic.

High above, the ball of light fell from the sky, so intense he had to shield his eyes, stopping twenty feet above the surface, remaining stationary, pulsing and silent before it sped up upward, then dropped into the middle of the water; a clean entry followed by a rumble under the surface. The entire reservoir lit up from below. A ring of water rose upward, forming a bulging circular mound, radiating, lifting outwards, exposing rock on the bed, creating a circular wave spreading from the point of entry, lit up by the glowing orb at the bottom. Rooted to the spot, he stared as a boom wave formed, then grew, twenty feet high, churning stone and silt as it surged toward the shore.

He dropped everything, turned and ran up the banking, through heather and bracken, tripping, scrambling, not daring to look behind, feeling the cold rush of air on his neck from the approaching surge. It struck hard, knocking the breath from his lungs, tumbling him head over heels, slamming him into the road fence. Twangs of thick steel wire snapping inaudible above the roar of water as the fence unraveled, easing the pressure on his chest. He tried to get to his feet but the force of the surge wave made it impossible as tons of slurry pulled in the opposite direction, dragging him backward down the bank with the retreating deluge, not knowing which way was up or down, his body pelted with stone and grit and knees scraped the bottom as he grabbed at a submerged tree stump to steady himself.

Aftershock waves battered him as they surged and retreated, knocking him over several times before the reservoir lost its energy. Standing chest-deep in cold swashing water kept him on tiptoes and after wiping brown slurry from his eyes, he coughed up filthy water, stretched his arms for balance and looked around at the bizarre sight of the reservoir, swaying, lit up from beneath like a giant, murky swimming pool. Something touched his fingertips on the surface. He dived sideways as his tackle box-seat floated past, eyes tight shut, in the silt laden water and with one arm looped through the box seat's shoulder strap, he broke the surface and began a lunging, twisted backstroke, towing the box and losing a shoe for his efforts. It was almost impossible to swim dragging the box seat full of water but determined he would not lose it a second time; he found a steady rhythm and made slow progress toward the shore when something strong and metallic gripped his ankle. He let go of the strap, reaching down his leg, screamed, and disappeared below the surface.

The mini drove into the rest-stop at the side of Cantref Reservoir, as Dianne Jones didn't want to be pulled over by the police a second time for using her mobile while driving. In mid-conversation with her best friend, she saw the pinprick of light on the horizon, which, within a second, grew into a fireball, exploding and splitting in two. She stopped talking. Her mouth fell open. A dazzling orb headed skyward, then dropped, hovered a hundred yards away, level with the mini for a second, and rose again before plummeting into the reservoir. She lifted one hand over her eyes to shield the glare. Water swelled upward in a huge hump, then fell back and outward. She dropped the phone in her lap. A man was running up the far bank, but the wall of water hit him in a mass of frothing slurry, then dragged him backward. He reappeared with arms flailing in the water, pulled out about twenty feet. It was a surreal sight, with the entire reservoir lit up from below, swaying back and forth.

The man steadied himself, paused, and, for some inexplicable reason, dived under the water. Why? He should just get out! She held her breath, praying he would come back up. He resurfaced and started swimming. She opened the door, tripped and fell onto her knees. Ignoring the pain of sharp gravel, she ran around the car and peered down. The man had vanished. Impossible for him to reach the banking in a few seconds. She would have seen him. He must have gone under again. Dianne watched, frightened, helpless to do anything. Too far from the other side. Hell, she couldn't even swim!

Time ticked by. Her head swung left and right, hoping for headlights in either direction. Nothing but darkness and silence, apart from the diminishing sound of breaking waves. She waited, scanning the luminous surface for any signs of movement. The light from the depths of the reservoir flickered and vanished, plunging everything into darkness. A man was dying and she, his only hope. Tears rolled down both cheeks.

A noise cut through the dark silence. A distant voice.

"Dianne? Dianne? Are you still there?"

She reached into the car, cut her friend off, and made the call to report a drowning man, who had not surfaced for several minutes.

TWO

Five days later

"There is a god!" exclaimed Alf, pointing ahead.

Jim lowered the newspaper and stared at the empty road.

"What am I supposed to be looking at?"

"Those bloody traffic lights have gone."

"Hallelujah" said Jim, settling his eyes back on the racing page. "Must have found him then."

Alf shook his head. "Wish they had found him sooner. It's been a pain in the arse this week making deliveries. We might beat the rush hour for a change."

Jim rolled the paper up and looked across at the glistening expanse of water. "Take some searching. Bet he's in a mess with all the fish chewing his guts out."

Alf grimaced. "Didn't see the logic in closing one lane. Bloody stupid. Health and safety gone mad. They could have kept both lanes open."

Jim stuffed the paper into the door pocket. "The press are a bunch of arseholes. Park where they like. Cops should book them all, and move them on, not set up bloody traffic lights. They'd have booked us and sent us packing if we decided to park like that."

"Still, I'm glad they've gone. It just seems that everyone else has to suffer when something goes wrong."

As they passed the dam wall, Alf took his foot off the gas, staring out of the side window.

"Thought you said we might beat the rush, Alf?"

"Can't you see that, or are you blind?"

Jim leaned across for a better view. "See what?"

The van slowed to a crawl and Alf wound the window down. "There's someone collapsed in the grass." He pulled over and stared at what looked like a pile of rags lying on the verge.

"Probably pissed up or on drugs," said Jim. "You should drive on. If it's a druggy, you never know what they'll do. My cousin Eddie, the copper, said you can never trust them. Might stick you with a used needle."

"Don't be bloody daft. We're not in the big city here. Let's take a look first. Maybe they've been hit by a car."

They both got out and crossed the road. The bundle of rags moved as they approached. Jim stepped back, watching the man's hands.

"You okay, mate?" said Alf, bending down. The disheveled man, lying on his side, looked up and shook his head.

Alf sat him up, propping him against the dry-stone wall behind. He ran a filthy hand through matted hair and looked up at the two men, his eyes flitting between them.

"Do you feel ill?" said Alf.

He shook his head again, white faced, gawking at the two men with a distant stare.

"Been in an accident?" said Jim, looking around, in case there was a wrecked car nearby.

The man swallowed. "No," he rasped.

"Have you been lying here long?" said Alf, putting an arm out to steady the man.

"Need to go home." He tried to crouch and fell headfirst into the grass. They picked him up, propping him back against the dry stone wall.

Alf continued. "Where's home, mate?"

"Cardiff."

"How did you get here?"

He pointed to the opposite side of the reservoir. "Drove. I parked it over there. Someone's stolen it."

"Sorry to hear that, mate. You called the police?"

"No phone."

"In the car, was it?"

"No," he said, coughing. He spat a lump of mud into the grass and wiped his mouth on his wet sleeve. "Phone in the box—it sank."

"Box?"

"Box floating past—"

"This guy's not making sense," whispered Alf. "He doesn't seem right to me. Let's get him to the hospital. It's only a couple of miles away. Perhaps we should call the cops as well."

"No, don't do that. I'm okay. A bit dizzy. Must be the heat. Need to get home."

Alf looked at Jim, who shrugged his shoulders and decided the man wasn't a crazed addict about to stab him with a used syringe, and crouched beside him.

"Okay. Alf, let's get him in the van."

They hauled the man up from the wall and received several strange looks from passing vehicles as they frog marched him across the road, lifting him high enough so his shoeless foot didn't drag on the tarmac. It took time to get him in the van with weak legs that kept sliding off the step. In the end, Jim pushed, and Alf pulled from the driver's seat, bundling him into the seat.

With the confused man seated next the passenger door, to stop him leaning onto Alf, and the central locking engaged, Alf fired up the van and it was on its way.

After a mug of stewed tea, the man got some color back into his cheeks.

"What's your name, mate?" said Jim, topping his mug up.

"Peter."

"Nice to meet you, Peter. I'm Jim and this ugly bruiser behind the wheel is Alf."

"Thanks."

"So, did you catch any fish, Peter?"

"Three but lost them all."

"Ones that got away, eh?" said Jim and laughed. Peter didn't crack so much as a smile.

"Not been a good day. Lost my tackle. Car's gone. Pretty shit all round."

"So, you caught nothing?"

"No, the wave took them."

"Wave?"

"Yes, the wave. Took me as well."

Jim looked at Alf and pulled a face. Alf stifled a laugh and tapped the side of his head.

"Do you want us to drop you off at Merthyr police station?"

"What for?"

"To report your car stolen!"

"No, I'll ring from home. Just need to get home. She'll be so cross. Said I would be home by eight."

"You will be. It's only four o'clock."

"What?"

"You'll be home by five thirty at the latest."

"Can't be right?"

Alf leaned forward and tapped the clock on the dashboard.

"Two minutes past four, mate."

"Why is it light?"

"Light?"

"It was dark when I stopped fishing."

"Well, it's gone four, but it doesn't get dark for at least another five hours," said Alf, glancing across at Jim. "What time did you think it was then, mate?"

The stranger didn't reply and fell silent for a few minutes. His eyes closed. He nodded forward and was snoring before they joined the dual carriageway at Merthyr.

"Alf, he doesn't seem right to me. What do you reckon? Should we pull into the hospital and get him checked out? He might be seriously ill and kick the bucket in the van."

"Nah, let's drop him off and get home. He doesn't look as if he's about to drop dead to me. Just looks knackered and think about it. If we stop at the hospital, we could end up there all night. You know what they are like, sat in a waiting room all night with every drunken drongo and his dog. Do you want to eat supper from a vending machine?"

"What if we take him to the hospital and leave him to it? The nurses will keep an eye on him."

"That puts an extra twenty minutes on the journey and we'd be wedged in the middle of rush hour traffic. Let's Keep going, drop him off home and his folks can take care of him."

"What if he has got no one at home?"

"Bloody hell, Jim! We'll drop him off home and we can get home on time for once."

Peter slept all the way to Cardiff with his head on Jim's shoulder. As the van approached the outskirts, Jim shook the stranger. He grunted, leaned to the left, and banged his head on the door window.

"Come on, mate. WAKEY WAKEY RISE AND SHINE!"

He sat up and rubbed his eyes. "Sorry. Dozed off. So damned tired."

"Don't we know it," said Alf. "Snoring like a buffalo, mate. Now, where can we drop you off?"

"Sorry about that," he said, trying to focus, rubbing his eyes. "Where are we?"

"Cardiff. Top end of North Road."

"Oh, I can see now. Not far to go. Do you know where the garage is before the Gabalfa roundabout?"

"Yes, do you live near there?"

"A short walk up the road from there."

"Short walk to where, mate? I Used to drive a cab for twelve years. I know every nook and cranny in Cardiff."

"Mavis Grove. It's about a mile along from Tesco and the garage. I can walk. I don't want to put you out. You've been so kind already."

"No problem, mate. I reckon your legs wouldn't make it one hundred yards, let alone a mile, and you can't walk up there with one shoe on."

He looked down at his feet in astonishment. "Where did my shoe go?"

"Dunno, mate. Found you like that. The other shoe was nowhere in sight."

The van turned off North Road and soon they pulled into a cul-de-sac.

"Thanks, gentlemen. You've been so kind. I don't know how to thank you."

"No worries, mate," said Jim, helping the man out of the van. "I'm sure you would do the same for us."

They watched him stagger toward a large detached house. "Bloody weirdo," said Alf, smiling and waving to the man as he turned the van around.

Eileen Slater pushed her fringe, stuck to her forehead, to one side and mopped her face with a tea towel before placing a steaming dish of spaghetti bolognese and garlic bread on a tray.

"Hot in that kitchen, is it, love? Why don't you open the window and get some air in?"

"If I did that, your supper would be like ice and you always moan your head off if your supper's cold. Do you want your cup of tea in there?"

"Aye, and don't sweat all over the cup."

She gave him the finger behind his back and retreated to the kitchen.

"Sugar or sweeteners?"

"Sugar. After the week me and Jim have had, I think I need some carbs to boost me up."

"Nice you're home at a reasonable hour for a change. Watch," she said, passing him the cup, "it's boiling!"

"Splendid stuff, my little dove. This looks great. I'm starving," he said, sitting up straight, pouring ketchup over the spaghetti.

"If you'd rung me on your way home, I'd have had it ready when you came through the door."

"Don't go on. It's been a long old day without winding me up. Nice it's cooked fresh though. Fed up with dried-up grub. I was early because they shifted those bloody traffic lights above Merthyr."

"Don't you dare get anything on the sofa or I'll go apeshit!"

"Yes, love."

"Work go okay?"

"Pretty much. Deliveries went tickety-boo. Picked up a weird hitch-hiker on the way back. Well, not so much a hiker. Me and Jim had to pick the weirdo off the deck."

"Male or female?"

"Odd guy. Thought he was drunk or drugged up at first. Dirty looking bugger with a shoe missing. Seemed a bit of a nutter at first, but after a cup of your paint stripper, he perked up."

"Cheeky sod. You can make your own in future."

"Only kidding, my little dove! Your tea puts hairs on my chest—and yours," he said with a wry grin and dodged a slap.

"So who was he?"

"Didn't find out much. Said his name was Peter. Unsociable sod. Slept most of the way to Cardiff. He looked bloody knackered. Lives in one of the posh houses near Tesco. Remember the ones you fancied before we bought this, but out of our price range?"

"Nothing wrong with this house!"

"I didn't mean that," he said, twirling his fork around the spaghetti. "He can't have been a tramp to afford a gaff like that, now could he?"

"Your brother rang. Said he'll be over at the pub tomorrow night if you want to play darts. They're one short on the team."

"Out of money, more like."

"Thought he was working down at the stadium as a steward?"

"Nope. If you remember, they sacked him for selling tickets on the black market."

Eileen turned the news on and disappeared into the kitchen.

After the weather report, the regional news came on and a photo of Peter Jenkins filled the screen.

"Bloody hell, Eileen! Come here quick. That scruffy bugger we picked up. It's him on the telly!"

Alf tipped half the spaghetti over the cushion as he lunged for the remote to turn the sound up.

Breaking News—Thirty-nine-year-old Peter Jenkins from Cardiff, who disappeared last Sunday, believed to have drowned in Cantref Reservoir in Powys following a suspected meteor impact has been found alive and well. A spokesperson for the police said his disappearance, which caused a huge search of the reservoir and surrounding area, is under investigation—

"Jeez, look what you've done. I said to be careful and don't spill anything. How many times—"

"Eileen! Do me a favor. Shut your trap and pass me the bloody phone."

THREE

Ben Sharman ran his fingers over the cool, chrome surface, savoring each of the thirty letters, smiled and stood back.

"Moreton Scientific Investigation," he whispered, his grin getting wider. "Moreton Scientific Investigation. Who would have thought it." He chuckled to himself.

It never ceased to amaze him he owned the business, after years of academic study, failure to find a job in scientific research after university, plus the unpleasant four years and three months in the army and now, despite everything, he couldn't believe he controlled a globally recognized business, and all down to a chance meeting with his old university lecturer and the luckiest of breaks.

"You seem quite pleased," said Claire, unlocking the front door. "You coming in, or are you going to stare at that plaque for the rest of the day?"

Ben stroked the sleek metal plate once more. "You must admit it adds an air of class to the building," he said and laughed. "I'll be there in a few minutes, after I've finished admiring it."

"How much did this one cost the company?"

"Had to be done. Plastered all over the news after the last case and we haven't got a bloody sign outside the door that people can see. Stands to reason that we should take full advantage of our celebrity status. I was considering changing it to include my initials 'B.S. - Scientific Research', but as my dear girlfriend pointed out, 'Bull Shit' didn't quite sit right, so I changed it to Moreton, which shouts out where we are on the planet."

Claire laughed. Three months earlier, she would have verbally jousted with her boss. After the recent alien encounter, she'd backed off the repartee, just glad to see him alive and happy!

"I'll leave you to your self-glorification. Just remember, we have a backlog of tests to catch up with."

He waved her away as he breathed on the plaque and polished it with the cuff of his shirt.

"Morning, Kath," said Claire as she stepped into reception. The center cleaner jumped, holding one hand on her chest.

"Jeez, you scared me half to death, creeping up on me like that."

"Sorry, Kath," said Claire, "How was your weekend?" Then wished she hadn't asked.

Kath leaned on the vacuum cleaner and switched it off. Her green eyes sparkled, mischievously.

"Quite good, apart from Patrick."

"Oh?"

Kath took a large breath. Claire exhaled and looked at her watch.

"It's his back, playing up again. It's amazing how it always seems to happen when I need him to mow the garden and do some painting. He's been putting it off for too long. The bloody grass is up to my knickers and I am sick of looking at magnolia walls. I'd like the grass clipped nice and short and a pea green living room. Soft I am and he takes full advantage. I should have put my foot down with a firm hand. If he spent as much time on a Saturday in the garden as he does in the Black Bear, my garden would be as rosy as his cheeks. What's worse is the gambling and the lies—"

Kath, about to plunge into her usual lengthy monologue of various ailments and her husband's legendary drinking and betting, was interrupted when the office phone rang, bringing her tongue to a temporary halt.

"Been red hot all morning," said Kath.

Claire smiled with relief at being given an escape route. "The press again, I expect, wanting another interview. I'd better answer it."

"Ben certainly put us on the map," said Kath, clicking the vacuum cleaner back on and singing a mysterious Gaelic song in an unfathomable key.

Claire darted away, in awe and despair the diminutive Irish woman who could talk for hours, with no sign of taking a breath. She wondered how many hours Kath had talked at her since she began working as Ben's assistant. Kath O'Brian, at her verbal best, had all the time in everybody else's world.

After taking the call, Claire opened the office window and leaned out, craning her neck to see Ben still taking photos of the new sign on his cell phone.

"Ben, phone call for you—urgent."

He took more shots, flicked through the photos with the same satisfied grin, and stood back to take more.

"Ben!"

"Who is it?" he said, not taking his eyes off the plaque, lining up another angle with the phone.

"Ben, I'm not discussing details out of the window," she hissed, as a woman walked past, tutting as she had to steer her pram around Ben.

"Tell them I'm in a meeting. I'll ring them back."

"Ben!" she shouted. "They are saying it's urgent."

He slouched into his office, clicking his fingers for a pen and paper, then dismissed her with a single flick of his hand.

She bit her tongue.

Over an hour later, he joined Claire in the lab.

"Ben, I put a truckload of letters on your desk and are you aware your laptop's repaired? Kelly brought it in. You may need to pay her a bit more this week."

"Great stuff. No, she will invoice me for any added hours. I don't directly employ our IT staff, remember? She's self-employed."

"I keep forgetting she's not on the books. She's like part of the furniture. Anyway, what was that phone call about?"

"Have you ever been to Wales?"

"Wales? Not been there for years. I once had a holiday in Swansea with my parents, when I was a kid. Why are you asking?"

"Fancy a trip out?"

"Not really. I've a million things to do and don't forget. You wanted samples from that illegal dumping site tested by close of play today?"

"This is far more important so you can forget the tests for now. We're going to South Wales this afternoon." He handed her a note with an address scrawled on it. "We'll be staying at least one night. so you need to book a hotel close by."

"So, whether or not I fancy going, I'm going?"

"I've already committed us to go, so I'm afraid so."

"But Dave's taking me out tonight. We've booked a table at the Manor House!"

"I apologize, Claire, but you need to reschedule. Or, he can come with us if he likes. In fact, that would be a great idea. At least I would have someone I can have a proper drink with."

"Ha ha, I could drink you under the table. And I don't know if Dave would want to come."

"Either way, you are coming with me this afternoon."

"What's so important you need me to come?"

"Remember that guy on the news last Sunday who disappeared after a meteor strike?"

"Nope. We've been on holiday and watching the telly is the last thing I want to do when I am lying on a beach!"

"Okay. A small meteor landed in a reservoir I can't pronounce in the Brecon Beacons. A witness said it split in half before impact and a bright light shot out from it into the sky and fell into the reservoir."

"Did it kill him?"

"No, it caused an enormous wave that pulled him in while he was fishing. The witness watched him go under and he didn't come back up."

"The poor man."

"Well, not so poor. He's turned up since with amnesia. Can't remember anything after he went under the water. Someone discovered him on the side of the A470 five days later."

"A470?"

"Sorry. The A470 is the main route from North Wales all the way down to Cardiff and runs along the side of the reservoir."

"Why are we going there?"

"Come on! Moreton Scientific Research. You are looking at the best scientific detective mind there is on planet Earth. I make world news, remember?"

"Oh, I forgot. If H. G. Wells was alive, he would have written about you! Come to think of it, he already did. The Invisible Man!"

"What do you mean, invisible?" he said with a pained expression.

"You're never to be found when we need you. Anyway, what's the score with this Welsh trip? Why are we being dragged all the way down there?"

"Something odd about the whole thing. They found meteor fragments and put the pieces they could find together and want me to look at them. There are unnatural indentations in what they've reassembled."

"In what way unnatural?"

"Marks which do not appear to be of the natural world. Man made, or should I say alien made. He's sending video footage and stills. He would have settled for that, but I insisted on visiting the site."

"And he being?"

"Sorry. You recall the team from Cambridge that came to the Center for our last extra-terrestrial investigation?"

"Of course."

"Remember the geeky looking one? The one with the massive glasses who was always sniffing in the lab. Got on your nerves?"

Claire's face changed to a grimace. "The walking plague. Remember him? That disgusting creature left used tissues on every worktop. How could I forget?"

Ben laughed. "Knew you would remember him. He asked for my second opinion after being sent by the Cambridge team to investigate. It sounds too interesting to just comment on photos, so I asked him to meet us at the reservoir. Now, we have little time. If you want to take Dave, not a problem, but we need to make tracks."

"Perhaps I won't bother asking him," she said, fluttering her eyelids. "A cozy hotel with my beloved boss. Mmm, now let me see."

"I'll ring Dave myself," he said, shaking his head. "Can you imagine Amy's face if it were just us two? Now go home, get your glad rags on, and be back here at one o'clock at the latest. We'll need the full field kit and bring a flask of coffee. It'll take a good couple of hours to get to this Welsh reservoir and I haven't got time to stop for a break on the way."

FOUR

At eight in the morning, the chatter of staff and clattering breakfast trolleys filled the corridor, but failed to wake the latest patient. The ward sister let him rest but needed him washed, fed, and ready for the consultant at nine, even though she knew the doctor looking after Peter Jenkins would be unlikely to arrive on time. She tapped on the ward desk as the clock edged to the top of the hour.

"Dr. Hernandez is a busy man, Nurse Evans. Rouse Mr. Jenkins and make sure he's prepared."

Carol Evans nodded to her colleague, who spoke like a robotic nursing textbook. 'Prepared', she thought. Like an oven ready chicken about to be basted.

"Will do sister. I made sure we kept back some breakfast before the catering staff took the trolleys back and its still hot enough for him. The poor man must be starving. Shall I give him his breakfast before preparing him?"

The ward sister carried on staring at the monitor on the nurses' station desk, without acknowledging her. Carol turned and walked away, muttering to herself.

"Nurse Evans. Do you think I am deaf?"

"No, Sister," said Carol, cursing the woman's acute hearing. Without looking back, she walked to the other end of the ward corridor, thinking, but not daring to whisper more expletives.

Through the observation window Peter Jenkins appeared to be in a deep slumber, so she nudged the door, wide enough for her to slip through, ensuring it wouldn't engage the hold open device that always made a noise. A sigh escaped her lips as she contemplated the hospital's need to operate like clockwork, despite the potential harm to patients' well-being. Should the hospital wake someone up just because the doctor has to do rounds at nine? And, considering Dr. Hernandez's habitual tardiness, it was almost comical how important he considered himself, exempt from adhering to the rules.

Carol closed the door behind her and approached the bed, observing Peter's eyes moving rapidly beneath closed eyelids, lost in the depths of a dream. His muscles twitched, and he emitted a soft moan as he shifted to one side, lips moving in silent conversation with an unseen presence. Curiosity got the better of her and she leaned in to eavesdrop on his sleep-induced musings. Peter's head arched backward, and Carol instinctively reached out to steady him, placing her hand on his forehead. Startled, he recoiled, thrusting both arms upward, causing the bedsheet to lift off his body. His left leg, freed from its cover, kicked her hard in the thigh, triggering a sharp pain that made her drop to one knee.

Hoping to avoid any onlookers witnessing her awkward retreat from the bed, Carol pulled herself into a nearby chair, nursing her throbbing leg in silent discomfort.

"Mr. Jenkins, can you hear me?" she said, moving as far from him as the chair would allow. "Time to wake up for breakfast." There was no response and the twitching in his arms spread to his legs, making the bed sheet look alive, about to take off. She watched, rubbing the top of her throbbing leg again, which was coming back to life, as his eyelids opened, revealing just the whites of his eyes.

A voice. A familiar voice. A distant voice calling from the light above. He struggled upward from the deep, cold brown water. Every time he tried to break the surface it gripped his ankle and when he kicked out at the clamp with the other leg he howled in pain, scraping skin off his shin bone on the sharp metallic edge. Deeper and deeper into the earthy swirling depths, his ears popped and gurgled. The voice, still there, calling him upward. Two more metallic snakes wriggled out of the brown mire, locking on, twisting around his torso, turning him over and over, constricting, like a giant snake crushing its prey. Panicking, fighting, searing red hot burning in his lungs, wanting to breathe and daring not to inhale the filthy water, he tried to pull the tangle of metal serpents away, but they held fast, biting deeper into flesh, sucking him deeper into the blackness. From below, foam bubbles filled a rising transparent sleeve, engulfing his body and thin tubes slid up his nose, making him wince in agony as they forced their way down the back of his throat, making his nose bleed.

"Mr. Jenkins, time to wake up," she said, giving his shoulder a rough shake.

He lurched backward as a metal claw held the back of his head firm while another gripped his throat. He gagged and wretched as the tubes fed, inch by excruciating inch, down the trachea, into his lungs and took his first breath since being submerged in one huge gulp. As he exhaled, a sharp stab in one ear gripped every muscle in his neck and back as a dark, living needle pierced through the soft tissue, sending pain searing through his entire head as he sat up in bed and screamed.

"Mr. Jenkins, Mr. Jenkins. Can you hear me?"

The ward sister joined her, and both pushed down on his shoulders as he convulsed. As quickly as it started, the episode was over and Peter Jenkins relaxed, soaked in perspiration, eyes wild and bloodshot. He stared from one nurse to the other.

"Where am I?"

"Hospital, Peter," said Carol, mopping his brow with a tissue.

He stared around the room, taking in plain walls, warm air with a hint of antiseptic and the starched uniforms.

"Must have been an awful nightmare, Peter," said the ward sister, taking his temperature and checking his pulse. "Let's get you sitting up in the chair. Cup of tea and breakfast and you'll be as right as rain."

Weak, drained, but thankful to be awake, Peter managed the hint of a smile and leaned forward as the nurse held a glass of water to his lips because his shaking hands couldn't hold it.

It was the second identical nightmare and as vivid. The first time, at home, occurred while he slept on the sofa. Jill cried when he knocked on the door after having been missing for so long. Her tears of joy flowed, and after the initial shock and emotional reunion, she called the police, but he fell into a deep sleep for a few minutes while she talked on the phone and woke screaming and crying after feeling the strange clamps around his legs and razor-sharp stab in the left ear. When the police arrived, he was asleep again and Jill insisted he got checked out and instead of waiting for an ambulance, the police took him to the hospital in Cardiff, where he remained unconscious on the ward until the second nightmare.

Dr. Hernandez stood at Peter Jenkins' bedside at exactly nine o'clock, which amazed Carol Evans and the rest of the ward staff. Renowned for his casual approach and lack of time management, Dr. Hernandez disrupted most wards on his rounds, having little respect for hospital protocols or day-to-day routines. She wasn't sure if it was sheer arrogance or he was oblivious and although she respected the status he carried, Carol loathed his disregard for the smooth running of the ward. She guessed Peter Jenkins' media frenzy and high level of interest in the hospital caused him to arrive on time for his rounds.

"How are you feeling this morning, Mr. Jenkins?" said Hernandez, thumbing through the chart at the end of the bed.

"Weird if I'm honest."

"In what way?"

"Nightmares, so real."

"You've been through a traumatic experience. Vivid dreams are normal after such events."

"They're not normal."

"Nightmares never are normal, Mr. Jenkins. We're just going to do some routine tests."

"I've had nightmares before, but never like this."

"Okay. Other than the nightmares, how are you?"

"Exhausted. My head is pounding. When can I go home?"

"I won't know that until we have run some more tests, Mr. Jenkins. You have lost five days of your life that you have no recollection of. We need to find out why."

Peter Jenkins shook his head. "What do you mean, lost five days?"

"You were fishing last Sunday. They found you lying on the verge at the side of the road near the reservoir and brought you home yesterday.Yesterday was Friday"

Peter shook his head. "There has to be some mistake."

"I can assure you there's no mistake, Mr. Jenkins."

"There must be."

The doctor left the room and came back with a copy of a newspaper. He pointed at the top of the front page. Peter Jenkins stared at the date.

"As you can see, six days have now elapsed since you went fishing and you were missing for five of them."

"But it can't be—"

"Mr. Jenkins, I am not in the habit of forging national newspapers for a practical joke. I can assure you the date on the paper is today's date." Carol nodded in agreement. The situation perplexed Peter.

"But—I don't understand."

"You lost your memory for the entire time. Total amnesia. As you recover, I am confident you'll regain some, if not all, the missing memories. Severe shock can do this and you almost drowned, which is a significant factor.

"But for five days!"

Hernandez moved around the bed, pulled a chair sideways and sat facing Peter. "You are quite a celebrity, Mr. Jenkins. Local volunteers, tracker dogs, helicopters, and even the army searched for you, but you evaded them all before reappearing a few hours after they abandoned the search. Hundreds of people were looking for you from dawn till dusk. Everyone thought you'd drowned in the reservoir, myself included. It's a lot for you to take in and we need to make sure you are fit and healthy before we can discharge you. The nurse will take a blood sample, and then you can rest for a while before we do some scans."

"Scans? Why would I need scans?"

"Because of the unusual circumstances of your disappearance, I want to run a full and thorough medical check on you, head to toe. You have several unusual scrapes, cuts and bruises, and I need to be certain you are healthy on the inside and outside."

After breakfast, they wheeled Peter to the scanning suite and an hour later Felipe Hernandez and his staff pored over the images.

"Are you sure about this?" said Hernandez, staring at the image on the screen.

"Absolutely. We've been over this so many times, checked and double checked every image," said the technician.

"But this is ridiculous. Impossible! Have you talked to the contractors who installed the machine? Is there some sort of anomaly? Could it be a shadow or something wrong with the scanner itself?"

"They are sending someone right now to run a diagnostic check. A waste of time in my opinion, but I expected your question and asked for the check, anyway. I am certain that what we are seeing is free from any mechanical malfunction or interference."

"So, what are you saying? That thing on the screen is real?"

"What we are seeing is accurate," said the technician, pointing at a dark object on the monitor.

The monitor, sharp and clear, showed a tiny, solid sphere resting on the top of Peter Jenkins brain, with thin strands radiating out in all directions, not unlike a spider. Hernandez compared a dozen separate images of the brain cavity. It became obvious, from slight variations of strand length from frame to frame, that the spider like object inside Peter Jenkins' skull was moving.

FIVE

The extra-terrestrial crisis at Moreton a few months earlier made international news, headlining every media channel on the planet. So many lost their lives to an ancient alien causing terror from its lair, right under everyone's feet in an uncharted cave complex. Like all headlines, the media moved on to other new shiny things and the biggest media scramble in the town's history had all but gone. Ben made the most significant contribution to end the crisis, and now tried to put it well behind him. It made a welcome change to work away from Moreton in Marsh for a while.

"How did Dave wangle out of the trip? I thought he would jump at the chance," said Ben. He set up the GPS, put Moreton in the rear-view mirror and realized he hadn't told Amy that Dave wouldn't be accompanying them. Hopefully, she wouldn't find out he had gone on an overnight trip with just his stunning assistant, a rival in Amy's eyes, who nurtured a streak of jealousy that often made life difficult.

"I only have eyes for you. I thought you knew that," said Claire.

"Ha ha, funny girl. So why didn't he come?"

"Duty calls. Bodyguard work for some Egyptian billionaire in Mayfair, and isn't back till Saturday. He sends his apologies and said he would have loved to have come, but money's obviously a bigger draw than me and you. I'm not complaining. He earns a big paycheck to spend on me and I get a trip to Wales with my favorite boss. Win, win!"

"Is he enjoying his new job? I thought he might have second thoughts about quitting the army?"

"The top-brass bullshit got to him in the end. His last boss was a real jerk. Micro-manager, checking and questioning everything Dave did, and being a puppet on very short strings wasn't Dave's thing, so he had enough time served to get out. He loved the army, but between Major Kemp, that arsehole of a boss, and losing men to the bloody alien, it got to him. Being his own boss seems to suit him. Besides, he gets to live with me. What more could a man want?"

"Pity he's working. I could use a bit of male company."

"Cheers, Ben. Love you too."

"You'll do," he said, patting her on the head. "You're the next best thing."

"What do you mean?"

"You should have been a man."

"What?"

"You're the only woman I know who tells her other half to turn the TV over halfway through a film to watch darts, or was it Manchester United?"

She laughed. "Been talking to Dave, have you?"

"Yep. He said you'd go to church if the vicar wore a Man United scarf."

"Did he now? I love sport. What's wrong with that?"

"Perfect woman, I suppose?"

As they climbed the Heads of the Valleys road from Abergavenny, the sky lost its brightness with thickening clouds when they descended through the outskirts of the old iron works town, Merthyr Tydfil and the weather steadily changed for the worse, with the sky almost black by the time they reached Cantref Reservoir. Ben pulled into a lay-by overlooking the vast expanse of water just as a cloud burst leached all color out of the scenery.

"Pity this weather. Could be stunning," said Ben, admiring the magnificent views through rain spattered glass. The windscreen lit up, followed by a clap of thunder that shook the car.

"Bloody hell, that was close," said Ben, now barely able to see out of the car.

Claire drummed the dashboard with her nails. "If this turns out to be another visitor from another world, do you think it could be something to do with our last encounter?"

"God help us if it is," said Ben, having to raise his voice above the hammering rain on the roof of the car.

"But what if it is?"

"Speculation is fine, but aren't scientists supposed to work on facts?"

"It doesn't sit right after seeing off one deadly alien, and within a few weeks, another alien has turned up. Hell of a cosmic coincidence, don't you think?"

"I agree. But we have to go on facts, not assumptions or coincidences at this stage. Let's just see what Ron has to show us."

She carried on drumming her nails.

"What if—"

"Look out, Claire, here comes your runny-nosed friend now."

"Put the wipers back on. I can't see him."

"He's behind us, that's why."

She jumped as the back door opened. Ron Logan slid in, dragging damp air behind him, laced with stale wet tobacco. Claire moved forward in her seat, widening the distance between her and Ron.

"Good to meet up with you again, Ron. You remember Claire, my assistant?"

"Couldn't forget that pretty face," he said, taking his glasses off and wiping them with a tissue. "Gorgeous!"

Claire watched over her shoulder and shuddered. Without his glasses, Ron looked different, like a soggy, anemic mole. She wondered what else the tissue had been used for and made an obscene gesture with her left hand to Ben, who scowled back at her.

"Ron, I have the gist of the incident. The images you sent me were okay, but I would like to have a look at the real thing. Nothing wrong with looking at photos, but I need everything first hand."

"Sure. Same as me. I'd rather get my hands dirty. You can't hear, touch, or smell anything in a photo."

"Is everything still in place, more or less?"

"Yep. We've taken all samples off site as a precaution, but the two impact sites are as we found them, unless there have been any nosey sods digging around. Good job we got it done when it was dry. Always seems to bloody rain in Wales. Me and my other half spent a fortnight in Pembrokeshire a couple of years back and it pissed it down the whole time we were here until we reached the Severn bridge on the way home.

He pulled out another tissue from a coat sleeve and dabbed his face, then clenched the tissue. Claire shuddered as drips of water seeped from his fist.

"I wanted to show you the landing sites. One halfway up the mountain, over there to your right, and the other in the forestry on the other side of the reservoir."

"Surely you don't want to do that now?"

Ron sniggered. "In this downpour? Not a cat's chance! It's supposed to brighten up in the morning and the forecast is good after daybreak, but it's going to piss down all night, tonight, so we'll give it a miss for now, unless you and your charming assistant want to get drowned?"

Claire shook her head. "No way am I stepping outside in this. Tomorrow sounds good."

Ron smiled back at her and winked. Claire tried to be polite and tried to smile back, but her face wasn't receiving the message.

"How did the Cambridge team get drawn into this?" said Ben.

"The boss found out from one of his mates in the shaky hand club, who is on the board that selects companies and individuals for this type of work and a heap of other stuff. We got onto the government's approved list for scientific consultation and all that caper. From now on, any weird stuff like this, serial killings, terrorism, anything ghastly happening in the UK, and sometimes abroad and the big-wigs pull us in. I shouldn't be telling this, but you should get on the list yourself."

"Thanks Ron. I'll check it out when we get back."

"You may have to do a bit of creeping and slip someone a back-hander, but the rewards are massive if you get on their approved list. Just remember, there is a downside. There always is."

"Oh?"

"When something interesting passes their way that they want us to investigate, we have to drop everything. Literally everything, regardless of any other work we have on the go, including holidays and weekends. We got called to investigate an incident in Uganda and the boss had to leave in the middle of his brother's funeral, so it can be a pain in the arse, but it must be worth doing, for the director to sign up for it."

"Passport to print money, eh, Ron?"

"I wouldn't know, Ben. I just do the legwork at the sharp end. Our desk jockeys looked after all the money stuff in finance."

"Come off it, Ron. You're like a bloody ferret. I bet you even know what your boss had for breakfast this morning."

Ron put his glasses back on, which steamed up, and grinned, showing a full, yellowing set of teeth. "Let's just say that he's ordered a brand new, top-of-the-range Bentley on the strength of it."

"Does that mean I can order a new car on the strength of the Cambridge team's good fortune? I could do with a new Bentley myself."

"You'll get some more work put your way, that's for sure. You and your team impressed the boss on our last excursion, even though that army idiot pulled us off the job before it was done."

"Well, thank you. Glad to hear it. Tell him likewise when you get back to the office."

"Does this mean I get a pay rise by any chance?" said Claire.

Ben shook his head. "See what I've got to put up with, Ron? Staff always on the take!"

"Where are you two staying?"

"Where did you say we were staying, Claire?"

"The Lodge Hotel. A couple of miles from here."

Ron opened the door to get out. "I fancied that one, looks upper class, but our finance section looked at the price and booked me into some three-star guest house in Brecon. There might be more money coming in, but the boss is still as tight as a camel's arse in a sandstorm. Meet me here in the morning, say nine thirty?"

"Sounds great, Ron. See you then."

Claire watched him run back to his car through sheets of rain in the wing mirror. "He's even more creepy without his specs. Good job he's not staying in our hotel. I would have to stack furniture up against my bedroom door with him slithering along the corridors."

"He's alright, Claire. There's more to Ron than you think."

"Sorry. I'm an excellent judge of character and he's a creep—one hundred percent."

"Poor old Ron. Judged and hung by a jury of one."

"You should have brought Jen instead of me."

"Why would I bring a trainee lab technician instead of you?"

"Because she has a thing about ugly men."

"I assume you're referring to Ron as the unattractive male?"

"Well, let's be fair. He's no male model. Jen would like him. Remember that sales rep with the scar?"

"The one with the Scottish accent?"

"Yes. Scar down his cheek, skin like a walnut."

Ben laughed at her accurate description. "Jen fancied him? You're kidding me."

"Hello, Ben Sharman. You are a bit slow on the uptake. She slept with him a few times. Every time he came down with more test kits, he was staying overnight with her in the village. A charmer, that's for sure."

"I wondered why he was at the lab every five minutes. I didn't see her going for someone like him!"

"Well, there you go. Ron better look out or Jen will eat him alive!"

"Ron? No chance!"

"Anyway, forget about him. I'm starving. I hope they're doing some decent food when we get there."

"How much was this Lodge Hotel per night?" said Ben, pulling out of the lay-by.

"About a hundred and eighty with breakfast."

"Each?"

"No. One double room."

"Yeah right. If that's the case, you get to sleep in the car."

"It was three hundred and sixty quid altogether, for two en-suite doubles."

"Bloody hell, Claire. It better be good. What about food tonight?"

"Are you asking me out on a date?"

"Shut it or I'll find a local fish and chippy."

Claire winced. "Stop the car."

"What the hell for?"

"Just stop the bloody car."

"I was only joking about the chippy."

"It's not the chippy."

Ben pulled up at the side of the road.

Claire pointed over her shoulder. "Logan left one of his stinking tissues on the back seat. Get it out of here before I throw up!"

SIX

So many shades of green on the mountains, broken only by the shadows cast by moving clouds, flocks of sheep grazing in dappled sunlight and rocky outcrops, turning the mountains into a verdant patchwork quilt on a much grander scale than the rolling Cotswold hills they were used to. The hotel receptionist insisted that the Brecon Beacons were 'magnificent and not to be missed'.

They set off early, following her instructions to take in the view from the Storey Arms car park at the foot of Pen y Fan, the highest peak in the Brecon Beacons. Ben, glad he'd given in to Claire's pleading, smiled at the breathtaking vista of unbroken views toward the outskirts of Brecon and beyond, cradled by old red sandstone giants bathed in green baize. The receptionist's recommendation had been gold dust.

"I never thought Wales would be so stunning," said Claire, pivoting around and squinting to keep the panoramic shot on her mobile steady. "I always imagine coal and wet, miserable weather, when I think of Wales, but this view is as good as anything in the British Isles."

"Almost as beautiful as Moreton-in-Marsh, but then I'm

biased," said Ben taking in a deep breath of mountain air, tinged with wood smoke, drifting up from a whitewashed farmhouse far down on the valley floor. He cupped his brow, staring at the distant, hazy hills. "It puzzles me why more people didn't observe the meteor on a cloudless night. It must have passed right over Brecon's town center. Odd there were no witnesses, apart from those at the reservoir."

"Perhaps it dropped out of the sky at a more acute angle?"

"If that were the case, everyone in Brecon and half of South Wales should have seen it. No, there's something not sitting right with this. We should interview the witness who watched it from the lay-by."

"Getting ahead of yourself?"

"Sorry?"

"We're here to investigate meteor fragments. Did Ron mention anything about interviewing witnesses?"

"No, but an eminent scientist should consider every angle. You must always get the full picture to be able to make a rational deduction."

She stopped taking photos and turned to him. "Is that a fact?"

"If you want to be great in this career, you must think holistically."

She laughed. "Ben, you can do better than that."

"What?"

"Buzzwords! I bloody hate them," sneered Claire.

"Holistically! Why don't you just say 'consider everything'?"

"Less effort. Holistically is one word and says it all."

"Please don't. Fashionable words spread around by people trying to sound clever make me sick. People who use phrases like 'blue sky thinking' and 'very much so' should be given a fair trial and then shot."

Ben smirked. "Thinking outside the box, let's stay on the same page and move on. Mr. Logan awaits!"

Claire scowled. He scowled back as she tried to maintain the look of disgust and they faced off like two cats about to do battle. Claire cracked first, snorted and descended into hysterical laughter.

"Any other weird turn of phrase that offends you, Miss Manson?" said Ben, as they drove back to the reservoir.

"Not really. I wish people wouldn't latch onto buzzwords, it's so one dimensional."

"Haven't you just contradicted yourself?"

She sniggered, then frowned. "I've just thought, does Amy agree with you being here with me and staying overnight in the same hotel?"

"She doesn't know."

"You didn't tell her? Why ever not? Hell, that'll make it worse for you when we get back."

"Couldn't. She's on a bit of a downer and I didn't want to wind her up."

She looked across at him, shaking her head.

"What?"

"I don't believe you," said Claire. "You're telling porkies, aren't you?"

"How did you know?"

"Women's intuition. I can sniff out a lie a mile off and there's one hell of a stink coming from your direction. Now, why didn't you tell her?"

"Nothing sinister. I simply forgot."

"You forgot? Bloody hell, Ben, I remember being at the sharp end of her tongue the last time she suspected there was something going on between you and me. I wouldn't mind so much if were true."

"Sorry. I would have told her, but in the rush to get ready—well, it sort of slipped my mind."

"Sort of?" She crossed her arms, leaned forward, and stared across at him. "What are you going to tell her?"

"The truth. With an eencie weencie twist."

Claire frowned. "Hope you're not planning on dragging me deeper into your cesspit of lies?"

"I'll tell her I've been on an investigation to South Wales with yourself and Ron Logan, and forget to tell her that Ron booked into a different hotel for the night."

Claire rolled her eyes. "Do you believe Ron's fictitious presence at the hotel will stop her from assuming the worst? This is ridiculous anyway. I work for Moreton Scientific Investigation and she has to accept that I will go with you, and other members of the team and stay at hotels from time to time. It's not as if we are sharing a bloody room, is it? I suppose I would be tetchy if the roles were reversed, but hell, is she expecting me to sleep in a tent on the side of the Brecon Beacons while you kip at some posh hotel? She slammed back in her seat. He looked across and they both laughed.

"Sorry," said Claire. "Pissed off at having to tread on eggshells. Anyway, how is she?"

"She was fine after the treatment. It worried me that her increased resistance to antibiotics would prevent all alien traces from being removed and I couldn't sleep in the same room with her for a while after she did that vampire number on me. Thankfully, it looks as if they have all been eradicated from her system, but the high dose rate and different concoctions of medication took it out of her.

"I can understand that. It must be knackering with that level of treatment."

"Her mental state concerns me more. She eventually caved in and had psychotherapy. So bloody stubborn — stiff upper lip and all that. The chief constable insisted, before she went back to work. The one person she couldn't argue with."

"And is it working?"

"It'll take time. You don't get captured by an extra-terrestrial, taken underground and subjected to the most horrific experience of your life without having some lasting effects. But she's getting there."

As they rounded a long sweeping bend, the first of the three reservoirs came into view.

"That's the Beacons reservoir," said Ben. "Cantref reservoir is next, then the largest, Llwyn-on. Cardiff Corporation Waterworks built them in the 1890s to supply Cardiff."

"How do you know all this stuff? You didn't have time to look up the history of the area?"

"I did a paper on water purity in South Wales as part of my final year at uni and had an internship with Welsh Water. Believe it or not, water is interesting. For example, Cantref is teeming with rainbow trout, such is the water quality. I hope this incident has done nothing to upset the balance and thankfully, I saw no fish floating when we looked at it yesterday."

"Interesting." Claire yawned. "Where's Booger Logan?"

Ben shook his head. "You should stop referring to him like that before you slip up and say it to his face."

They arrived at the lay-by shared with a burger van and a Harley Davidson, chrome glinting in the sunlight and looking in pristine condition, unlike its owner. An extremely hairy biker, in scuffed leathers, wiping the grease off his chin with a gloved hand, and pulling on a battered helmet, about to saddle up.

"It's not quite half past. Let's get out and case the joint before Ron gets here," said Ben, drowned out as the Harley roared into life, like the lion at the start of an MGM film.

The biker headed off toward Brecon and silence descended as the noise of the Harley's two-cylinder piston engine vanished around a distant bend in the road.

"What a difference in the weather since yesterday," said Claire, adjusting the sunglasses on her nose.

"Wales is like that. I used to come here a lot a few years back."

"What drew you here?"

"University in Cardiff and a woman — what else?"

Claire looked at him over the top of the sunglasses, her eyebrows raised. "Ooh, I love a bit of gossip. Who was she?"

"Girl I met in uni. She lived in Sennybridge, about ten miles west of Brecon."

"And what happened to her?"

"Nothing. I live with her."

"Amy's from Wales? She sounds so English! Can she speak Welsh?"

Ben laughed. "One day you'll stop jumping the gun. You'll never make a scientist if you keep 'assuming'."

Claire took her sunglasses off, tapping them on her palm. "What do you mean, assuming?"

"Amy lived in Sennybridge, for a while,. Her father was based there in the army."

"Ah. So she's not Welsh?"

"And I'm not Afghan, even though I was stationed in Afghanistan for a while in the army."

"You must know this area pretty well, then?"

"Some of it, but back in the day I wasn't here to sightsee." Ben screwed his face up. "Let's get upwind of that bloody burger van. That stink of fat is making me feel ill."

They crossed a stile and walked down the loose banking to the water's edge. Ben opened a leather file and pulled out an Ordnance Survey Map.

"Let me help," she said, holding one edge as the large map unfolded.

"According to Ron, the meteor approached from the north and split just before the reservoir and one half hit the mountain over there."

"Ben, you're pointing the wrong way," she said, pointing in the opposite direction toward the mountainside. "That's where it impacted, below the trees halfway up."

"Right," he said, gazing up at a dark gray scar on the right-hand slope.

"The other half entered the forestry on the other side of the reservoir. Missed the trees at the edge. No sign of damage until you get deeper into the trees, according to Ron."

"Over there," said Claire, pointing to a stone arch in the far bank road. "The police incident tape's still in place. Must be the entry point into the forestry."

"Okay. So, it splits in two and something really bright ascends and then drops into the middle of the reservoir, causing a large concentric wave which radiates out from the point of impact and catches up with our angler and the backwash drags him into the water."

"Where was he?"

Ben pointed. "To the right of the stone culvert arch over on the other bank, where one half of the meteor crashed into the trees."

"Must have scared the crap out of him."

"Eloquently put, Claire. The wave hits the bank, goes up so far, and pulls him back. The witness says he was under the water twice and on the second time and she didn't see him come back up and assumed he'd drowned."

"Obviously mistaken," said Claire, taking her sunglasses off and placing them on the top of her head. "She just failed to see him surface. What time was it?"

"Ten to eight, give or take. The emergency services logged the witness's call at five to. She'd been watching from the layby where we're parked, for a few minutes, hoping he would surface." said Ben.

"Would it still be light just before eight?"

"Barely. Sunset's around eight thirty."

"Mmm. Bet it was almost dark. When is dusk?"

"I told you, eight thirty," said Ben. "Keep up, Miss Manson."

"Dusk is half an hour later than sunset."

"Touché, you're right."

"The sun would set in the west, which is behind the far bank. The mountains and forestry blocking out sunlight would have made it difficult, if not impossible, to see him in the water."

"Don't forget what the witness said." Ben pointed to the middle of the reservoir.

"Remind me."

"The whole reservoir was lit up from below the surface after impact. She was certain she would have been able to see him if he made it out."

Claire pondered this for a while. "How long was it lit up for?"

"A few minutes after impact. She was certain he didn't surface before she rang the emergency services, after the light went out in the water."

Claire shook her head. "He isn't a bloody fish. He must have got out. She either didn't see him or the light disappeared quicker than she imagined. A person witnessing a brilliant white light from an exploding meteor landing in a reservoir and a man being dragged underwater is pretty traumatic. I bet she was so shocked she had no sense of time. Maybe the intense light interfered with her sight for a while. You know what it's like when you see fireworks or full beam on headlights, you can still see them after they've gone? If that light was as intense as she claims, it could have affected her vision for several minutes.

"That's why we need to speak to her."

"Puzzling how he could go missing for five days and turn up out of the blue."

"It's possible he wandered for days or stayed hidden in the forestry. There are mountains and moorland for miles and plenty of tree cover. He could have gone anywhere. He tapped his finger on the map.

"What dominates this map?"

Claire stared at the detailed markings. "Wilderness," she said without hesitation.

"Exactly," said Ben, who never ceased to be impressed by Claire's sharp mind. "You can practically walk from this point all the way to North Wales off grid. They localized the search for Peter Jenkins around the forestry, mountains, and Merthyr Tydfil. I reckon he tried to get to his car or home but, confused and shocked, walked totally in the wrong direction. He could have been walking for the entire week without seeing a soul."

"Poor man. Outdoors for a week, freezing and starving."

"Should have lost a substantial amount of weight, but that wasn't the case. He's in good condition, all things considered, and must have found food and shelter and simply can't remember a thing. My guess is he found his way back to the reservoir, realized he was in the right place after wandering for days, and got as far as the main road before collapsing with exhaustion. I told you not to assume anything, and lo-and-behold, I've made several assumptions myself. Based on logic, I can't see other explanations for his disappearance. Can you?"

He got no reply.

They stood for a while, taking in the scene. Both trying to visualize the strange events. A meteor splitting in two in the sky, sending two halves in opposite directions. A brilliant white spherical something ejecting from the meteor crashing into the water. An enormous wave. The. reservoir lit up from below. A man being dragged down the banking then wandering the Welsh hills and mountains for days before returning, found collapsed at the side of the road. A movie trailer to a blockbuster science fiction film would have been more believable.

Gravel crunched as an approaching car slowed, pulling up behind the burger van.

"Look out, Claire, here comes the man of your dreams!"

SEVEN

Ron, wearing combats and hiking boots, leaned over the stile and beckoned them to the side of the road.

"He looks like a ferret in fatigues," whispered Claire.

"Didn't know you were in the SAS, Ron?" said Ben.

Ron's nose twitched, but he didn't crack a smile.

"I'm dressed for the occasion. So, unless you both want to get ripped apart by gorse, stung by a million Welsh nettles, or bitten by an adder, and there's plenty of all three on this mountainside, I suggest you change into something more appropriate," said Ron, lighting up a battered, half smoked Marlboro.

Ben flicked the tailgate of the car and pulled out a plastic crate containing thick canvas boiler suits and safety boots.

"I was hoping we wouldn't have to resort to these," said Claire, slipping off her shoes. "Never been used before by the feel," she said, pushing her foot into the stiff leg of the boiler suit.

"I'd check for spiders before you put them on," said Ben, winking.

Claire grimaced and pulled her leg back out, shook the heavy garment and stared down the trouser legs.

"They bloody stink Ben, where did you get these from?"

"I didn't. Inherited them when I bought the business. They've been in the attic store for donkey's years. Stop whining and get them on."

Claire tucked her trousers into her socks, rolled her sleeves down, and did all the buttons of her blouse up to her neck before thrusting her leg back into the leg of the boiler suit.

They'd only checked half their equipment when Ron strode off across the main road, in a cloud of tobacco smoke, shouting instructions. "I'll show you the mountain impact site first and then we'll drive to the other site, on the other side of the reservoir. Tread carefully. There are dips and holes all over the place, easy to sprain or even break your ankle."

Claire was about to follow until Ben reached out and held her back by the shoulder.

"Let the silly bugger go ahead. We'll catch up when we're good and ready. He was like this when in the lab with the Cambridge team. Brilliant, but sometimes oblivious to others, so let him wait."

She watched Ron march through thick tussocks of grass, following a sheep trail winding up to the impact site high above. After checking through every item in the field kit, Ben slammed the tailgate and gave Claire the thumbs up.

Ron hadn't been exaggerating. The trek up the mountain wasn't easy, and both were glad they changed clothes.

"Jeez, it didn't look that bloody steep from down there," said Ben, eyes locked on the ground, checking every inch of the rough ground ahead.

"Not far now, boss," said Claire, overtaking him. "You need to get yourself fit, old man."

The gorse, like razor wire, and marsh grass, which grew everywhere, felt like pins pricks, even through the thick canvas. They caught him up as they reached the gray scar on the mountainside.

"We're here," Ron wheezed and sat down, pulling another half-smoked Marlboro from behind his ear.

"How the hell can you smoke that crap after hauling yourself up here Ron?" said Claire, standing up wind to him. Ron winked and took a large drag on the cigarette.

Ben studied the impact site. Rocks and dirt strewn for twenty yards, fanning out from the lip of a small crater which measured barely ten feet deep from the outlying soil surface.

Claire rummaged through the kit bag. "I'll take samples and readings, or would you rather I take photos?"

"I'll do the photos. You do the rest and video the whole site in as much detail as possible."

Ron settled on a large rock and chain-smoked while Ben and Claire took samples, photos, and made notes.

"Ron, did your guys move anything apart from the fragments of meteor?" said Ben.

"Nope. Apart from the fragments and soil and rock samples, it's as we found it," said Ron, putting one cigarette out and lighting another.

Ben peered into the small crater. "Anything jump out at you as odd, Claire?"

"Background radiation reads the same in the impact area as the undisturbed areas of the slope, which isn't what I expected. But it's the lack of impact damage and the angle of entry that doesn't make much sense."

"That was my first thought. This wasn't a conventional meteor strike. Not that I'm an expert. Something traveling at thousands, maybe hundreds of thousands of miles an hour, should have created a much larger crater with far more impact debris."

"It'll be interesting to see what's on the other side of the reservoir," said Claire, pulling the top of the boiler suit down and tying the arms around her waist. "Bloody frying in this. We all done up here?"

"Almost," said Ben and, after combing the immediate area around the crater, it was time to move to the other site.

Ron marched down through the long grass tufts like an old steam train, with clouds of smoke following in his wake.

After parking up on the other side of the dam wall, they moved slowly through trees toward the second impact site. Branches of sharp pine needles raked their faces and hidden rabbit holes, tree roots and dead branches made it lethal underfoot. Claire cursed as pieces of twig and needles collected in her hair and found their way down her blouse collar, despite it being buttoned to the top. A path of sorts meandered through the undergrowth from recent investigations, but until they almost reached the point of impact, they had to bend double under low-hanging branches.

Ron stopped next to a numbered disk pinned to the base of a pine trunk. He was about to speak when a sneeze erupted. A dog-eared tissue came to the rescue as he sneezed again. Claire's eyebrow twitched.

Ron continued. "This is the point of entry into the trees. This first tree has about six inches missing from the crown. From this section, the trees show progressive damage, as if someone has sliced off their crowns at an angle. The last group of trees have been uprooted."

Ben looked up, but branches hid the top of the tree. "How wide is the damage path?"

"A tree's width."

They stepped forward, pushing under branches until they could stand where large parts of the trees were missing.

"It cut through, throwing the top parts of each tree skyward."

When they reached the impact site, there was a similar crater to the first, but not as deep.

"Bloody strange," said Ben. "Such a narrow flight path. Must have been a tiny piece of meteorite. It doesn't add up. Pieces breaking up would continue through the atmosphere in a constant direction. The witness stated that it split close to the reservoir and each part went in a different direction, which would suggest either an explosion or something weird, particularly with a third component ending up in the middle of the reservoir."

Ben stood on the lip of the crater. "Almost the same depth and extent of impact. Seems like this meteor had slowed down before it hit land. Makes little sense."

"That's why you're here, Dr. Sharman. This looks like an impact of a few hundred miles an hour. A meteor would travel at between twenty-five to one hundred and sixty thousand miles an hour when entering Earth's atmosphere."

"So, even with air friction slowing it down, it would still strike at tens of thousands of miles an hour. This one didn't, that's for sure. Did the divers search the whole reservoir?"

"Yes, a thorough search. Took days. It's not deep except in the middle, but as you can see, it's a big search area."

"Anything unusual?"

"In the center, about two-thirds of the way back from the dam wall, there is a depression on the bed about thirty feet across and twelve feet deep. According to an official from the Welsh Water Authority that depression does not exist. Divers checked it but nothing in it apart from rock and shale. There's no sign of whatever created the depression."

"Sure it wasn't there before?"

"Positive. Welsh Water Authority has photos of the reservoir bed drained, and it didn't look like that two years ago."

"Don't you find that odd?"

"Yes. No debris from whatever hit the bottom or impact damage."

"This is getting interesting."

Much to Claire's relief, they made their way back to the small access road above the far bank, and over a stile to the water's edge.

"The angler stood here," said Ron, stamping on the sandy gravel. "Looks like the wave washed him up the bank into the barbed wire fence behind us. We found part of his coat pocket impaled on a barb and his rod bag wedged in the fence. The receding wave would have drawn him back out into the reservoir."

"How do you know where he was standing on impact?"

"From another angler who left earlier. He said Peter Jenkins was here at his usual peg."

"Peg?"

"It's an angler's position when there is a fishing competition. Marked with a wooden peg."

"Fishing peg! of course. This wasn't a fishing contest, though, was it?"

"Sorry no. Ignore my angling terminology. We believe he was about to leave when the wave struck, as the rod bag was found, fastened with a buckled strap with his rods secured inside. He may have been carrying it."

"Anything else retrieved?"

"Yes, a box seat with several bait and tackle boxes found about twenty yards out at the bottom."

"Are there any indications on the shoreline to show where Peter Jenkins exited the water?"

"Follow me." Ron walked back toward the dam wall.

After a few hundred yards, he stopped and threw his jacket on top of the fence.

"Sorry, no stile but you can straddle over the jacket."

Ben looked at Claire. "I'll go first and help you over."

"No thanks. I'll be fine," she said, pushing Ben out of the way. Another twitch of the eyebrow and her leg was over the fence, quickly followed by the rest of her, landing on a ledge of loose banking that collapsed. She slid forward, surfed across the shale, staggered, then fell sideways before sliding on her backside into the reservoir feet first. She leaped up as her boots filled with icy water.

Ben and Ron looked on, expressionless.

"Okay, guys you can laugh if you want to," she said, beetroot faced, pulling the first boot off to empty it, at which point they erupted.

After emptying the second boot, she started laughing herself. Tears ran down her cheeks, laden with mascara, making the situation more ridiculous. Ben, still laughing, put her hand on his shoulder to steady her while she pulled the boots back on.

"Cheers, boss, what an idiot!"

"You said it."

The moment disappeared as Ron blew his nose so hard it made his eyes water. Claire stopped laughing and looked on in disgust as Ron wiped his eyes, folded the handkerchief, and rammed it up his sleeve. "We found. Peter's left shoe here yesterday morning. It's been in the water, but the interesting thing is the footprints in a section of mud on the road, which match his right shoe and left footprint."

Ben pointed "Isn't this the nearest point on the shoreline to the impact in the middle of the reservoir?"

"Not quite. It's farther back. This is the part you'll find interesting. I had a dog handler who tracked Peter from the edge of the reservoir to where the two deliverymen found him at the side of the road and took him home."

"But he might have walked into the shallow area farther up or down from another location before he exited here?"

"I got the dog handler to walk the entire perimeter of the reservoir. Not a trace."

"How accurate is a dog search?"

"The dog handler said he was one hundred percent certain that Peter Jenkins came out of the water here, with no other entry or exit elsewhere around the perimeter. The only other explanation is that he exited after the boom wave pulled him in and then re-entered the reservoir five days later through the tributary that discharges into the reservoir at the north end on both occasions."

Claire took her sunglasses off and scanned the far end of the reservoir. "Let me get this right. He got dragged into the reservoir after impact them swam all the way to the inlet stream up there," she said pointing to the distant north shore line, "and after days of wandering around, re-enters the reservoir from the same stream?"

"Seems to be what must have happened when you put the footprints and dog search together," said Ron.

"If that were the case, he must have either waded or swam to reach this point?"

"That's right. Must have swum for most of it, as there are several lengthy deep sections. The thing is, his wife said he's not a strong swimmer and couldn't have done it."

"Can we talk to the dog handler and is there any chance of meeting this Peter Jenkins?"

Ron shook his head. "I was hoping we could all speak to him. Peter Jenkins left the hospital in Cardiff and no one can find him."

"He wasn't well enough to be discharged after this happened?"

"They didn't discharge him. He left the hospital of his own accord and nobody's seen him since."

EIGHT

Dr. Richard Parker checked his watch. The next train to Taff's Well was still five minutes away and platform six, at Cardiff Central station, was already full to bursting with shoppers and nine-to-five workers on their way home. Another five minutes of arrivals would mean a severe delay in getting home and a very uncomfortable journey with carriages rammed to the gunwales. He checked the announcement board, and the train held up for an additional six minutes, made the decision easy.

Outside the station, expecting to join a queue in the taxi rank, it amazed him to find several available. The extravagance of a cab for such a brief journey irked him, but the thought of having to ask his wife to pick him up outweighed the cost, tenfold. Greeting him in the cab, the strong smell of tobacco made him regret not having his car repaired and the driver, seeing him waving a hand under his nose, flicked of the half-smoked cigarette discretely into the gutter.

"Where to Boss?"

"Drop me off opposite the gates to Whitchurch Golf Club."

"Nice," said the driver, starting the meter and pulling away from the station. "Here on business, boss?"

"No," said Richard, his tone killing any further conversation.

Grateful that the man in the front had got the message, Richard eased back into the frayed seat, contemplating the eventful day at the hospital with its intriguing fresh case. In all the years he had worked in the sector and throughout his tenure as critical care manager, no case surprised him, until today. The scans gave him the shivers, revealing something grotesque, alive and incredible inside Peter Jenkins' skull. His doctorate on parasitic invasion in humans had researched every aspect of the subject, or so he thought. The life cycle of the human botfly, that captures and lays eggs on mosquitos which then transfer the botfly's spawn to humans, had been one of the most complex parasitic cases. The thing living inside Peter Jenkins' head made the life cycle of the human botfly look mundane.

Richard Parker's car failed to start for the second time in a week and was on his way to meet the vehicle recovery driver in reception when Felipe Hernandez paged him for a second opinion on the strange object on the scans. When Richard saw the images of Peter Jenkins' brain cavity, he forgot all about his car and the Mercedes remained immobile in the hospital car park. He examined the patient from head to toe, making sure he had every fact first-hand and spent a long time staring at the strange intruder inside Peter Jenkins' head on the monitor. A unique parasite, unlike anything he had ever encountered before.

Sat in the chair next to the patient's bed making notes, Richard was so far deep in thought that didn't see the tiny black legs extending from Peter Jenkins' left ear or notice the tiny alien crouching on the pillow with legs extended. He was so engrossed in writing a thorough account of this unique parasitic invasion that he didn't sense its grip on the elbow of his white coat. The pen stopped writing and dropped to the floor when razor-sharp legs penetrated the tympanic membrane in his ear. An excruciating pain jolted across his jaw and neck, accompanied by spangled, flashing lights in the periphery of his vision. His head fell back in the chair and temporary blindness turned his world black. Peter Jenkins stared up at him for a second.

Richard's sight returned after a few brief moments. The darkness receded and flashing lights reappeared, then faded. He returned Peter's stare, nodded and left the room. An unexplainable compulsion drove him to walk back to his office, where he unlocked a secure metal cabinet. Why was he looking for something that had nothing to do with Peter Jenkins' condition? He asked himself the question several times, realized from some dark place at the back of his mind what he was about to do. He tried to resist reaching into the cupboard but could not control his hand as it pulled out a syringe. Then he selected a small bottle of clear liquid.

"I don't feel well," said Peter, trying to get up. The nurse propped him up with two pillows.

"What's the matter? Do you feel sick?"

"No, I need water. I'm so thirsty."

She eased his head to the right. "Your ear's bleeding. Lie on one side while I get something to clean it up. I'll be back in a second."

"Don't forget to bring me a drink, please," he shouted as she hurried out of the room.

She returned to a room with an empty bed and no patient. The ward cleaner, polishing the tv monitor, looked up and smiled. "Hello Kathy, how are you?"

"Have you seen Peter Jenkins?"

The cleaner stopped polishing. "Sorry?"

The nurse checked the en-suite bathroom. "Where is he?" she said.

"Where's who?"

"Peter Jenkins. The patient who was in the bed two minutes ago?"

"He passed me as I came in to clean. Thought he must be going to the day room."

"He must be confused and shouldn't be wandering about in his condition. We need to find him."

The news spread fast, escalating into a full-scale search of every floor of the hospital and the grounds, except for the hospital's underground car park.

Dr. Richard Parker found himself back at the side ward and couldn't understand why he led Peter Jenkins down the seldom used staircase, instead of the lift, to the doctors' parking bays in the sub-basement, or why he took him there at all. There was also no rational explanation for injecting more than enough morphine to in Peter Jenkins' arm to kill him. A strange detached notion, as though he were a spectator, not responsible for his actions, dispassionate, without remorse.

"Twelve quid, sir," said the driver as the taxi pulled up outside a large detached Victorian house. Richard snapped out of his thoughts about his earlier, disturbing actions. He couldn't remember the last time he used a cab and as the cab driver pulled away, he turned and the familiar sound of crunching gravel leading up to the front door filled his ears. Why didn't he care? A man murdered by his own hands. He shrugged his shoulders, slid the key into the lock, and pushed the door open.

"Is that you, Richard?" shouted his wife from the kitchen.

"Mary, I'm in the study for the next hour. Something important's cropped up. I need to do some research."

"Hint taken. I'll do tea later."

He didn't know why he said that to his wife or why he turned the laptop on in the study. Richard looked down at his fingers in anticipation, not knowing what they were going to type. 'UK sources plutonium' appeared on the screen in a Google search bar. He read with bemused interest as pages from old newspaper headlines from 2013 appeared on the monitor. 'Britain has a plutonium problem.' Britain has the largest storage of plutonium on the planet, costing seventy-nine million pounds a year to store—

The searches continued. Hotels, maps, Companies House, and a corner of Britain he had never been to before. He didn't acknowledge his wife two hours later when she came into the study, then retired to bed. His cooked supper sat, cooling, congealed, on the edge of the desk.

More searches. Online route maps, plotting distances and fastest routes to somewhere in Northern England he had never heard of, plus a multitude of reports on plutonium storage across the UK. All interesting, but the relevance to him meant nothing. After more searches on world history, politics, and social history, he took his eyes off the screen and looked to the side, pushing the plate away, laden with gravy skin, shrouding stone cold food. The searches continued until at four in the morning. His fingers switched the machine off. Richard wasn't tired but climbed the stairs, got into bed, and fell asleep straight away, waking three hours later.

He rose, dressed in the same clothes, and walked to the study, picking up the laptop. Why was he doing this? He couldn't answer the question. Opening the French windows, he stepped out onto the patio into a garden filled with birdsong. Robins and hedge sparrows in full voice. A Beautiful morning with a slight mist in the air and dew laden grass. Droplets, clinging to the surface of the manicured lawn, soaked through his socks, cold but not uncomfortable and made him laugh. He would never venture out without something on his feet. Was he dreaming?

The loud splash disturbed the chorus of birdsong as it broke through water lilies and sank to the bottom of the pond, confirmed to him his state of consciousness. Concerned but not alarmed. A two-thousand-pound Apple Mac submerged, how strange!

Back in the kitchen and opening the fridge, Richard selected eggs, bacon, cheese, and ham, consuming them voraciously. Fascinated that he had cooked none of the food and didn't register taste or consistency. He recognized the need to stop this madness but lacked any motivation to act.

After writing a note to let his wife know he would be gone for a few days to London, he took the Aston Martin and headed north and didn't know where he was heading, but suspected Cumbria to be the most likely destination after the internet searches he made earlier. four and a half hours later, he passed the sign for Kendal on the outskirts of the Lake District.

NINE

The monitor showed a steady pulse rate. It slowed after being treated with naloxone, a powerful opioid receptor blocker and the blue skin pallor faded as the naloxone and oxygen ventilation began to take effect.

"He's over the worst of it," said Dr. Hernandez. "If he hadn't been found so quickly, he might not be with us."

"Who found him?" said Ben.

"One of the hospital cleaners on their way home. He was lying in her parking space as she reversed out. The poor woman was in shock and assumed she'd run over him. Either he stumbled and fell, or someone put him there."

"In front of the car?"

"Yes, between the front and the concrete wall. There's a gap of around three feet."

"So, how did he get such a high dose of morphine?"

"The truth is, I don't know. It wasn't part of any treatment he was receiving from me. He disappeared from the MRI suite before being put through for another scan. Peter said he was feeling unwell, and the nurse left the room to fetch him a drink of water. I can only assume he gained access to morphine in the hospital, but there are no reports of anything missing, so how he got hold of it is just bizarre, unless of course someone administered the morphine, which to me is equally bizarre."

Ben looked at the unconscious patient. The poor man had been through hell in the last week, and the MRI scans were more than strange.

"Any thoughts on what's inside his head, Doctor?"

"When you have studied and practiced medicine for as long as I have, you think you have seen just about everything. But this is something I cannot explain. Can you?"

"That's what I intend to find out."

"What's your view, Miss—?"

"Claire Manson. Please excuse my boss. He's not good at introductions. I also work at Moreton Scientific Investigation. I don't like speculating without the full facts," she said with a beaming smile that Dr. Hernandez reciprocated.

"Watch her, Dr. Hernandez. Remember the Disney song 'Never Smile at a Crocodile'?" Hernandez laughed.

Claire flushed slightly but carried on her interrogation.

"Do you have CCTV in the area he was found and all other parts of the hospital?"

"Yes, virtually throughout the hospital site, although some cameras might not be working. The police are teaming up with our security guys, so they should have some answers pretty soon."

Ben thumbed through the MRI scans. "You said this thing inside Mr. Jenkins' head was moving. Can you elaborate, only I can't tell from these scans?"

"If you look at the legs on the first and sixth image, you can see that they've slightly retracted."

Ben compared the two slides. "You're right. Amazing!"

"It is, but you wouldn't be saying that if you were Peter Jenkins."

"When do you think will he be able to talk?"

Hernandez looked thoughtful. "A day or two and after the week he's had, I don't want him stressed any more than is necessary. The police are eager to talk to him as well. Would you like to speak to his wife? I asked her to go to the relatives' room while you were here, so we could talk freely."

"That would be useful. Has she been told about the hitchhiker inside his skull?"

"She has. I told her myself."

Jill Jenkins wasn't what either Ben or Claire expected. In sharp contrast to her slight, and nondescript husband, Jill Jenkins was of Amazonian stature, well-toned, and strikingly good looking. Claire was getting mixed emotions; empathy, and jealousy at the woman's perfect skin, cat green eyes, and turned-up nose that gave her an elfish air, with perfect lips and enough pout without overdoing the Botox. Quite an intoxicating combination. For all the effort, the makeup was unsuccessful in hiding days of turmoil, tears and suffering from her husband's misfortune.

Their introduction—'Dr. Ben Sharman and partner Claire Manson' caused a raised eyebrow and a surge of willpower from Ben to suppress a laugh. Under normal circumstances, he would have corrected the introduction with a friendly jibe, but this situation made it inappropriate.

"I'm sorry that this has happened to your husband," said Ben.

"Thank you," she said in a whisper.

"We're looking into the incident at the reservoir and wondered if you would mind answering a few questions if you feel up to it?"

"Okay," she said but looked reluctant, staring down at her hands, clasped together on her lap.

"Does he go fishing often at Cantref Reservoir?"

"Not often. He's been a few times over the last couple of years."

"Did you ever go fishing with him to the Reservoir in the past?"

"Oh yes, but I got bored sitting there all day, so I stopped going after the first couple of times."

"Did he always fish from the same place, or did he move around the reservoir?"

"No, it was always the same spot. The first time, he bagged a dozen trout and didn't want to move from there. I tell a lie. He moved on one occasion, a bit farther round the reservoir, because somebody came early and took his usual place."

"You must have been so relieved when he came home after being missing for five days?"

She nodded, turning her wedding ring round and round on her finger. "At first I didn't think it was him. He looked such a mess, and I had already convinced myself he had drowned when they couldn't find him."

"What was he like when he came home?"

"Confused. Tired. At first, I wasn't taking much notice of what he was saying. I was just so pleased to have him back."

A tear appeared in the corner of one eye. Claire offered her a small box of tissues from her bag.

"Thank you," she said, taking one and dabbed it away.

"What did he say to you before you called the police?"

"He was talking over and over about about a wave that hit him and a metal clamp on his leg pulling him down."

"A metal clamp?"

"At first I didn't have a clue what he meant, but I've been thinking about it. There's probably a lot of junk dumped in the water and his leg got caught in something."

"That could be it an old bike." remarked Claire.

"He said little else apart from that. I called the police to let them know he was safe at home. Then he fell asleep on the sofa and wouldn't wake up. The police took him to the hospital."

"And has he spoken to you since he has been in hospital?" said Ben.

"Yes, of course. I've been here the whole time he's been here."

"And has he mentioned this clamp again?"

"No, but he seems distant. Not his usual self. Shock setting in I suppose."

She looked up at Ben and stared with her vivid green eyes for a second. "What's inside his head, and please, be honest about it?"

The question from Jill Jenkins broadsided Ben. Claire rescued the temporary silence. "At this moment, it's a mystery, and that's why we're here—to find answers."

"Is it some form of parasite?" she whispered.

"We're still looking at every piece of information," said Claire.

"What if it kills him?" The corner of her eyes glistened with tears.

"Jill. Sorry, do you mind if I call you Jill?"

"Of course not."

Claire gently took hold of her hands. "Just because there is something inside Peter's head does not mean it's going to kill him. If it is parasitic, it's not in its own interest to end his life. Try not to worry and we will get to the bottom of this as soon as we can."

Jill offered Claire a card. "I have to go to my husband. Please keep me in the loop."

Claire, surprised, took the card. "Of course. I promise."

As they walked out of the hospital, Claire pulled the card from her pocket. Jill Jenkins—Freelance Journalist.

"Did you get any vibe off her Ben?"

"Like what?"

"She doesn't ring true to me. The caring wife bit."

Ben shook his head. "Seemed genuinely upset to me. Wouldn't you be?"

""I think it was a mask. I caught a glimpse of what's underneath in her eyes, when she handed me this card and no wonder she wanted to be kept in the loop. Look."

Ben read the card and laughed. "Claire. Do you think she would be sitting in a hospital for a week with her nearest and dearest if her job was her priority?"

"I suppose not."

"On the other hand, it could be good for us."

"You mean you."

"No, us. As in Moreton Scientific Investigation."

"Did you just offer me a partnership, Ben Sharman?"

"In your dreams. No, I meant for the business as a whole."

"You are unbelievable! Perhaps she's a journalist for the local rag?"

"She looks too sophisticated for a local paper."

"Now who's being naïve?"

"Here, she has her own website," said Ben, shading the screen of his phone from the sunlight.

"People have websites for their cats. That proves nothing," said Claire.

"Says here that she has won the Features Writer of the Year at the UK Press Awards. Does that sound like a local scooper?"

"Let me see," said Claire, pulling his arm toward her.

"Mmm—she's also won a host of other minor awards. For once, you may be right. Might be good for us. Or if we don't get this right, it might be bad. Very bad!"

TEN

Richard Parker hated driving long distance, but the drudgery disappeared once the magical mystery trip unfolded as the car headed north up the M5 and M6 motorways. He guessed, from the earlier Google searches, Sellafield to be the destination, but didn't have a clue which route the car would take him once it exited the motorway toward Barrow and Kendal. Villages came and went as the Aston Martin purred along, many places he'd heard of but never been to before. This part of northwest England, featuring on his bucket list, was somewhere he always intended to visit but never got round to it, and now here he was, visiting the place on the most bizarre trip of his life.

The strange journey continued through Cumbria, on A roads and dual carriageways, bypassing towns and villages with strange and some quite appealing names. Beck Head, Lingdale, and Newby Bridge appeared and disappeared as the car progressed through breathtaking scenery of the Cumbrian landscape, with never-ending mountains, river crossings and glimpses of the Irish Sea, making him wonder how long it would take for the car, driven by him using a mysterious automatic pilot, to reach the final destination.

Frustration grew as he tried to analyze this irresistible need to drive hundreds of miles with no clear, logical reason. Could he be having the ultimate nightmare? Was this just a mind blowing hallucination, and if so, what caused it? He wound the window down, allowing the moorland breeze to fill the car and the cool buffeting of his hair and taste of raw bacon still in his mouth from the earlier uncooked breakfast spelled out reality, not fantasy. Far too real and vivid to be dreaming. He stared at the winding road ahead, going over and over the previous 24 hours, looking for a reason, but all he could detect was growing dread. A trickle of information seeped into his consciousness from an unknown source, growing into a flood of what would unfold in unstoppable detail. He could not believe he was possible of committing such vile atrocities.

Along a stretch of flat road, he had the urge to slow down and look across at towers and sprawling industrial buildings, a mile from the road toward the coastline. Was this the Sellafield nuclear site? Had he arrived? Passing the distant industrial landscape, the car sped up and twenty minutes later pulled into the car park of a small hotel which looked familiar as one of the many searches made online during the early hours of that morning. Instinctively moving to the trunk of the car, Richard stopped, realizing he had no luggage to lift out, and turned toward the hotel main entrance, being guided by an unspoken force inside his mind.

The alien took full control in the hotel's reception, deactivating Richard's conscious mind as he had served its purpose and, for now, was no longer of any use.

"Can I help you, sir?" said the smiling, bald man behind reception. "Do you have a reservation?"

"No reservation, sorry. It's been a bad day. There is an intermittent fault with my car's electrics and it'll take time to fix. Can I book a room for a couple of nights?"

The man checked the desktop computer for vacancies. "Yes, we have a room available. Would it be just the two nights?"

"Not sure at the moment. Maybe more. It's a real bother as I've left my bank card at home. I have plenty of cash. Are you okay with cash?"

A gleeful smile appeared on the man's face. "I can't remember the last time someone wanted to pay with cash but, unless there's been a change in the law, it's still legal tender," he said and laughed.

Richard forced a smile, which looked more like a sneer than a genuine, pleasant response, but the man wasn't looking at him as he searched and pulled out a small, battered cash box, hidden beneath a pile of newspapers under the desk, and didn't notice the odd grimace to Richard's lips, exposing one half of his teeth as the alien got used to controlling facial movements.

"Do you want me to pay for the extra night now?"

"Would you like a receipt?"

"No, that won't be necessary."

The smile widened as the man unlocked and opened the cash box. "Sixty pounds a night for cash and I'll keep the room available for a third night until the day after tomorrow at four pm. Just let me know by then."

Richard nodded without expression.

The receptionist handed over the room key and carried the cash box into the office behind the reception.

Richard lay on the double bed, closed his eyes, and fell asleep in a few seconds. Sleep, an annoying human necessity to recharge the body, gave the alien time to review the series of the events leading up to this point and progress had been better than expected, allowing more time to locate and secure the target. Being on a specific mission, remote from the ship, in total control and off-grid from the demanding clutches of the ship's commander, was exhilarating and although speed dictated everything for the mission to succeed, the alien hoped to use every available second before becoming just one of the crew again, with constant orders to follow.

That evening, Richard arrived in leafy Elmwood Drive, a well-to-do area filled with spacious detached houses, and remained in the car, parked across the street, for an hour before a man in a dark tracksuit, carrying a kit bag walked from house number twenty-five to the blue Land Rover Discovery on the drive. Richard checked the photocopy in his pocket, against the face behind the wheel as the Discovery drove past, confirming he had the correct address.

A car pulled up behind and Richard reached for the newspaper on the passenger seat and opened it, with both eyes locked on the rear-view mirror. He watched with interest as the driver behind tried to make himself less conspicuous, putting on a baseball cap and pulling the peak down to cover his face while talking into a large hand-held radio before getting out and hurrying across the road into the driveway of number twenty-five, where a middle-aged woman in a dressing gown opened the door, peered over the man's shoulder, then pulled him inside. Richard saw the curtains above the entrance door close through binoculars.

An hour later, the same man left the house and drove away. Richard leaned over, pulling the sealed bag out of the glove compartment. With the road clear of cars and pedestrians, he walked casually to the front door of the house and knocked.

The same woman, now dressed in jeans and a sweater, opened the door with a look of surprise.

"Oh, hello," she said.

"Sorry to disturb you. I saw the man who just left your house dropping this in the middle of the road," he said, holding a yellow cloth. "He drove off before I could tell him."

She blushed and was about to take it from him when he lunged forward, wrapping a hand around the back of her neck, pulling her forward, forcing the yellow cloth over her mouth, then pushed her inside. By the time she had overcome the shock of being assaulted, she slumped in his arms, unconscious.

For a slight woman, her weight surprised him and he had to lower her onto the parquet floor and drag her into the living room, before lowering her onto the carpet. He pushed her away from the wall and lay down next to her, shuffling close so that his right ear touched her left ear. Once settled, he screamed as the excruciating pain lanced through his head and neck as the transfer took place and a trickle of blood dripped from her left ear onto the carpet, spreading out in a small, dark patch.

Richard Parker, now aware of his surroundings but having no control over his actions, stood and stared at the woman lying beneath him on the carpet. He knew her from the previous evening's intensive research and wanted to rouse the woman, to pick her up and warn her but though no longer hosting the creature, it still controlled him, overriding all logical actions, setting him on a course he could not deviate from.

Surreal but so real, with no control over any of his functions apart from thought, the next stage in this macabre journey horrified him. Unlike the journey. north from Cardiff, he knew where he must go next and why, and pulled by some unseen force, Richard closed the front door of number twenty-five, walked across the road to the car, and drove south.

Scared and nauseous, Helen Groves dragged herself onto the settee and listened for her attacker. Silence filled the house. Had the intruder gone? What had he used to overpower her? The scent clung to her nose and mouth. Ether? Not dissimilar to the bottles of pure ether in the lab store, but not quite the same. It had to be chloroform or some other powerful sedative. She wanted to call the police, but something stopped her. What was wrong with her? Why couldn't she get help? Paul would be home soon, but it made no difference. She wouldn't be able to tell him, either.

Richard Parker took seven hours to make the long drive south, stopping only once to refuel, arriving an hour before dawn at the empty car park.

He left the car with the door open after he got out. Pointless, closing it as he wouldn't need the car again. Cool, crisp air filled his lungs as the hot engine metal ticked as it cooled and, like watching a film, he observed himself walking forward. The crunching of his own footsteps vanished as he stepped from gravel onto the vast green carpet that stretched all the way to the edge.

The odd twinkle from passing cargo ships and hazy moonlight danced upon the expanse of cold black water that spread out across the huge panoramic seascape of the English Channel and when he reached the last of the soft grass, the breeze ruffled his hair from the sudden updraft. Richard, unable to resist, took a final step forward and six seconds later joined the waves and rocks, five hundred feet below.

ELEVEN

Ben stuck the aerial photo of Cantref Reservoir to the whiteboard and stood back. The pieces were coming together, although he still hadn't formed a hypothesis.

"Claire!" he shouted. "Can you come back?"

She returned to the lab carrying two mugs of coffee.

"You only just sent me out to make these!" she complained.

"Sorry. Is there anything I've missed?"

She scanned the board. A4 photos of the impact sites plus several close-ups in and around each crater. A photo of Peter Jenkins. A map pinpointing the reservoir, Peter Jenkins' fishing peg, and the lay-by where witness, Dianne Jones, parked her car. Lower on the map, more pins in the hospital and Peter Jenkins' house in Cardiff.

"Has there been a murder? Looks like a police incident board, without the long number under Peter Jenkins' mug shot."

"No, it just makes sense to have the key elements visible in one place. Scattered facts create scattered thoughts!"

"What about photos of the meteor fragments?"

"I just had a call from Ron. He's delivering pieces of the meteor from both impact sites, which are far better than any images he might send. I would prefer it if we created our own images from the samples."

Claire knew what was coming next. Ben had used the royal 'we'. "You mean images I will create?"

Ben shrugged his shoulders. "Let's be fair. You are much better at photographic stuff than anyone else here, so why not you? Anyway, those can wait till Ron gets here."

"If I'd known he was coming, I would have dressed down," said Claire.

"Stop it! Ron is alright. You just haven't got used to him yet and it will be good to examine the cause of this mystery first hand."

"What tests do you want me to prep?" said Claire

"The usual, and can you set up the posh camera and lighting for macro shots? Oh, and we'll need the electron microscope. Is it working or is it still on the blink?"

"Of course it's working. I called in the engineer last week. You stood next to him while he looked at it."

"When was that?"

"Last Wednesday. You were in research fairyland."

Ben smirked. "My amazing concentration. Blocks everything out. It's one of my assets."

"Caractacus Potts."

"What?"

"The mad professor in Chitty Chitty Bang Bang—Caractacus Potts. He lived in a world of his own, just like you."

"Bloody hilarious Claire. You're splitting my sides. Better get ready. Ron will be here soon."

"Can't wait. I'll get the bleach spray ready for the worktops."

To Ben's surprise and disappointment, Ron arrived with quite a small box.

"They wouldn't let me bring the lot," said Ron with a sheepish smile. "There are two boxes inside. One from each site."

"Cup of coffee, Ron?" said Ben, taking the box from him and placing it on the lab bench.

"Yep, just the ticket. I'm bloody parched after that drive from Cambridge."

"Great. Claire can't wait to make you one."

She scowled. "I suppose you'd like another?"

"Please," said Ben, waving her away with one hand and opening the box with the other. "Sugar this time, those cheap sweeteners Kath buys for us are disgusting."

The first box had a section of Ordnance Survey map taped to the top with the mountain impact site highlighted.

"I'll start with this and Claire can test the other. How long can we hold on to these little beauties?"

"They didn't stipulate a time. They were so busy arguing about how many pieces to give you they forgot to mention a deadline to me, so I'll leave them with you. As far as I'm concerned, it's at least a week, unless they remember and ask for them back sooner."

"Cranking your mileage claim up, eh, Ron.? You must be making a fortune between us and your visits to that Welsh reservoir."

"Not with the price of motion lotion at the moment. But every little helps, and it's nice to get down here more often. I'd love to live down here."

Ron necked his coffee down and made his excuses. He was gone in twenty minutes, much to Claire's relief.

"He's getting better. Not a tissue in sight," she said, spraying the worktop and looking at every shelf and cupboard top.

"Keep that away before you contaminate everything!" As he stared into the eyepiece, he grinned and pointed to the floor next to Claire.

She leaped sideways. "Dirty bastard. I knew he would leave something behind," she said, picking the tissue up with a pair of test tube tongs.

Ben looked at each of the six sample pieces and turned to Claire.

"Incredible!"

"What is it?"

"What I haven't seen is parts of a naturally formed meteorite. Pass me a magnifying glass."

He laid each piece out on a sheet of paper on the worktop.

"Look at the largest piece. Notice anything strange?"

Claire moved the magnifying glass over the piece of rock.

"It's got rough and smooth patches, but apart from that, it just looks like a piece of rock."

Ben placed three pieces in a row.

"Now, what do you see?"

The surface of the three pieces had a common smooth area with a distinct pattern running through.

"My god! This is man-made! But that's not possible."

"Doubt if it's man-made. More like little green man-made. We'll do some analysis of its makeup, but I think this meteor is, in fact, a molded casing. Dianne Jones stated the meteor split and something else flew out of it into the sky. I think that whatever was ejected was in the middle of, or formed part of, a molded structure."

"This puts a different slant on the whole thing," said Claire, her eye almost glued to the magnifying glass.

"Can you do a spectral analysis of a sample," said Ben, putting his hand over the samples, blocking them from Claire's view, "while I analyze the samples from the other impact site?"

The eight pieces in the second sample box were larger and more revealing. Ben's theory appeared to hold good as more detailed indentations, which could not have occurred naturally, became clear. He experimented with the pieces and found two, which fitted perfectly together. Under the magnifying glass, there were other markings too small to make out. He switched to the low-powered microscope, staring in disbelief.

"Claire, you need to see this."

"Won't be a second. Results coming through now."

She stared at the screen as the results appeared.

"You're right. It isn't rock. It's a form of silica in a fine mixture of another substance that the database doesn't have a record of. My guess is it's some type of cement or molding compound. Not natural rock apart from aggregates mixed into it."

"Never mind that. You really need to look at this."

Under the microscope, the detail was clear. The imprint of part of what looked like a hatch door with symbols or text that no earthly being had written.

Claire's excitement grew as she retrieved the spare, low-powered microscope and expertly affixed the camera. With meticulous precision, she began capturing photographs of every component from both boxes. As the clock approached ten in the evening, the whiteboard and half of the surrounding walls were adorned with a multitude of crystal-clear images. These images collectively unveiled a portion of a spaceship's hull, and by extrapolating dimensions and angles from the data, they estimated it to be a spherical object measuring two meters in diameter.

"Claire, I think we should call it a night. I won't be able to sleep after this. I just hope it has nothing to do with our friend in our last encounter with alien life."

"Shouldn't you call Ron and tell him?"

"I've sent him a text. He'll be down first thing tomorrow. Poor sod. He hasn't long got home, and his house is on the other side of Cambridge. He got hold of the rest of the samples. Not sure how he did it, but we might be able to reverse engineer the sample pictures you will produce and see what this UFO looked like."

"Sure it's a UFO?"

"Has to be. Either that or the best spoof in the history of alien encounters.

"If you're right, it makes you wonder."

"Wonder what?"

"Where it is?"

"I have a hunch it's still in that reservoir."

"A hunch based on what?"

"Based on nothing. Just a strong feeling. Come on, we're back in here in a few hours. Go home and get some shut-eye."

Claire smiled. "I can't believe what's happening. This is the best job in the world!"

Ben smiled. For once, he couldn't agree with her more.

TWELVE

"Anything worth looking at in the fridge, love?"

"Why don't you have a look yourself? I'm drying my hair."

"Oh, come on, I'm starving. It takes it out of you in the gym."

Paul Groves pulled his training shoes off and threw them through the door into the hallway. He was about to crash out on the sofa, but stopped and stared down. He bent forward, reached out, touched the carpet and inspected the sticky red smudge on his finger.

"Helen. Why is there blood on the carpet in here? What's been going on?" he shouted.

"I had a nosebleed earlier and forgot to clean it up. Don't panic, I'll sort it out in a minute."

"You never have nosebleeds. Are you sure you're okay?"

"I'm Fine."

"Why are you drying your hair?"

"I've got to spruce myself up. I have to go to work."

"At half eight at night? You're kidding me?" He threw his socks into the hallway and lay back on the settee, flicking through the TV channels.

"There's a panic on in the lab. Do I have to remind you I'm never off duty?"

"So, you weren't kidding about the fridge?"

"No, so get off your fat backside. You have eyes!"

"What time will you be home?"

"I Don't have a clue and won't know till I get there. If it's nothing serious I might me straight back, but who knows? I might be there all night if it's something major."

"Either way, I'll wait up for you."

"Don't bother. There's beer in the fridge. Gallons of the stuff, fill your boots and by the time I'm home, you'll be out of it."

"Where's the bottle opener?

"Get off your bloody backside and find it. Stop asking me stupid questions so I can dry my hair in peace."

Paul slumped onto the sofa, ramped up the sound on the TV to overcome the drone of the hair dryer, and spent ten minutes scrolling through Tic Tok and Instagram on his mobile.

Helen peered around the corner of the door. "Your stinking socks go in the wash basket. I'm not your mother." She muted the TV, kneeled and scrubbed at the bloodstain with a damp cloth.

"Hey! I was listening to that."

"No, you weren't. You were looking at that mindless crap. Aren't you too old for Tic Tok? For God's sake, grow up!"

"It would surprise you what you can learn from this mindless crap," he said and looked up. "Watch the carpet. You'll shred it the rate you're going."

She didn't respond, attacking the stain with even more gusto.

"About time you got one of your minions to do the unsociable hours. Thought you were supposed to be running the show?"

"One of my minions would only end up calling me out anyway," she hissed. "I'm the only one with security clearance to deal with this. I am head of the department and it's my responsibility if there's a problem." She shook her head. "It's a nuclear power station, not a bloody golf club."

"Well, I wouldn't put up with it if I were you."

She glared at him. "Well, thank God you're not me. I'm responsible for anything that goes wrong in the lab. Being conscientious is in my nature. You—"

"Hurry with that cloth. The match is about to start," he said, pressing the un-mute button.

She threw the blood-stained cloth at him, missing the top of his head by a whisker. It stuck to the wall behind the sofa before sliding and dropping, leaving a long streak of crimson soaking into the wallpaper.

"See you whenever," he said, turning the TV volume up to maximum.

Grabbing her coat and keys from the hall rack, she slammed the front door, marched across the gravel drive and then slammed the car door after getting in, cursing him all the way.

Conflicting emotions filled the brief journey with boiling rage and bewilderment at her lack of control. Why was she going to work? There was no reason, but she was compelled and couldn't stop herself. Why was there blood on the carpet and what had the stranger done to her? Her mind whirled as she drove into the entrance.

At the barrier, she lowered the window.

"Working late, Helen?"

"Got some urgent stuff to deal with. You know how it is."

"I'll deactivate the alarm for the lab. Call me when you're in and I'll reset it. If you need to get out—"

"It's okay Mick, thanks. The door has an override switch from inside."

"Either me or Jeff will do our rounds in about an hour. Will you still be here then?"

"Should be." She wondered how long it would be before she went home, still not having a clue why she was there.

"One of us will call in to make sure you're okay."

"Oh, thanks. I appreciate that. I'll keep the kettle on the boil."

"See you later," he said and watched her drive to the main lab section, lit up like a Christmas tree.

Helen sat and looked around the silent lab. Why was she here? She didn't want to be here. She didn't want to be at home either. Was she going nuts? Dread crept into her thoughts and a horrible reality surfaced. A vivid picture of blood spraying up a wall flashed across her mind. What the hell was that about? A familiar wall with a wallpaper pattern of green and red flowers she knew only too well. The image disappeared as fast as it had arrived and she assumed it must be a flashback of the blood stained cloth she had thrown in anger at her husband. But it wasn't the same, or was it?

She re-ran her earlier rant with Paul, reliving the sequence. Drying her hair, stopping to argue, walking to the kitchen to fetch a wet cloth to clean up the stain on the carpet. The cloth missing his head, sticking to the wall with the same green and red flower pattern, sliding then dropping to the floor, leaving a red smear of diluted blood soaking into the wallpaper. She hoped her lazy husband would have the sense to clean it off the wall before the paper stained for ever and needed replacing.

No. It wasn't the same as the image that flashed across her mind a few seconds ago. That was a spray of blood spattered upward, all the way to the ceiling. Her stomach churned as the image she recalled revealed blood from her husband's head. As reality set in the vision became clearer and she now knew why blood sprayed up the living room wallpaper. Sweat beaded on her forehead.

The blood sprayed wallpaper churned through her mind as she stared out of the lab window when the entity inside her head shut her consciousness down. It gave it time to think without the constant dialogue going on in Helen's mind. So far, the latest events in the plan were progressing perfectly. One more switch and taking care of loose ends would make it absolutely perfect. It just depended which security guard showed up at the lab.

At ten thirty, Jeff Randle knocked the lab door.

"Hello. Helen, are you here?" The lights were all on, but there was no sign of her. He stepped in and walked toward the back rooms. The alien reactivated Helen Groves' mind.

"I'm in here." she said, from the galley kitchen.

Perched on a high stool at the breakfast bar of the small kitchen, she patted the seat next to her. He walked over, put his arms around her, and kissed the back of her neck.

"We're chancing it a bit too much," she said, pushing him away.

"You're kidding me? Your old man wasn't anywhere near the house today. What time did he come home?"

"Ages after you left. It's not that. The street's quiet and that old bag over the road is always on the lookout for her next bit of gossip. The neighbors might spot us."

He sat down and put his arm around her.

"Why don't you come to my place instead of me having to sneak around? I haven't got a wife to worry about. Just me and the dog, and he isn't going to tell anyone. Stay all night. In fact, I'd love it if you'd spend a night with me. Please?" he said, kissing her neck.

"Don't tempt me." She pushed him away again. "And I mean that. I'd love a night of TLC, but, Someone might see me. I can explain why you're coming to my house. A visit from a colleague about work is legitimate and can be easily explained. But me, a high-profile head of department coming to your house? Why would I be doing that in the eyes of anyone watching and asking the question, and there are people living in your street who work here? If I was one of your neighbors, I would assume you were having an affair, not consulting a colleague about a problem at work. Can't you see that?"

"Yes, but is it something else?" he said, and laughed.

"What do you mean, something else?"

"Do you want to shove two fingers up at your hubby? Me and you at it in your marital bed and all that?"

She smiled. "Shut your face and come here," and wrapping her arms around his back. "Hold me. I need a cuddle."

She gripped him tight around the nape of his neck and kissed him before snuggling up, bringing him closer. He pulled away and looked into her eyes.

"I can stay here for a while," he said and winked, kissing her cheek, the tip of her nose, then her forehead. "If you know what I mean?"

"No chance. Not in work, and definitely not in the lab!" She pulled him closer. The alien seized its chance, shut Helen's mind down, and tilted Jeff Randle's head down. With both hands clamping the back of his head, it aligned their ears, gritting her teeth as the pain hit. It was over in a second, and after the initial scream, Jeff Randle stood rigid, holding his bloodied ear. Helen slid off the stool and walked through the lab, terrified of what she was about to do. She couldn't stop it. Her mind wasn't controlling any physical movement. She was in a floating trance. A mere spectator. She pushed the override button on the door to the car park and ran across the yard. The engine started, and she watched her arms lift to the steering column, knowing she was not controlling them.

As the car approached security, Mick raised the gate and was about to walk out as she passed straight through and drove off without a sideways glance. He watched the rear lights turn at the junction and vanish down the long, dark road. Mick shook his head, lowered the gate, signed her out in the register and un-paused the Netflix film on his phone.

Jeff Randle couldn't understand what was happening. Why had she left and not come back and what was the blinding pain that disappeared just as quick as it arrived? He contemplated the small silver flask. What was so special about it? He didn't know and didn't care. It had to be delivered. To where? He lifted the flask from the lab workbench and walked to the door, turning all the lights out, resetting the alarm and locking the door. When he reached the security van, he slipped the flask under the passenger seat, not knowing why he had done it and with no resolve to stop. After the usual checks, he drove to the staff car park, making sure there was nobody watching him transfer the flask to his own car.

Helen arrived home to find Paul fast asleep on the sofa and opened the cabinet in the study, pulling out a double-barrel shotgun. With the top drawer of the study desk unlocked and opened, she removed two cartridges from a box of twelve and loaded both barrels. She couldn't believe that she would go through with it, but, unable to resist, she entered the living room. As predicted, Paul was out of it, surrounded by empty bottles of lager on the sofa. He looked half human asleep, as the sneer had gone. Peaceful, she thought. In fact, he looked quite serene. Such a pity to end their marriage this way. She was sure an acrimonious divorce would have given her far more pleasure, watching him lose everything. She raised the gun, thinking only of the noise and not the consequences, screwed her eyes shut and fired. The first discharge blew most of Paul's face away. She stared impassively at the blood sprayed up the floral patterned wallpaper before pushing the barrel under her chin and slid her hand down to the trigger.

"I'm not too clever, Mick. Guts been playing me up all night. Any painkillers in the first aid box?" said Jeff.

"No. Plasters, bandages, and all that kind of crap, but no medicine, which is bloody stupid. But there you are, company. health and safety shit. You can have your broken arm put in a nice, tidy sling, but give the poor sod some pain relief!"

Jeff grimaced. "None in your locker, mate?"

"Sorry. Thought you looked a bit on the rough side earlier. Did you pop in and have a chat with Helen? She blanked me as she left."

"Yes, saw her in the lab. Too busy reading something to talk so I left her to it. Didn't realize she was gone. I've been over the other side checking the outbuildings."

"Women, eh? Bloody strange sometimes. You take my missus.

Right as rain one minute and as nasty as a polecat the next. You're lucky you're single."

"Sorry, Mick. I think I'm going to have to go home. Stomachs like a washing machine. Dose of the trots and a headache. I can feel it coming."

"Stay away from me. You can't go till you a replacement's organized. You know the score."

"I'll sit here till you get someone. Hope I don't shit myself while I'm waiting."

Roger called the control center, and a replacement arrived an hour later.

"I'll help you to your car. Are you okay to drive?" said Mick, pulling his coat off the rack. "You look bloody awful."

"Feeling rotten, Jeff, but I don't need a carer. Think I can get to the car on my own. But thanks for the offer, anyway."

"Suit yourself. Sign out, get yourself home, dose yourself up and get some sleep. Good job. It's your day off tomorrow. You look like a bloody ghost."

When Jeff arrived home, it was a quick change of clothes and back into the car. It mystified him. Where was he about to go and why?

THIRTEEN

Classical music was not Peter Jenkins' preferred choice, but Vivaldi's winter provided a soothing tonic against the intense humming of the MRI. It seemed an eternity since the flat motorized bed fed him into the scanner and he'd got used to laying still and was enjoying the experience.

After his time in the hospital, the fishing trip seemed a distant memory. A traumatic blip in his life with five days of memories erased. But the unease lingered with growing conviction that whatever had invaded his body was out to harm him.

The music from the headphones changed to pan pipes and gently flowing water, drifting him off to sleep. Waves soothed and calmed as the pan pipes meandered from the trees across the reservoir. Water grew restless and swept toward him, angry, growing, surging. Huge brown waves broke the banking, chasing him up toward the road, flattening the gorse and long, reedy grass. A metal hand reached from the crest of the lead wave as he stretched both arms out for the wire fence. Muddy, slimy metal fingers gripped, pulling, wrapping around his ankle. Sliding backward through uprooted gorse and slurry, he gagged, inhaling thick, oozing mud, flowing, searching, blocking ears.

The smell of wet dirt creeping up each nostril. The metal hand pulled deeper and deeper. His eyes opened, and a coiling pipe climbed up to him from the blurred sphere below, forcing his jaws apart, pushing the mud lodged in his mouth down his throat. Suction drew the brown slurry backward into the pipe. He choked, blackness beginning to shroud his peripheral vision, interrupted by bright flashing lights. More silver tubes snaked up from the sphere, forcing their way into his mouth, nose, and ears. Warm liquid flushed through. Senses dimmed, and the small sphere below faded into the brown mire.

"Mr. Jenkins. We're all done for now. Can you hear me, Mr. Jenkins?"

He woke, tense, and wide-eyed, taking a huge breath and lay gasping as the nurse pulled the headphones apart and lifted them away.

"Would you like a cup of something? You've been quite restless for the last five minutes."

He couldn't speak until his breathing returned to some form of normality. Moving his tongue around his mouth, he was sure he detected the tang of mud. It faded away and all he registered was the rapid thumping of his heart.

"Please," he said, blinking as the dimmed lights brightened. The short sleep clouded everything and although he felt better, the horror from the depths of the reservoir lingered.

Back in the side ward, Jill Jenkins was waiting.

"Well, Doctor. Any change?" she said, taking a pace forward, staring into his eyes.

Dr. Hernandez nodded, and tried to shrink backward, but he was already flat to the wall. "I can't see anything abnormal. It's quite astonishing that it has gone from the brain. I'll do more total body scans tomorrow to make sure we have removed it and it has not moved to another part of the body."

"Moved?" she said, leaning forward.

"Sorry. We need to ensure it has gone from all parts of Peter's body. The scans will take an hour or two."

"If there is any chance of it moving, shouldn't you do another scan straight away?"

"Mrs. Jenkins—"

"Please call me Jill," she said, placing the fingers of her right hand gently on his arm.

He looked down at her hand, willing her to remove it, but she left it there. "Sorry, Jill. I think your husband has been through enough trauma for one day."

"But what if it hasn't gone? Surely you need to find out for definite?"

"I'm confident that another twenty-four hours' rest will be more beneficial for your husband."

"Alright. If everything is okay, when can my husband come home?"

"Should be okay for the day after tomorrow. This is an unprecedented case, and I don't want to let him go just yet."

She gripped his arm. "For his benefit or yours?"

"His welfare is my major concern."

"You didn't answer my question, Doctor."

"There are other tests I wish to run while he's here. Yes, it will be for general medical benefit, but as I said, Peter's well-being is paramount and every test I carry out is for his welfare and well-being."

"What sort of other tests?" she said. releasing the grip, with fingers still lingering on his lower arm.

"Jill! Will you stop interrogating the good doctor or I'll tell him not to discuss anything with you," said Peter. "I know what you're up to, and I don't like it!"

"Sorry, Doctor. Occupational hazard. You were about to say something about tests?"

"Enough, Jill! Please excuse my wife. She is a journalistic predator first, concerned wife second."

"It's not a problem," said Hernandez. "The tests will be blood, urine plus blood pressure, sight, hearing, reflexes, and, of course, the additional scans. Blood and urine tests will be the most important to see if there have been any effects or changes resulting from this parasitic episode."

"Thank you, Doctor," she said with a gleeful smile. "That's what I wanted to hear, and when will you have the results for me?"

Peter shook his head as he watched her verbally devour the doctor.

"Can't give a definitive time for Peter's test results. This process can sometimes take a couple of weeks, but because of the unusual circumstances, it will be quick, likely within twenty-four hours of the tests. That's why I want Peter to remain in hospital to be on the safe side."

"Thank you, Doctor." She released the doctor's arm, turned, blew Peter a kiss, and walked out.

Peter shook his head. "See what I mean, doctor? Got what she wanted and then disappears. She'll be on her way to the coffee shop right now to write up her story for tonight's deadline."

Hernandez stepped away from the wall, glad to have his personal space to himself once more. "I asked if you wanted me to share your medical status with your wife. I can always cancel that permission if you wish. It doesn't concern me either way. It's your choice."

"Don't bother, Doctor. Even if I wanted our doctor-patient confidentiality, restricted to you and me, she would find a way around it. She's ruthless and bloody good at what she does."

The doctor stepped half out into the corridor to check who was there and stepped back in, closing the door.

"What I would say is that I think you shouldn't rush home. If you wanted to stay for an extra week, I will arrange it."

"A week. Why would I want to do that?"

"I'm giving you my best advice. You have to admit there aren't many patients that come here who have had a parasitic spider roosting in their skull. It's off the medical charts and I'm concerned that there may be some side effects we haven't expected. I'm being upfront here. This is not for my benefit."

The doctor left, and Peter considered his options. If the tests revealed that his six-legged stowaway had gone and proved there was no other cause for concern, they should discharge him. Being able to go home ought to be something to look forward to, but Jill wouldn't let him go to work and would be on his case every waking hour, making as much capital out of his story as possible, dragging him screaming and kicking through the media or wherever she could make money from his amazing story.

An extra week in the hospital suddenly seemed quite appealing!

FOURTEEN

The ship had been dispatched to survey the last planet, which was almost fully explored, marking the culmination of a meticulously executed mission to investigate this remote sector of the cosmos. Shielding devices, cloaking the ship, meant no sensor that Earth possessed, could penetrate the exterior. Even with high-powered visual devices, the hull of the ship would appear as a small piece of space rock debris.

Data collected had been mind blowing after exploring many worlds with little or nothing to offer. The dominant race on Earth achieved remarkable technical progress and had already traveled beyond their planet, but it was the variety of other lifeforms that astonished everyone on board, as did the strange and illogical way that such an advanced race treated their home planet with absolute contempt, and although advanced physically, mentally, and technologically, they were a species that disregarded their future. Earth provided the perfect place to establish a new outpost, but only after removing the current inhabitants at the top of the food chain.

It considered the wonders that Earth had to offer and the disastrous malfunction that almost ended their lives. With energy draining, it shut itself down while the car traveled to the final destination. The human, programmed to drive without stopping, left nothing for the alien to do. With all preparations made, the precious cargo, located under the seat, would soon be on board, ready to use and allow them to complete the last planetary survey, rejoin the mother ship, and bathe in the glory of a most successful mission.

The car traveled to the speed limit, making good progress, with very little traffic on the road, reaching the Welsh border by daybreak. The dual carriageway leading to the outskirts of Monmouth wound its way down past the fields to the left, shrouded in low mist, running next to the River Wye and the Forest of Dean beyond on the English side of the river. As the road bent to the left, a lorry a hundred yards ahead, began braking because of the increased incline, and the driver eased the car into the outside lane to pass, maintaining the speed limit of seventy miles an hour. As the nose of the car reached the huge black tires of the rear double axle the lorry braked hard, and without warning veering to the right as a badger ran across the carriageway. The lorry over-steered to correct itself and the tractor unit snaked outward into the outside lane striking the front of the car, forcing it headlong into the central verge, several feet higher than the road. In the battle of the two vehicles to regain control, there would only be one winner. The car slewed left, then right. Jeff grappled with the steering wheel as the car twisted, and careered sideways toward the steep banking on the left as the lorry's released its grip. The car off over the barrier and plunging down the hillside, turning over and over, end to end, pieces breaking off, flying toward the approaching river, and coming to rest upside down in the middle of a steep field.

The lorry took another hundred yards to pull up. After a frantic call to the emergency services, Jakub Lipska leaped from the cab, rushed back up the carriageway, vaulted the fence, and part ran, part fell down the slope, through wet grass tussocks and thistles. When he reached the wrecked car, the driver, thrown from the vehicle, lay crumpled twenty feet farther down the field. Jakub turned him over, pulled the collar of his shirt open, and placed his fingers on the driver's neck. No pulse. He checked again, tried to calm himself down and began CPR, a skill learned in the Polish army. He compressed the man's chest and the rib cage gurgled on one side. A stream of crimson streamed down the side of the driver's shirt, soaking into Jakub's overall trousers. The warmth on his thigh and the metallic smell of blood made him gag. He tried to block out his own thoughts and feelings, but the blood-soaked man lying in front of him was all his fault and should have remembered his heavy goods training in the Army and ran straight over the damned animal. The man's chest cavity seemed punctured to Jakub, and he believed his efforts to revive him would be futile, but he carried on, even though he was on the verge of passing out himself from the stench of blood and the realization that he may have just killed a man.

It seemed an age before the welcome sound of sirens in the distance broke the sound of his own exertions as the chest compressions and gurgling blood continued. He tried the man's pulse again and again, but there was nothing to show any sign of life and even though he knew the man was dead, Jakub kept trying with tears streaming down his face.

He stopped and leaned down to give two quick mouth-to-mouth breaths. Something sharp pierced his top lip and a blinding spasm ripped up through his nose, making him recoil. He tried to pull away, but his mouth, impaled and joined to the other man, was stuck fast. He tried to scream, but all that came out was a muffled screech as bubbles of blood frothed between the two men's lips. The more he tried to pull away, the more intense the agony. For a few seconds, he lost all sight and something scurried across his face. When he tried to brush it off, another surge of pain jolted through his hand between his thumb and index finger as a razor sharp black leg pierced all the way through. He passed out, slumped over the shattered body of Jeff Randle, and lay still. Tiny legs folded together in a swift pincer movement and burst through his inner ear.

Jakub opened his eyes to a sea of blurred flashing lights and struggled to get up.

"Whoa there. Take it easy."

The woman's concerned face came into focus. He looked around at the bright interior of an ambulance.

"How are you feeling?"

"Awful. I feel so cold," he said. She wrapped a woollen blanket over his shoulders and pulled the sides close around his chest.

"It's the shock. You'll soon warm up. What's your name?"

"Jakub."

"Okay, Jakub. Did you put the call in? Were you driving the lorry?"

"Yes. How is the man in the car? It was all my fault. I braked too hard for an animal running across the road. Is he okay? Is he alive?"

"Not sure yet, Jakub. The other crew is making him secure and bringing him up now. We will be taking you to the hospital to be checked over in a minute."

"My vehicle?"

"The police are here. Road accident investigation will be here for hours, so don't worry about your lorry. They will take care of it. Have you any pain?"

"Just my face and hand."

"You took a few bumps and scrapes. You went down to the car to help?"

"Yes. Then something crawled across my face and bit me."

"Where?"

"On my hand."

"I can only see one puncture mark at the base of your thumb and quite a few scratches. Was it a snake?"

"No. It was like a spider, I think. It ran over my cheek and eye."

"Okay, we'll check this out when we get to the hospital. If you have taken a bite, then you'll need a tetanus injection."

She turned his hand over and back, checking for swelling.

"Looks like he didn't make it then?" said Jakub, pointing out of the ambulance doors. Four firefighters, carrying a sealed body bag on a stretcher, walked past to the other ambulance.

"No, it doesn't," she said, placing her hand on his shoulder. He turned away and cried.

A police patrol officer leaned in. "Any chance of a quick word before you take this gentleman to hospital?"

The paramedic stepped out and after a brief discussion, the officer climbed in.

"Just a few details, and have you got your vehicle's keys? We'll take it to Monmouth until you are ready to fetch it. It's going to be here while the crash investigation team does their thing and before you ask, they could be here all night and maybe into tomorrow morning as well." Jakub wiped his eyes with the back of his hand and pulled the lorry keys from his pocket.

It was satisfied that it made the transfer without too much effort, but the new host was far from ideal. Not being native to this island was a tremendous disadvantage and would make him stand out. Another host had to be found quickly that could blend in and complete the mission.

FIFTEEN

Jolted from temporary stasis, the alien tried to take control but wasn't quick enough to prevent the car from careering sideways and flying over the barrier. Both frightening and interesting because the host's level of adrenaline at the point the car flew in mid-air was exhilarating.

Impact with the slope didn't occur immediately due to the steep downward gradient toward the River Wye far below. The front end of the vehicle bit into the turf after being airborne for over fifty yards, jarring on underlying rock, setting up a vicious end to end rotation, making the host's head whip backward, snapping his neck. For the rest of the car's destructive path, the alien's sensors were on full alert as the host's brain function all but ceased. It retracted legs, antennae, and brain connections to the host to prevent damage and unnecessary pain to itself, hoping the host's skull would provide a layer of protective armor.

The car smashed into the field several times and on one sideways rotation, the host's body left the vehicle through the windscreen, airborne for a second, before landing face down.

The other interesting aspect was what it discovered when it

reconnected with the host. Not expecting to find activity, it was stunned that the human, apparently deceased, was performing a strange and intense function, flooding chemicals outward from one part of the brain. Another wave of euphoria and images of flashing lights swept through the alien as the chemical passed through the connections into its body. It lasted for less than a few seconds before fading to nothing when all human brain activity ceased. Fascinating. The man was clearly dead, but a strange last function of the brain kicked in. It absorbed a trace of the chemical, similar to the one used to control the host's mind, for later analysis. A notion crept into the alien's mind as it sensed a distinct, but intangible force leaving the host's body. Could it be a side effect of the chemicals released? Were humans's strange beliefs that there is life after death true? The alien discarded the notion as ridiculous. An unfounded conviction based on false gods. A lie to control the masses, but an interesting phenomenon to be thoroughly investigated at a later time.

It scanned the immediate area for human life forms, detecting several creatures that the humans called cows moving toward the man's body. Their inquisitive nature drew them to something different from their normal, mundane existence. The beasts were quite close when their mood changed to fear and backed away as their natural senses picked up the strange force field coming from the alien's body. The scan of the field continued and another life form appeared further up the slope, moving at speed toward the body of Jeff Randle. A human, running and falling down the slope toward the car, gave the alien a fresh sense of hope. Knowing that humans either buried or cremated their dead, either method of the body's disposal would mean certain death if it stayed within the current host, so it extended and folded its legs in a state of readiness, waiting for an opportunity to switch hosts.

A male human turned the man over and started trying to revive him. The alien's usual route through the auditory system was impractical and risky. With skillful maneuvering, it cut through the back of the dead man's optic nerve, around the eyeball, and passed unseen with two razor-sharp legs lying just under the skin below the eye. Jakub Lipska bent over to make a seal over the mouth and the alien struck, piercing the dead man's cheek and lancing through Jakub's top lip. A chemical release from a leg tip fused a small patch of the two men's lips together. While Jakub struggled to free himself, it broke through the cheek and crawled across Jakub's face and into the ear canal. Jakub almost brushed the alien off as his hand swiped the side of his face, but the alien's evasive action sent a razor-sharp front leg through his hand. Jakub tore himself free with heavy bleeding from the tear to lip and the hole in his hand, then screamed in agony as six legs, folded together as a single spear, punctured the tympanic membrane deep inside his ear.

With control of the brain established, and the emergency services arriving on the road above, it deactivated Jakub's mind and the frightened man passed out, lying face up next to the body of Jeff Randle.

The temptation to get far away from the incident before the authorities could reach Jakubs unconscious body almost overwhelmed the alien. It weighed all the available options and made the right decision to stay at the scene. Cooperating with the authorities provided more opportunity to stay on mission without raising suspicion. Running away would complicate everything and currently being ahead of schedule meant that time and opportunity were on its side.

The journey in the ambulance proved disappointing. Jakub Lipska spoke very poor English, wasn't familiar with the geography of the British Isles, and would not be a suitable host, but on the flip side the female paramedic proved the opposite. She tried to make the journey to Nevill Hall Hospital in nearby Abergavenny pleasant by telling Jakub about her connection with Poland. How she and a friend drove across Europe and stayed a month in Warsaw and asked him many questions about his homeland, but it took a long time for him to comprehend and answer. The Polish language proved difficult to translate when information from Jakub's core knowledge needed extracting to answer her many questions. Preparation for the mission had included all languages with the focus on Welsh and English, which were pre-programmed into the alien's brain, but Polish had been unnecessary until now and proved difficult. Another English-speaking host, who would be familiar with the geography of the British isles, was necessary. Jakub looked up and smiled at the woman because that new potential host sat less than two feet away.

The alien engineered an opportunity, making Jakub slump down on the ambulance gurney and slide over to the side. She leaned across and pulled him up, tucking her chin over his shoulder, dragging him up onto the trolley. With both their heads touching, it made its move, transferring from ear to ear as she heaved Jakub backward. Blood-curdling screams were loud enough to be heard in the front compartment and the driver did an emergency stop, sending his two passengers sprawling across the floor. He ran to the back of the vehicle, yanking open the door, looked inside at Jakub and Sue Dean, staring up at him as they tried to get up.

"Are you okay?" he said, mystified at not finding a problem.

"Everything's fine. Why the hell did you slam the brakes on like that? You could have hurt both of us?"

"You were screaming!"

"Not me," she said. "Not either of us. Now, get us to the hospital, please, before a car runs up the back of us. You've parked in the middle of the road."

"But I heard you scream. Your ear is bleeding," he said, pointing at her.

She put her hand to her ear and looked at the blood on her fingers.

"Must have happened when I was scrambling down the bank," she said, wiping her hands in a tissue

"But you screamed."

"No, I didn't," she shouted. "How many times have I got to tell you?" she said, shaking her head.

The driver stared at Sue's livid face for a second and was about to climb into the back of the ambulance and continue the argument when her eyes narrowed in a harsh, feral stare. He stopped, thought the better of it, and backed away. She maintained the frightful glare until he shut the door.

Jakub Lipska didn't mention the hand bite at the hospital, as he could remember nothing of his ordeal. Sue Dean didn't find it necessary to inform the duty doctor, because she knew it wasn't a bite, and trying to explain the real reason for the wound would sound absurd. As much as she wanted to say something, she couldn't, and after finishing her shift, still wearing her uniform, she drove back to the crash site outside Monmouth to retrieve the silver flask, puzzled, but unable to stop herself.

SIXTEEN

The team gathered in the lab for an update.

"Before we begin," said Ben. "You all know Ron Logan from the Cambridge team and we also have the pleasure of Detective Inspector Sarah Birch and Detective Inspector Gwyn Churchman, who are representing the two police forces involved. Would you like to go first, Sarah?"

A diminutive shrew of a woman stepped forward with her equally pointed and pin-eyed colleague. They could have been twins if it weren't for the obvious age difference.

She proceeded with a lengthy PowerPoint presentation which was not only boring but showed a complete lack of understanding.

"Do we look like we're members of the public dragged in off the street?" whispered Claire.

"Shhh! Just play the game. I'm sure she'll get to the good bit—"

"Eventually?"

"Shush, for goodness' sake!"

DI Birch explained the boundaries of both forces, their rank structures, and a host of crime statistics, arrests, and successful convictions.

Ben shot a few threatening glances around the lab when murmurs and shuffling began to compete with the speaker.

"It's an advert for their police forces. Feels like a bloody careers lesson," said Claire. "She's oblivious."

"Button it!" Ben hissed.

"Shall I make coffee before I die of boredom?"

"Good idea, but do it quietly."

The other uniformed shrew took over after twenty minutes and changed the mood.

"First, can I say what a pleasure it is to be here, and second, can I just correct your assumption, Ben? There are now over ten police authorities involved."

"Sorry?"

"There have been some developments since we last spoke to you. I'll fill you in. But, before I do, I must insist that what I am about to tell you all is not to be repeated outside this building and you will understand why."

There was a tangible charge in the room. His piercing stare darted from one person to another till he had eyeballed everyone in the room.

"The incident at Cantref Reservoir led to Peter Jenkins being hospitalized and almost murdered. We believe that another member of staff was involved."

Claire handed Ben a mug. "Have I missed anything?"

"Shut up and listen."

"They found Dr. Richard Parker, who was the last person seen with Peter Jenkins before he was given a potentially lethal overdose of morphine, at the bottom of the cliffs at Beachy Head, a renowned location for suicides. We found his car in the car park at the top of the cliff. It is our belief that either someone threw Parker from the cliff top or he jumped."

"Is he dead?" asked one of the lab technicians. Even DI Birch had to laugh at the question.

"Exceedingly!" said DC Churchman, which received a ripple of laughter around the lab.

"We tracked his movements leading up to his death, and so there are now multiple police authorities involved. Parker booked into the Excelsior hotel in Whitehaven, which is in Cumbria, and told the hotel's owner that he had left his credit card at home, which was untrue, and his car had a mechanical problem that prevented him from returning home, which we also believe to be untrue. We interviewed his wife, but she could not provide any logical reason for her husband to have driven to Whitehaven. We traced his car and phone to several locations in the Whitehaven area. One location was a street where a man was murdered and a female attempted suicide on the night that Parker was there.

"This is more like it," said Claire loudly. A few of the staff looked around, and Ben poked her in the back.

"The lady who attempted to end her life is an employee at the nuclear power plant at Sellafield. On the night of the murder, she went to work, which was not unusual as she was one of the top scientists on site and occasionally worked after office hours. What was unusual was that a security guard at the plant felt unwell and left work early. He was subsequently found deceased at the scene after a road accident just outside Monmouth in South Wales. These would normally be a series of unfortunate unrelated incidents, but there are far too many coincidences. I don't believe in coincidences, especially when it involves suspected murder, fatalities, attempted suicide, and suspected suicide."

Claire raised her hand.

"Yes, Miss Manson?"

"Can we see timelines for all these apparently related incidents, and what are your thoughts on why this has all happened?"

DI Churchman pulled a wad of notes from a briefcase and waved them in front of him. "Hard copies of the investigation summary. I'll also email a copy to Dr. Sharman."

Ben walked to the front, took the notes, paused, and turned to DI Churchman before handing them out.

"I appreciate your update, but for future reference, could I ask if the police would provide information in real time? We've been told this sizeable chunk of vital information after the horse has bolted. We can be far more effective if we are keeping abreast of events as they happen."

DI Churchman pushed his glasses further up his nose and looked down at Ben. "You appreciate that it takes time to gather and collate everything before we can release it?"

"I appreciate that, but this isn't a release for the press or the public. We are here to help you and we can't do that if you've closed an incident. For example, what is the status of the incident at the house in Whitehaven? Is the accident site in Monmouth available for us to examine?"

"We have teams at both sites dealing with it."

"With respect, DI Churchman. What is the point of you being here if you are inviting us to the party after the candles on the cake have already been blown out?"

"We are keeping you in the loop," said Churchman, whose voice had developed a slight tremor.

"For what purpose?"

Churchman looked toward DI Birch for support. She bent her head and looked at the floor.

Ben could see that it was getting uncomfortable and changed tack.

"From our perspective, we have an unidentified flying object breaking up over a large reservoir. The outer casing, which at first appeared to be a meteor, is, in fact, a manufactured molded casing for a small orb-like flying craft. We believe that this may be at the bottom of the reservoir."

"I can confirm that a thorough search of the bed of the reservoir was carried out by a team of police divers and they found nothing resembling a small orb," said Churchman.

Ben nodded. "Agreed. I do not doubt that. I've informed you of these facts already. Have you considered my proposal that you should do another search with sonar and divers, as there may be something down there that you can't find because it doesn't want to be found? It has either buried itself under the lake bed or moves to evade detection."

"We looked at it, but to be honest, a UFO seemed ridiculous. Our chief wouldn't commit the resources."

"So, what your chief is saying is that the scientific facts count for nothing?"

"No. I didn't say that."

"I beg to differ. That's exactly what you said."

Claire saw the redness rising from Ben's neck and walked to the front.

"Teas and coffees are ready." She stepped between Ben and the DI, facing Ben.

"Would DI Birch and DI Churchman like to join you and take coffee and biscuits in your office? Ron, please join them. I will be there shortly."

She walked to the kitchen, hoping the telltale sign meant that Ben wasn't about to blow his stack.

After an unproductive twenty minutes, the police duo left the building. Ben gripped the arms of the swivel chair and kicked the waste paper bin through the door of the office.

SEVENTEEN

"I think your obstacle is about to be removed," said Ron with a smug grin.

"What are you talking about?"

"The comedy act that just left."

"How?"

"I just made a call to my boss, who talked to an Old Etonian school chum in the Home Office, who fired a rocket up the backsides of certain high-ranking officers in Cumbria and Dyfed-Powys police who are the leading the police investigation."

"Really?"

"Ben. You can sit there smoldering for the rest of the day or you can get your arse in gear and visit the incident sites that are now available for us to examine. The crash site at Monmouth is the obvious starter as it's on your doorstep, then Whitehaven in Cumbria. Sussex police have impounded and secured Richard Parker's car at Beachy Head, so that can wait."

Ben smiled and slapped Ron on the back. "Great work Ron. You're not just a pretty face." He looked at Claire over Ron's shoulder, willing her not to make a comment. She didn't need to say a word, as her face said everything.

"Both forces have given you the green light to work with them. No surprise there," said Ron.

"Common sense prevails at last! Right then. Let's get this show on the road," said Ben, rubbing his hands.

Stopped from re-entering the incident scene under the guise of leaving a piece of medical equipment behind, the police sergeant informed Sue Dean they would find it for her and she could pick it up later from the station. She drove back into Monmouth, took the bridge over the river to an elevated bank hidden behind a large weeping willow tree, overlooking the River Wye, where the alien observed fresh activity on the other side of the river bank and reflected on its new host. Sue Dean proved troublesome to manipulate, apart from her driving skills and local knowledge, and was of little actual use, so the alien shut her conscious mind down to make unhindered progress. The other hosts had been easy to control, but medical issues and drugs for her depression were an unwelcome interference and another new host would need to be found.

The more pressing issue was the flask, still in the car. Being denied access was frustrating, but the police would eventually remove the flask or it would remain at the crash site until they removed the car from the field. Hopefully, one or the other would take place soon and there would be an opportunity to retrieve it and take it to the ship as planned. Apart from the unforeseen accident, good progress had been made so far, and the alien was confident in its ability to see the mission through to a successful conclusion.

At the same time the alien watched from the far bank of the river, Ben stood on the dual carriageway, taking in the entire scene, studying scrape marks and distortions on the barrier where the car cleared the verge. Fifty feet of undisturbed field before the first point of impact, deep with a large brown rut. Gouges and dirt from subsequent impacts. A door impaled in the ground. Wing mirrors, rear window, pieces of chrome trim, and a ripped out headlight peppered the field. The tire, torn from its axle, retrieved from the River Wye far below, rested on the side of the riverbank. Paper and other ejected contents scattered showed the route of the vehicle's last violent journey and the remains of the car itself lay upside down and broken, a stark lonely figure at the end of a runway of terror. Jersey cows, about to be herded into the next field by an approaching tractor, chewed and watched with mild interest as Ben stepped warily over the twisted crash barrier onto the wet, grassy slope.

"Careful as you go, it's slippery as hell all the way down, till it levels out," said the ruddy-faced sergeant as he helped Claire over the barrier. "One of our senior officers already went flying on his backside all the way down," he said with a small chuckle.

"Were you here at the scene after it happened?" asked Ben.

"Yes. A difficult one, as you can see. The call came in at— hang on a second." He pulled out his notebook and almost tripped over the first impact rut. "Sorry. First call made at four twelve am by Jakub Lipska, the driver of a goods lorry, traveling from Poland. Brave man. Almost killed himself running down here to get to the car. Can you imagine it? Just getting light, running down this slope. How the hell he didn't break his neck is beyond me."

"Where is he now?"

"Checked out of hospital around eleven this morning. They thought he was concussed, but it turned out to be shock with no recollection of the accident when we interviewed him.

"Has Jakub Lipska left yet?"

"No, he checked his vehicle over at the local garage where we took it after the accident and is staying the night at the King's Head

Hotel in Monmouth. Off to Dublin, first thing in the morning, to finish his delivery, or so he thinks. Our crash investigation unit won't let him turn a wheel till they have finished looking at his vehicle. Reckon he won't be sailing across the Irish Sea for at least a day or two."

"You say he can't remember the accident?"

"Can't remember a thing. Still can't recall anything, last time I spoke to him."

"The deceased man. Where was he found?"

He turned, walked back up the field, leaned out over the barrier and whistled to one of the PC's stood in the coned off area at the edge of the dual carriageway. "Take over here until I get back and keep your eye out for any more press. They've been around here like flies around shit and seem to think the road verge is their own personal parking space."

He walked back toward them with both arms outstretched waving them slightly for balance. "Okay, follow me. I'll show you and be careful. It's as slippery as hell." The Sergeant led them down the steep slope and around the car to a patch of flattened grass. "A paramedic found the lorry driver slumped over the deceased, blood all over his hands from the dead man."

The surface of the field in this area gave little away, with footprints mashed into mud from a multitude of emergency service personnel.

"He tried to resuscitate the deceased man. Got to give it to him. He did his best. Most folks would've stood back, leaving it to the paramedics, assuming they can perform miracles after it's too late."

"Can we take a peek at the car, inside and out?" Said Ben.

"Be my guest. We've done our thing. Waiting for you to do yours before it's removed. You must have quite a pull with the higher ups. We were supposed to wrap up here hours ago until we were told to meet you here and offer you every assistance."

Ben winked at Claire. Ron had certainly pulled the right strings.

While Ben took photos through the gaping driver's side, where the door had been ripped out during the car's flight, Claire started sketching the field, the car's location, and the position of the body, outlined in yellow spray paint.

From the other side of the river, binoculars tracked Ben's every move to see if he found anything in the car. The police hadn't discovered the flask under the seat, confirmed by the telltale low-level radiation source the alien could detect within the wrecked vehicle.

Claire walked in a grid around the field dodging thistles and cow pats. Something glistened in the grass to the left of the first rut, so she bent down and teased out four intertwined metal circles embedded in grass and mud. The Audi badge from the front of the car, where it nose-dived into the field.

Ben pulled on neoprene gloves and climbed in through the door opening. Nothing unusual in the car, apart from the catastrophic damage. With the roof partly caved in, it was an awkward squeeze at a neck twisting angle to get inside and as he swung around in the driver's seat, soil from the back of the sun visor dropped into his hair. He brushed it off and lost his grip on the camera, which slid behind into the back seat well. He bent over to retrieve it and something caught his eye glinted on the back of the seat. Wedged between the seat and backrest the top of a silver flask protruded out. Ben took several photos, pointing the camera in the flask's general direction, finding it impossible to get into a position to line the shots through the viewfinder. He prized the flask out of the tight gap, laid it flat on the seat and took more photos. The contents of the glove compartment revealed a service book for the car and a torch. The accident had either ejected any other loose contents or the police had removed everything else from the car's interior.

"Am I okay to take some articles for analysis?" asked Ben.

"I don't see why not," said the sergeant. "Our investigation is over. I'll need to log everything, though. Anything removed belongs to the deceased's family and will need to be returned to us."

"Of course."

"Do you think you will be much longer?" said the sergeant,

cupping his hands and blowing into them. "Bloody freezing stood in this damp field, and the lads are starving." he said and chuckled again.

"No, were all but done here," said Ben, starting to shiver himself.

They bagged and logged several items retrieved from the trail of debris for analysis before Ben, Ron, and Claire left the scene, bound for Cumbria.

Sue Dean, parked in the garage near the roundabout they would have to pass, waited for the BMW to arrive.

EIGHTEEN

The Blue BMW vanished just after the turnoff for the A55 into North Wales and even though Sue Dean pushed her car to the limit, she couldn't keep up with it but felt an overwhelming urge to keep going, guided by the unseen force within.

"Are we nearly there yet?" said Claire.

"God! Are you really twenty-five?" said Ben, glancing at the screen. "The GPS says it should take another two hours, give or take, but that's after we stop for coffee at the next services, six miles up the motorway."

"Unless you are busting for the little boy's room, why don't we just keep going?"

"It's alright for you. You're not sitting behind the wheel. Time's not a problem and, just to keep you happy, there's a Costa drive-through at the next services."

Ron started snoring gently in the back, but after a couple of miles, after his head slumped forward onto his chest, wheezes turned into a roaring bellow.

Claire poked his shoulder. He opened his eyes for a second and fell asleep. Within thirty seconds, he was snoring again, even louder.

"Don't go through the drive-through. I can't stick that bloody racket. We'll go in and leave him here."

The services cafe section was empty apart from a couple of truck drivers.

"So glad we stopped. My legs are seizing up," said Ben, sprinkling sugar on the fern pattern in the cappuccino froth. "I didn't realize how far away the Lake District is and that traffic near Manchester—what's all that about? Another two hours of driving and I'll be a bloody cripple. "

Claire stared out the window. "Is he married?"

"Who?"

"The ugly one in the back making all the racket."

"Interested in him are you?" said Ben. "Mmm—Claire Logan, now there's a weird thought."

"Ugh! Don't!" she said, screwing her face up and waving like she was trying to ward off a persistent wasp. "I was only wondering if any poor sod would want to wake up next to that?"

Ben stared over his cup with a twinkle in his eye.

"Well? Is he married or not?"

"Yes, he's happily married and has been for the last five years."

"What's his wife like? I just can't imagine anyone being desperate enough to live till death us do part with that sweaty, creepy man."

"Graham is a real nice bloke," said Ben, waiting for her reaction with a grin.

"Graham?"

"His husband."

Claire put her cup down. "You're kidding me."

He laughed. "Nope."

"Ron's gay?"

"Ever heard of a woman called Graham before?"

"You're having me on Sharman."

"Deaf are you? I said he has a husband, or do you believe Ron is the most convincing drag king on the planet?"

"Seriously?"

"Yes, he's gay. He just doesn't sing it out from the rooftops."

"Bloody hell. That's the first time my gaydar hasn't gone off. Hang on. I've caught him leering at me a few times, and he's quite flirty."

"So? Perhaps he's bi-sexual. Play your cards right and you could be his bit on the side."

"Please, don't."

Ben took another sip of coffee, enjoying Claire's facial expressions at this new revelation.

"Well, I'm flabbergasted! You sure you're not winding me up?"

"Ask him yourself."

"As if I'm going to do that!"

"Ask Kath O'Brien when we get back. She bumped into Graham in the Black Bear last time Ron Stayed down and you know what she's like. She had the guts out of them both. I have known for ages and I went to the wedding."

"Don't tell me. You were the bridesmaid?" said Claire and they both laughed.

"Anyway, it's no big deal. Ron's a nice guy and very good at what he does, despite what you think."

Claire shook her head.

"Enough of Ron's sexual preferences, what's this hotel you booked us in like?"

"It looks seedy on the website," said Claire. "Old, tired and tatty, as if it could do with a total refurb."

"Oh, crap!"

"Hey. You wanted to stay at the same hotel as Dr. Richard Parker."

"Just hope I won't regret it."

"You won't. I checked it out online and rang the hotel manager and interrogated him. My guess is that it's not the Ritz and isn't quite the pits, so don't panic. Whoever did the web site photos was clueless. I looked at the reviews and apart from one idiot, who gave it a one star review because the weather was bad while they stayed there, the rest are three and four stars, so it should be okay.""

"Has it got a bar? I could murder a beer."

"Is that all you can think of?" said Claire. "Bar or no bar, we need to be bright eyed and bushy tailed in the morning. We're meeting another cop to look at the house on Elmwood Drive."

"The Groves house?" said Ben.

"Yes. After that, we're going to see the lab where Helen Groves was working at Sellafield."

"You have been busy, Miss Manson. Bit of a Busman's holiday."

"Busman's what?"

"Never mind. Can you check our email? "

"Hang on. Let me fire up the phone."

"Looks like Ron has arisen," said Ben, looking out through the window and sniggering. "God, he looks ghastly white."

"Shit—he's getting out and walking over."

"Well, at least you know he won't be hitting on you!"

Ron walked in, combing his hair.

"Cold in the ground, was it Ron?" said Claire.

Ben burst out laughing.

"Funny girl! Why didn't you wake me up?"

"You looked so peaceful, and I didn't want to disturb your beauty sleep, Ron," said Claire.

"Have I got time for a coffee? I could do with something to wake me up."

"Yes, and you can get me another latte, please," said Ben, passing him the empty cup.

Ron mopped his brow with a stained, wrinkled handkerchief as he made his way to the servery. Claire watched, her mouth almost resembling the letter n.

"Stop it, Claire," said Ben. "The trouble with your face is it tells me and the entire universe exactly what is going on inside that judgemental head of yours. He'll catch you out one day."

"I don't care if he does," she said, picking up her mobile and flicking through several emails. Her eyes widened. "This is interesting"

"What?"

"Dr. Hernandez wants to talk to you about the toxicology report for Peter Jenkins."

"That's good. I didn't expect the report back this quick."

"The next message is also from Hernandez. He's received the toxicology report for Dr. Richard Parker and says there's a link between both men."

"Did he say what it is?"

"No, but it must be interesting. He said to ring him day or night."

"Call him up and pass me your phone."

Ron reappeared, looking much refreshed after a trip to the gents and a face full of cold water. "What's happening? Who's he on the phone to?"

"Dr. Hernandez has some important info."

"About what?"

"Don't know yet till he gets off the blower. A link between Dr. Parker's and Peter Jenkins' toxicology reports."

They sat in silence, ear-wigging Ben's conversation but not getting much from the one-way conversation. Ben, saying nothing, being the listener.

He passed the phone back to Claire. "Have you ever heard of scopolamine?"

"Mmm. Rings a bell from my days in uni," said Claire.

"Does devil's breath ring any other bells."

"Yes! Now I remember. It's a mind-altering drug. We had a narcotics lecture about the drugs trade in South America. It comes from the nightshade plant and can allow someone to control a person's mind so much they can manipulate them into committing crimes. Even murder."

"Not conclusive. But yes, that's the one I'm talking about."

"What has Hernandez found?"

"The toxicology reports in both men have confirmed traces of a drug very similar to scopolamine. They're still working on it, but Hernandez said it has qualities they haven't seen before or have located on the National Database register. What do you think, Ron?"

"Sounds like somebody or something drugged the victims and controlled them."

"What about you, Claire?"

"My brain's doing cartwheels here. I'm trying to tie all this together. Let's assume that aliens in a crash landed spacecraft triggered the sequence of events. Let's also assume that they've administered the drug to get humans to do something for them. If I'm right, the burning question is, what do they want our victims for?"

"What do they want or need?" said Ben.

They sat in contemplation.

Claire broke the silence.

"Bloody hell. I see what they are up to. A spacecraft lands in a lake in the middle of nowhere. Why? Not for a sightseeing trip. Because it has a problem. A malfunction? They've run out of fuel or had a mechanical malfunction or both. What's on the doorstep of Whitehaven? The biggest storage of nuclear waste products in the country, where two people involved in the sequence of events, just happen to work. It has to link this all this together."

"A plausible theory," said Ben, rising from his seat. "Which we'll discuss further in the car. Let's crack on before today becomes tomorrow before we have even got there."

The Blue BMW pulled out of the services and rejoined the M6. Ben kept the speed down as they discussed the possibility of alien mind manipulation and didn't notice the green Ford Fiesta that closed in behind and slowed, maintaining a reasonable distance, following them all the way through Cumbria to the Excelsior hotel at Whitehaven.

NINETEEN

Both divers searched sector eight for almost half an hour as visibility had improved since the last dive in the same spot almost a week before and even through the small amount of haze on the bed, caused by their own exertions, lingered they could pick out every the stone and piece of shale at the bottom of the reservoir.

For Russel Fox, on autopilot having chalked up hundreds of diving hours, this dive was a luxury. Deep water, no dumped debris, and almost clear visibility, which was in complete contrast to his usual experience of wading across broken bottles, old bikes, bricks, and an assortment of dead cats and dogs. A swimming pool compared to the usual horror swamps he had to search.

His partner, Jane Clancy, a newbie on the team, loved the thrill of only her third dive. Fresh out of training school and over-enthusiastic about everything to do with work, she, the playful puppy and he, the hard-nosed, seasoned instructor, made an unlikely pairing.

Russel towered over her, with shoulders almost as wide as she was tall with a dark complexion, piercing brown eyes and full wiry black beard, in sharp contrast to his blond-haired, blue eyed 'apprentice'. Jane Clancy's curvaceous figure and stunning Scandinavian looks turned heads wherever she went, and it didn't take long for the rest of the diving team to label them 'Beauty and the Beast'.

The grid search in operation, drawing to an end for the day, had a small area of the reservoir bed left to survey. Above, on the police RIB, other members of the team were as wet as the divers below the surface as fine rain swirled across the reservoir in an icy cloak, making the temperature feel ten degrees lower.

"You okay down there, Russ?" said the sergeant of the surface team.

"Yes. Almost done. Another two lines of search and we'll be up."

"Gauge check?"

"Fifty bars. What about you, Jane?"

"Same."

"Yes, we're both okay on the air front. Both on fifty bars."

"Copy that."

Jane swam nearer to the bottom. And lifted some stones.

"Anything down there?" said Russel.

"No, thought something moved. Reflection from sunlight and clouds makes everything look as if it's moving."

She lifted a few more stones, stirring up the mud. The water clouded.

Something large and silver streaked past her visor. She lurched backwards, arms and legs flailing.

"What the—?"

She could hear Russel laughing as a huge rainbow trout disappeared from sight.

"You wouldn't be much good at tickling trout!" he bellowed into his facemask.

"Frightened the life out of me. Big one wasn't it."

"Best you come up a bit before you lose visibility."

As he looked down, mud swirled up in a vortex, blocking out the bed of the reservoir.

"Jane, come up now. I've lost eye contact."

"Hang on a minute. I think I may—"

"Jane?"

A sudden surge from beneath lifted him upward, making him breach the surface.

"Jane?"

She felt her torso being swept sideways by a powerful force that almost ripped the mask off her face. Her neck arched back as the current dragged her at high speed above the bed of the reservoir for a few seconds, then stopped. She sank to the bottom and kicked through the swirling mud for the surface.

"Jane?"

"Over here."

He turned to her, waving at him seventy feet away.

"How the hell did you get there?"

"Current took me along the bottom."

"But there is no current."

"Well, there was down there. Strong undercurrent. Thought I was going to break my neck!"

The RIB moved toward her.

"Come over here. We haven't finished yet," said Russel.

"Perhaps we ought to get out?"

"We will when we've finished."

As she swam towards him underwater, a mass of brown clouds swirled below marking the trail she'd been hauled across. Silt floated downwards, hitting the bottom, settling and fanning outwards. Water below appeared still again, with no current. She continued, eyes fixed on the bed below. Several tiny fish swam next to her, keeping pace with her steady underwater front crawl, just below the surface.

"Hurry, we haven't got all day," said Russel.

She kicked for the surface, but before she got there the tiny shoal if fish darted in all directions. Below her, something round rose out of the murk, revolving, vibrating, surrounded by twirling streams of silt. She twisted her arm so the wrist camera pointed down, but in a flash of metallic silver, the round object was gone, leaving the remnants of a spherical silt ghost behind.

"Russ, did you see that?"

"What?"

"Object below me. Round, metallic, about six feet across. Moving under its own steam."

"Can't see it. Where is it now?"

"Shot off to my left in your direction."

"Keep your eye out for it. I'll come over to you."

"Will do Russ. I think we've found what we've been looking for. Can you see it now? It must have passed you?

"Yes. It flashed right below me. Hell it's quick."

She saw a blur heading toward her at high speed before it disappeared again into another large plume of silt and mud that billowed upward. She watched and waited for Russel. The silt settled again with no sign of movement from the spherical object. With her eyes fixed on its last position, Jane kicked, letting herself rise upward. At the surface, she removed her facemask and looked all around, doing a complete circle. There was no sign of Russel.

She snapped the mask back in place and duck dived, but visibility had all but gone with a new silt cloud billowing upward, almost reaching the surface, blocking out any sign of the bed rock below.

"Russ, where are you?" Moving blind through the silt laden water, Jane lost all bearings, baled out and propelled herself upward.

The RIB moved alongside and one of the surface crew helped pull her out.

She ripped her face mask off and shut down the main valve.

"Where is he?" she said, looking all around the RIB.

"He must have dived again. We were monitoring you."

After calling him several times, a second RIB arrived at great speed following the distress call. Two divers were over the side and underwater in seconds.

A huge brown circle fanned out around the two ribs, making it impossible for the rescue teams to search by sight. Another RIB joined and four more joined the fingertip search of the bed. A series of giant bubbles erupted, causing the ribs to rock as the bubbles surged up under the boats, making the center of the reservoir appear to boil. The ribs had to make quick adjustments to stop them from capsizing. The turbulence stopped as quickly as it had started and a strange silent calm settled on the water.

"What the hell was that about?" said Jane, as all divers searching for Russel surfaced together.

One took off his face mask. "Stream of bubbles coming from one spot at the bottom. I could hear it and make out a solid gray sphere ejecting gas, which moved off at speed toward the dam."

"No sign of Russ?" said Jane.

There was no reply, and the diving teams disappeared under the water to resume the search.

The minutes ticked by, stretching out as the mood changed and Jane sobbed as reality set in. Another team arrived and ten divers frantically searched the bed, still unable to find their missing colleague after thirty minutes. Everyone assumed the search had changed from a rescue mission to body recovery.

Forty-five minutes into the emergency, the sergeant called for more backup cylinders, even though he knew that all hope of finding Russel Fox alive had gone. As he keyed the mic to make the request, a diver surfaced next to the boat.

"Where the hell did you go?" said Russel, pulling off his mask and looking at Jane..

Jane and surface crew froze.

"I said, where were you?"

She couldn't speak. The rest of the surface team sat gawping at him.

"Are you lot deaf?" he shouted

"Russ, I got on the RIB. You told me to swim toward you."

"What are you talking about?"

Other team members surfaced and six divers surrounded him.

"You can all get out now he's turned up," said the surface sergeant, staring at Russel.

"Russ, they've been looking for you for ages," said Jane, pointing at the other divers.

He pulled himself on board. "Is this some kind of stupid prank they taught you in training school?"

The sergeant leaned over. "Russel. You've been missing for forty-five minutes."

"What? I've been down there looking for Jane. You knew where I was."

"No, Russel. Not a peep from you for forty-five minutes. By my calculations, you should have run out of air about fifteen to twenty minutes ago. Let me look at your gauge."

Russel turned the gauge for him to read. The needle showed fifty bars.

The sergeant tapped the gauge, then rapped it with his knuckles.

"What are you doing?" said Russel, yanking the gauge away from him.

The Sergeant kept staring at him.

"What?" said Russel, looking from the sergeant to each of the other divers. He grinned at them. "Okay fellas. The jokes on me. What's the crack?"

When nobody laughed, Russel's grin ebbed away as he continued to look from one to the other in silence.

"Let's get back and discuss this further," said the Sergeant, swinging the RIB around and heading for shore.

The crews pulled the RIBs onto the bank and the divers assembled in the makeshift shelter.

The officer in charge tapped his watch. "Russel, how long have you been on your last dive?"

Russel stared at his watch in disbelief. Impossible. Nobody could do an hour and fifteen minutes on the cylinders they used and still come up with a load of air. He looked at the crew, waiting for someone to laugh. It must be a joke. But every one of them stood, stone faced, looking at him. He remembered doing the gauge check and checking the time. He'd only used thirty bars in over forty-nine minutes.

"Where have you been, Russel, for three-quarters of an hour while we had a full-scale emergency search team of over ten divers looking for you?"

"I was down there for a couple of minutes looking for Jane. I realize the time." He checked his watch again, then grabbed Jane's wrist, twisting it sideways till he saw the watch face. "But I don't believe what I'm seeing."

The sergeant wrapped things up. "Listen everyone. I'll need reports from all of you when we get back to base. For now, let's call it a day and get back to it first thing in the morning."

Russel pulled the thick neoprene head mask off, dropping it into its protective cloth bag. He sat back against the wall, confused and worried, and wiped away a trickle of diluted blood running from his left ear down the side of his neck.

TWENTY

The pounding on the bedroom door dragged Ben from an almost catatonic sleep. His hand searched for the bedside light, fumbled, found it, sat up, looked around, squinting in the harsh lamplight, not quite realizing where he was.

"Alright, alright I'm coming. Who is it?"

"It's me. Open up."

He opened the door, blinking and trying to focus.

Claire stood in the corridor in her dressing gown, then pushed her way past him.

"What are you up to, Claire?" he said, staring at his watch. "I've only been asleep half an hour."

She looked him up and down and laughed. "Nice boxer shorts! Get dressed and come downstairs. Someone's broken into your car."

Ben registered the distant sound of the car alarm. "Shit, perhaps it's just the alarm?"

"No, someone's smashed the passenger window. The manager just told me."

"Okay. Let me get dressed. Are you coming down?"

"Of course, but I better get dressed as well. I'll see you in reception and don't forget your car and room keys."

Ben, rubbing his eyes and yawning, reached reception where Claire was talking to the manager, looking radiant. She obviously hadn't been asleep when the manager called her.

They stepped out of the hotel main entrance into the biting cold mist where the car alarm filled the car park and the flashing hazard lights bounced off concrete walls, looked down upon by several other guests peering out of the upper windows.

The manager walked ahead with a torch, and Ben, wincing at the alarm, quickly silenced it as he followed.

"Sorry about this," said the manager. "We haven't had a car break-in for years!"

"It's not your fault," said Ben. "Can you call the police?"

"Already done it, but don't hold your breath. They probably won't turn up till the morning. They never do these days unless there's been a murder."

Ben peered in through the smashed passenger window but could see little inside the dark interior. He smiled ruefully, reminding himself that the trip to Whitehaven had gone too well, so far, and now this, a really inconvenient distraction when they needed to focus on the investigation. Was this the work of some passing opportunist thief, or someone with a more sinister purpose? On the plus side, the would be thief hadn't stolen the car, which would have been a real setback.

"Do you mind if I borrow your torch for a second?" said Ben.

"Certainly," said the manager, handing it over. Claire switched on her phone's torch app and walked around the car, looking for more damage.

The front seats had most of the glass on them from the shattered window. Ben could see the open glove compartment and the back seats pushed down, revealing the luggage compartment, empty apart for spare coats, which was how he left the car when they checked in. He shone the torch all around, being careful not to touch anything, just in case the police were going to look. He did a quick inventory in his head. Easy to remember, as very little remained inside the car after he locked it the night before.

"I think someone planned this," said Claire.

"How do you work that out?" said Ben.

"If it was an opportunist thief, how did they smash the window? There's no brick or anything else in or around the car, and that glass is very strong."

Ben walked into the street, shining the torch along the pavement on either side and onto the main road, finding nothing that might have been used to break the car window.

"They could have been carrying something to break toughened glass."

"Someone was looking for something specific in your car," said Claire. "I'd bet my wages on it."

Ben turned to the manager. "Can you contact the police again? The mobile signal's non-existent out here and I need to know if or when they are coming. I can't stand out here all night."

"Hang on a second," said Claire. "I can see blue lights."

A police patrol car entered the street in a hurry and, at the same time, the engine started on a car parked close to the hotel. A dark green Fiesta pulled away, with its front wheels spinning, and sped off passing the patrol car coming in the opposite direction.

"Gotcha," said Claire, peering into her mobile screen at a clear photo of the back of the Fiesta.

The patrol car sailed straight past the hotel at speed.

"Shit. Must be on the way to another incident," said Ben.

"I've got that car's registration here," she said, passing the phone to Ben.

The police arrived an hour later and logged the crime, but little else. The owner offered Ben a spare space in his lock-up garage to secure the damaged car and they got back to their rooms at just after three am.

Ben woke four hours later with his bedroom door being hammered on yet again.

"Hang on. Who is it?" He said, dragging his legs out of bed.

"It's me, Ron. I'm bloody starving. Are you ready for breakfast? You said to give you a knock at ten past seven, sharp."

Ron strolled in, appearing remarkably fresh, and looked Ben up and down with a puzzled look.

"Bloody hell, mate. You look like shite."

"Cheers, Ron. Claire and I have been up half the night. Someone broke into the car, about one in the morning. Surprised you didn't get woken up. Half the hotel guests were hanging out the windows watching. You must have been bloody dead to the world or deaf."

"Nope, didn't hear a thing, but I had my headphones on so I wouldn't have heard anything, anyway."

"Headphones?"

"Noise canceling headphones. Can't hear sod all with them in my lugholes Work a treat. Always use them when I stay away from home. You should try it if you have any trouble sleeping. It's the only way I can get some decent shut eye."

"I wouldn't use them. I'm always bloody knackered by about midnight, and sleep comes easy. Do us a favor Ron, go down and order me a full English breakfast and strong coffee. I'll be down in a minute. I need a quick shower and give Claire a knock while you're at it?"

"Was anything stolen?"

"No, I'm not that daft. I brought a few grands' worth of kit with us and brought everything in last night. The car was virtually empty."

"Bloody good job you did, Ben. Do you want me to arrange a hire car?"

"We'll see if they can fix it first. My guess is it will need to go to a bigger town to find a BMW dealer, maybe Kendal or Carlisle. I'll patch it up for now."

"Okay, but the offer stands," he said with a wink. "Let me wake the delectable Miss Manson," he said, rubbing his hands together.

"Best of luck. And Ron, strong coffee to bump start me!"

As Ben turned his mobile on, it pinged with several messages and rang at the same time.

"Morning, boss, sorry to disturb you. The police liaison officer has rung. They couldn't get hold of you."

"Hi, Roger, are we talking about the police in Wales or the local police up here in Cumbria? Only we are supposed to meet up with them today."

"No, it's the Welsh cops. It's about the new reservoir search. Something new has happened and they want your ear."

"How are you at work so early?"

"Kath O'Brien forgot her key and couldn't get hold of her hubby to bring it down."

"Joys of living and working in the same street, eh?"

"More like flogging a willing horse, I would say."

"Everything all right?"

"Yes, apart from Kath. It's everybody else's fault she left her keys at home. She's been ranting to me ever since."

"Best of luck with that! I'll ring the cops now, Cheers, Roger."

Ben arrived in the dining room for breakfast and the sight in the front bay window made him smile. Ron and Claire sat facing each other like a pair of weird, estranged lovers. She, young, beautiful, and refined. He, middle-aged, disheveled, and with a large tissue held to his bulbous nose. She turned to Ben and her face lit up.

"Your breakfast will be here in a minute. I sent it back once as you weren't here," said Ron, placing the crumpled tissue too close to the sugar bowl for Claire's comfort. She teased the bowl away with a teaspoon and pushed it toward Ben.

"Tea or coffee?" she said with a radiant smile.

"Coffee, as strong as possible. I'm bloody knackered."

Claire poured as a waitress arrived with the reheated breakfast.

She placed it in front of Ben with an apologetic nod. "Sorry, it's looking worse for wear but—"

"Just how I like it," said Ben to the young girl.

Ron pulled his phone out and scrolled. "There's a garage within a mile of here that can fix your car today. I've asked, and they can provide a courtesy car, but it won't be a beamer."

"How much?"

"Didn't say."

"Not much of a choice. Sod it — I'll go for that."

Ron got up. "Going for a ciggy. I'll sort the car with the garage while I'm outside."

Claire watched as Ben negotiated the curling bacon, dried mushrooms, and unpalatable egg. He pushed most of it aside and settled for toast.

"The reason I was late coming down is that I've been talking to the police about the reservoir search. They had a weird occurrence and one diver went missing underwater."

Claire's eyes widened. "Oh my God—drowned?"

"No, but they can't understand how he is alive. He had a cylinder with enough air for forty odd minutes and ended up underwater for well over an hour and had plenty of air left. There was a disturbance on the bed of the reservoir."

"What part of the reservoir?"

"The impact area with the deep indentation. The medics checked the diver and guess what??"

"Traces of a mind-controlling drug?"

"Got it in one. Two others saw a silver spherical object at the bottom of the reservoir which moved of its own accord. I told them to quarantine the diver. I also advised them to lock him up in a cell."

"Seriously?"

"Think about it, Claire. Peter Jenkins has something inside his skull confirmed by a scan and soon after, it has gone. He had also disappeared, feared, drowned, and now we have a police officer who thinks he's Marine Boy and can stay underwater longer than is humanly possible."

"So, the alien isn't influencing each person to carry out its goal externally. It's directing them from the inside."

"That's my latest theory, and if I'm right, the alien has transferred from person to person. Dr. Parker has a high level of the drug inside him but no alien. They have confirmed the same for Jeff Randle, who died in the car crash."

"Which means—"

"It must have transferred to another person."

"Could that person own a dark-colored Fiesta?"

TWENTY-ONE

Elmwood Drive stood out in complete contrast to the surrounding housing estates. Built before the Second World War for the top brass in the military, the surrounding farmland disappeared as a jungle of 70s suburban brick and concrete replaced it.

Ron tracked it down, with bloodhound precision, reciting every road memorized, which impressed Claire even though she gave no hint.

"Nice one, Ron. You should be a London cabbie," said Ben, who had just woken up in the back seat. As they crawled along the road looking for house numbers, a woman in a blue suit ushered them to park in the drive of the large house.

Ben wound the window down.

"Dr. Sharman?"

"Yes, that's me," he said, looking up at the smiling face.

"Pleased to meet you." She offered a hand. "DI Robyn Gates, Cumbria Constabulary."

"Likewise," he said, shaking hands through the window. Her youthful appearance surprised him, considering her rank, and guessed she must be nearer thirty than twenty. His gaze lingered for a little too long, mesmerized by her sparkling green eyes.

Claire coughed and poked him in the arm.

Ben took the hint and opened the door.

He introduced Claire and Ron as they got out and stood back on the edge of the drive to take in the imposing, wisteria-clad house. The multi-pitched roof with its weighty overhang added to the grandeur, with white rendered walls from another era, reminding him of his grandmother's house. The only scar on the face of this domestic beauty was the bay window, boarded up with ugly sheets of marine plywood.

"Very nice," he nodded. "Is the house empty?"

"Yes," said Robyn. "They will take Helen Groves into custody as soon as the hospital discharges her, which won't be for a few days."

"And her husband's body?"

"In the local morgue."

"Could you talk me through the events on the night of the incident here?"

She smiled and pointed to the front door. "Shall we go in?"

"In a minute. I'd like you to recall the events up to where your colleagues entered the property before we go into the house."

"Okay." She took a step back. "We received a 999 call from a neighbor, Don Caldwell, who lives opposite."

Robyn walked to the edge of the pavement and pointed out an even larger house across the road, visible above a thick laurel hedge.

"He heard a gunshot as he put the bins out for the weekly collection and walked across the road to investigate. Foolhardy, but also a brave thing to do. I certainly wouldn't have done it, but there again I have experience in firearms and he doesn't."

She walked across the gravel to the main front bay window.

"This boarded over window blew out from the gun that discharged inside the living room. Don Caldwell looked through the opening and saw Helen Groves standing over her husband. She was carrying a shotgun. He couldn't see Paul Groves' face, as he was looking in at the back of a settee, but with the blood spatter, which I will show you when we're inside, assumed she had shot him. He said she didn't see him and he ran back to his house, fearing she may try to shoot him as well."

"Wow! Must have been traumatic," said Claire.

"Extremely. We sent an armed response with backup. A patrol car got here first to observe. The armed response arrived and stormed the house, finding Paul Groves deceased on the settee in the front living room and—"

Ben interrupted. "Do you mind if you continue the account inside?"

"Of course."

She pushed the front door open, and they stood in the spacious hallway. DI Gates opened the door to the main living room.

The living room was modern and minimalist, with a curved leather sofa, many exotic plants, and a huge plasma TV in total contrast to the elegant tiled entrance hall. Apart from a few art déco sculptures, the living room had the vibe of a futuristic garden at the Chelsea Flower Show.

"We found Paul Groves seated on the settee at this end. She walked in from where we're standing and discharged one cartridge at almost point-blank range into his face."

Ron winced. "Nasty!"

"There was another cartridge in the shotgun which I believe she intended to use on herself."

"How did you know she intended to turn the shotgun on herself?" said Claire, taking notes.

"She intended to shoot him first and succeeded and then commit suicide with the shotgun, but when you have limited reach, it becomes difficult to kill yourself with a shotgun. Helen Groves is a petite woman. I think she failed to reach the trigger and decided in a panic to find a different way to kill herself."

"Bit of an assumption?" said Ron.

"Not just an assumption. I'll explain in a minute," said Robyn, stepping into the hallway.

"If you wanted to kill your partner with a shotgun and top yourself, wouldn't you plan it better?" said Ben.

"Yes, if it was premeditated," Ron commented.

Robyn moved to the side of the staircase, pointing up. "The second response team found Helen Groves hanging from a curtain tie-back from the stair banister above me. It was a bungled attempt, as the tieback failed under her weight. As she passed out, it unraveled, and she ended up lying on the floor at the back of the staircase with enough slack released from her neck to survive. The first team in would have seen her, except she lay on the floor out of sight here," she said, stepping around to the underside of the stairs. "She'd taken the cord from the living room curtains with Paul Groves' blood on it and used it to hang herself after shooting him. Does that sound like good pre-planning?"

"It proves nothing," said Ben, kneeling on a step halfway up the staircase, peering at the balustrades. "Who knows what goes through the mind of someone who just killed their husband?"

"The team released Helen Groves from the curtain tie and while they were reviving her, an officer noticed a red mark under her chin in the shape of a figure-of-eight. This was consistent with the shotgun's double barrel being forced upward against her skin. It all points to her trying and failing to kill herself with the shotgun. We'll confirm that with forensics, but I'm confident I'm right."

Ben considered the scene. Wife trying to commit suicide in the hallway. Husband dead in the living room, window blown out. He stepped outside and turned full circle on the drive, taking in the street, house, front courtyard and drive, then listened, hearing only sparrows chirping from the guttering above.

"Anyone else around beside the man across the road?" he said, picturing the gunshot shattering the tranquility of Elmwood Drive.

"She has inquisitive neighbors, but only the Caldwells heard the gun go off and recognized it as a gunshot. We've done a house to house and other neighbors were out, or heard nothing and the one family that heard it, about three doors down, thought it was a car backfiring. Jean Caldwell, wife of Don Caldwell, who put the call in, said that she knew Helen Groves was having an affair. In fact, the man she alleged her to be having an affair with was here in the house with her before Paul Groves arrived back from the gym. She said that he is a regular visitor and always parks up the road in the same place on the opposite side before he walks across. He never had to knock and was always let in quickly and only ever visited when Paul Groves was not at home."

"Could have just been a friend?" said Claire. "Doesn't mean he's her bit on the side."

"Jean is adamant he is her bit on the side. Every visit from this man results in the bedroom curtains being drawn after he arrives and opened as soon as he leaves. I'll leave you to come to your own conclusion."

"Has this secret lover been traced?" said Claire

"Not yet, but there are clues. Jean gave us a description of his car, a white BMW type. She said she wasn't hot on car makes but said it looked posh."

Claire laughed. "BMW posh, eh?"

Ben gave her a look of disdain. "Cars all seem the same these days, particularly if you aren't a car person. So, do you have anything else apart from a posh white car?"

"Yes. An excellent description of lover boy."

"Any CCTV available on the day of the shooting?"

Robyn laughed. "I find it astonishing that the Groves don't have any security measures in place, despite the high crime rate for break-ins and car theft in the area. We found nothing on the front of their house or CCTV from their neighbors."

"The report I received through email today said that there was a second blood trace in the living room," said Ben

"Yes, that was from Helen Groves. A tiny amount on the carpet right there." She pointed to a small patch set back from the rest of the blood spatter around and behind the settee.

"Can we take a sample?"

"Of course. We've finished our investigation."

"What's the likely outcome for Helen Groves?"

"I believe the evidence is strong enough for a guilty charge for premeditated murder. On saying that, you can never predict the Crown Prosecution's view or case outcomes."

"Would it be possible to speak to the lady across the road?"

Robyn laughed again. "I'm sure she would love to help. She seems to have been reveling in the whole thing!"

TWENTY-TWO

Claire collected samples from the living room and hallway while Ben and Robyn Gates crossed the road to number thirty-two, where a female figure watched them from an upstairs window.

Jean Caldwell couldn't contain the look of satisfaction as she welcomed them in, ushering them through to the conservatory, where tea, coffee, and an array of biscuits and cakes had been laid out well before they knocked on the door.

"He used to turn up every time Paul Groves went to the gym," she said, without prompting, pouring each of them coffee. "Like clockwork. She must have told him when her husband was going out. Stands to reason, doesn't it? How else could he have known?"

"How do you know Mr. Groves was going to the Gym?" said Ben.

She smiled, pushing the plate of custard creams towards him. "Dressed in his designer sports gear, carrying a posh gym bag. My son goes to the same gym, and he said Paul Groves goes there at least three times a week. When I gave our Nigel some dates he said that Paul was at the gym for two of them."

"Dates? How many dates?"

She pulled a well-thumbed notebook out of the coffee table drawer and opened a bookmarked page.

"Six."

Ben tried not to look at Robyn's raised eyebrows he saw out of the corner of his eye.

Ben started taking notes as she talked, but found it hard to keep up with her.

"He would drive through the street to check if her husband's car had gone, like he was on some sort of reconnaissance mission, then come back about five minutes later. He always parks in the same spot and sits in his car for a while before getting out and walking, bold as brass, across the road. Guilty as hell he was. I can see where he parks from my spare bedroom and when he's at her front door, I can watch him from my living room window."

Ben checked his notes. "You said he had a white BMW or a similar car?"

"Ooh Yes. Big white posh thing. We had one in the past but changed it as there's no need for anything fancy now that the kids have moved out. Just me and Don, now you see. We don't go out that much anyway and I like to keep an eye on my Don working in the flower beds." She swept her arm across the window overlooking the garden. "It's stunning in full bloom."

"You have a lovely garden, Mrs. Caldwell," said Ben, admiring a blaze of flowers through the French windows.

"Yes, it is wonderful," she said with a proud smile. "My Don's got green fingers. He only has to touch a plant to get it growing and flowering. I've won so many prizes for my roses and dahlias. I've lost count."

"So, an older car?" said Ben, steering her back to the reason they were there.

"Think so. Can't swear to it, though. I walked past it a few times while he was up to no good with her, when I took the dog for a walk, you know."

"Can you describe the man who visits Mrs. Groves?"

"Handsome toy boy, that's what he is, and at least twenty years younger than her, in his early thirties, I'd say. Black short hair with a bit of a mustache, slim, athletic, and towering over her. She's a shorty and old enough to be his mother. I told our Don that and he said she's well over fifty. It's amazing how a bit of hair dye and Botox can roll back the years."

Ben saw Robyn's sideways glance at Jean Caldwell's jet black hair, shiny forehead and wrinkle free skin.

"Amazing," said Ben. Robyn had to turn away. "What type of clothes does he wear?"

"Pretty casual most of the time. Jeans, polo shirt, that sort of thing. During the winter, he used to turn up in a great big coat with the hood pulled over. Lately, he's been more brazen. Sometimes wears sunglasses. Just looks pretty normal, I suppose."

"Can you think of anything else?"

"No, not really. It was a regular thing and has been going on since the end of last year. Parks in the same spot. Walks over and she lets him in. Spends an hour doing whatever they get up to and leaves," she said, rolling her eyes.

"Perhaps he's just a friend?" said Ben.

Jean Caldwell laughed out loud and shook her head. "It's obviously an affair, by the way she looks up and down the street when she opens the door. I stay well back in the shadows or pull the blinds and watch through the gaps and I always switch the light off so she can't see me. The curtains in the upstairs bedroom close a minute after he gets there and open just after he goes. Let's be fair. It's not rocket science to work out they've been at it."

Ben looked at Robyn and mouthed 'anything else?'. She shook her head.

"Thank you, Mrs. Caldwell," said Ben. "You've been really helpful, and these cakes are delicious. Did you make them yourself?"

"Oh gosh no. My husband does all the cooking in this house. I'm far too busy to make cakes. My Don is one in a million. Most of my friends moan about their husbands, but not me. My Don is so domesticated and can wash, clean, iron, cook and does everything in the garden and even goes to the supermarket for our weekly shop."

"Well, he does sound like one in a million. Please thank him for me and if you remember anything else, here's my card. Please call me any time."

They stepped out of the Caldwell's front door and Ben fancied that Jean Caldwell's grin was wider than anything Lewis Carrol could have conjured up.

"Her poor husband," said Ben. "No wonder she's too busy to cook, spying on everyone from her window!"

Robyn laughed as they crossed the road. "Yes, she is rather observant."

Ben looked over his shoulder. Jean Caldwell smiled from her living room window and waved. He waved back.

"She's still watching, I take it?" said Robyn.

"Yep. She's there all right, like she's on sentry duty. You can just see her with a whip in hand on the garden patio as poor old Don digs his life away in the borders."

"She might not be most people's cup of tea," said Robyn. "But I'm just glad there are people like her that keep their eyes open. Most folk would say they saw nothing, even when we know damned well they have."

"True. But I still think she's a nightmare. How much do you reckon she's spent on having her face and the rest of her done?"

Robyn snorted. "She's got to be seventy, if she's a day, with the figure of a twenty-five-year-old. The top lip, shiny forehead and perfect boobs must have cost a few quid. No wonder her husband does all the housework. She must be permanently under the knife!"

Ben continued past the entrance door of the Groves' house and peered through a gap in the temporary boarding on the bay window. Claire was still busy inside, swabbing the blood stains on the carpet.

"Do you think it's something to do with the boyfriend?"

"Not sure yet," said Robyn. "The strange thing is that her mobile phone records show no evidence of a clandestine lover. All the numbers we found are friends, businesses or work and there are only a few, so it was easy to check out."

"Surely there must be some communication going on between them?"

"You would put money on it, but no, nothing. They were careful, and we found no link between Helen Groves and a potential lover after checking her social media and email addresses."

Ben grinned and waved again at the house opposite.

Robin, sniggered, resisted the temptation to turn around.

"She's a nosey old bat." He waved again and turned to Robyn. "I bet old Don Caldwell spends all day in the garden out of her way. No wonder it looks so good! I'd hate to have her living opposite me."

"Better than CCTV and a guard dog," said Robyn. "At least she's given a half decent description of the toy boy."

"What about burner phones?"

"Possible, but we didn't find one in the house and Helen Groves was in no fit state to dispose of it, hanging off a curtain tie back at the bottom of the stairs."

"Unless she keeps it somewhere else?"

"We may never know unless she tells us."

Ben stopped on the drive and looked back. Jean Caldwell was still in the window.

"Could I talk to Helen Groves?"

Robyn nodded. "You can if her brief will let you. Helen's daughter has gone to town to get her mother a real high flyer from London. He's a Rottweiler, apparently."

"I'm used to fierce dogs. Jean Caldwell wasn't too difficult."

Claire was still taking photos and making notes when they walked into the house.

"Ron has just nipped out to get your car. It's done," said Claire, replacing the camera back in its case.

"Fantastic. How are you looking in here?"

"I'm finished. I was just double checking all the photos were in the order as I logged them down." She walked to the window. "Here's Ron now, with your shiny new window."

The blue BMW pulled up on the drive back to its pristine condition. Ben frowned, seeing Ron get out of the car with a half-smoked Marlboro hanging from his lip.

"I think we're all done here," said Ben. "Thanks, Robyn. You've been so helpful. I'm really grateful," he said, offering her his hand.

"You don't get rid of me that easily, Dr. Sharman," she said, taking his hand in both of hers. "You're following me to the gatehouse at Sellafield. I've arranged it, but we're having lunch first at the Wheatsheaf in Egremont, an olde-worlde village pub on the way. One of our senior officers wants to meet you. There's a table reserved, and he's footing the bill."

They stood, hands locked for a second. Claire winked at Ben behind Robyn's back.

"An offer we can't refuse," said Ron. "I'm bloody famished."

"Yes, that would be nice," said Ben awkwardly. "If you would like to show us the way?"

"Certainly." Robyn drew the living room curtains and locked up.

"Nice to have you back," said Ben, patting the roof of his car. "Great job, Ron. You can't tell someone smashed the window."

"It bloody well should be a good job at four hundred quid," said Claire. "You better put this through your insurance."

"I suspected it would be about that," said Ben ruefully. "Never mind, we're having a freebie on Cumbria Constabulary."

"Robyn's' nice," said Claire. "She got the hots for you."

"Don't be ridiculous!"

Claire laughed. "I can tell. She can't keep her eyes off you."

Claire looked with satisfaction as Ben blushed. He didn't respond.

After Robyn introduced everyone, they sat down in the dining section of the Wheatsheaf. Ben was curious why the chief superintendent insisted on wining and dining them. The chief superintendent assured Ben that they would receive any assistance Cumbria

Constabulary could provide. Ben smiled, impressed that a single phone call by Ron cut through a mile of red tape and brought the main man in Cumbria Constabulary to the table. After an hour of polite chatter, Ben thanked him for the excellent meal and hospitality and, as Robyn's boss gave his fond farewells, Ben felt the mobile buzz in his pocket.

When they pulled out of the car park, he put the voice mail on loudspeaker.

"Hello, Dr. Sharman. This is Jean Caldwell. You asked me to call you if I remembered anything and I remembered something after you left. Her fancy man came to the Grove once in uniform. Pretty sure he works at Sellafield. I remember walking past the car and seeing a staff parking permit for Sellafield in the window. Hope that helps. I'll try you again later."

TWENTY-THREE

The fire officer watched his crew wrestle with a large canvas tarpaulin, dragging it over the car and tying it down to hide the interior from rubberneckers. Satisfied that all was in place, he climbed into the cab, removed his helmet, and reached for the microphone.

"From alpha two six, Watch Manager Mackenzie, A595 near Howgate roundabout. Stop for car fire. One person reported in vehicle confirmed deceased by medical team in attendance. Awaiting instructions from police prior to extrication of body from car. Will remain at the scene. Can you confirm ETA of senior officer, over?"

"Stand by,"

He replaced his helmet and dismounted the cab.

"Joe. Keep your ear out for control. They're finding out something for me. I have a nasty feeling we might be here for hours. Isn't it typical. I'd booked the rest of the shift off tonight. I'm off on holiday in the morning and my Doreen is going to play hell with me, when I eventually get home as I haven't got the suitcases out of the attic yet for us to pack."

"When's the boss getting here?"

"I'm the boss here, sunshine."

"You know what I mean. The area commander?"

"Control will let us know. I'm guessing it'll be a while unless they mobilized him at the same time as us. They're sending the newbie from Kendal."

"Arnie bloody Felton? Better polish your boots and the wagon!"

"It's not a station inspection, Joe. He'll be too busy with the police to be bothering us."

"Bet he looks the wagon over, anyway. He can't help himself. The day shift at Kendal said he ran them ragged on the drill yard after he put his hand on the teapot and found it was hot, when they should have been doing their checks. His favorite trick is checking for dust on the roof of the wagon. He's a right piece of work."

"He'll want to know about the fire and the fatality, not us, so stop bleating on about Arnie Felton."

"Weird this one. He'll have his work cut out, working out how it started."

"Yes. Bloody weird. I'll give you that."

Distant sirens approaching grew louder.

"Felton was bloody quick. It's him alright in his red ŠKODA."

The pristine hatchback pulled in behind the fire truck and the area commander spent several minutes on the radio, dressing in fire-kit and checking every pocket on his fire tunic.

"Evening, sir, fair drag for you from Kendal?" said Mackenzie

"I was on my way to another shout at West Cumberland Hospital, which turned out to be a false alarm. Still trying to get to grips with the size of the patch I'm covering. Different to a London borough!" He pulled a clipboard from the passenger seat. "Okay, what's the score?"

"Bit of an odd one, sir. Female in the driver's seat covered in stains. Smells like brandy. Three empty bottles on the passenger seat and the whole car reeks of booze when you have a good sniff and ignore the burned flesh and plastic." He lifted the tarpaulin on the driver's side.

"Yes. I can smell it," said Felton, taking a couple of steps back. "Really strong."

"Looks like she poured the contents over herself and sat there burning till she died. Those are my initial thoughts, but I may be way off the mark. Might have been an accident as she was drinking from the bottle. Maybe smoking, igniting the fumes. Hard to say."

"Scenes of crime will be here in about five minutes and will be taking over the investigation. I take the usual has been carried out?"

"Of course, sir. Charged hose reel and extinguisher laid out, car battery disconnected. No need to chock and block the vehicle as the tyres are long gone and with the wheel rims welded to the tarmac, it ain't going anywhere. You might want to consider getting the rescue tender here to cut the roof off as the woman's body is stuck fast to what's left of the seat fabric. They'll struggle to move the body sideways through the door."

Felton nodded. "We'll get to that when the fire investigation team has done their work. For now, it's a waiting game. They should be here in the next fifteen minutes. Anything to add?"

"A driver witnessed the incident from two hundred yards back and pulled in to take a closer look. He said he saw a sudden flash inside the car. The seat of fire was on the front driver's side and the driver's window was open, with flames and smoke issuing from it. He also said he saw another car pull out from the lay-by further up the road as the car flashed over inside but couldn't be certain of the car make or color, as he was quite a long way back."

"That might be significant. Can you get his details and ask him not to leave until the police get here?"

"Already done."

"Good. Any idea who she is?"

"Not a clue, sir. Have to wait for the police to ID the number plate, what's left of it. Might need to find the chassis number. That's if it turns out to be her car."

He had been on his way home from work when he saw the woman waving him down in the lay-by. She looked frantic and after pulling into the lay-by and stopping in front of her car, she ran up to him and tapped his window.

"Can you help me? My car has broken down and I've no battery in my phone to ring the AA?"

He looked at her through the glass and wondered if this was a scam, as there had been several reports of car jacking in the area over the last few months. After checking his wing mirrors, satisfied there was no accomplice sneaking up, ready to yank his car door open, and noticing the paramedics' uniform she was wearing, he lowered the window.

"What's wrong with it? Perhaps I can fix it?"

"It's happened before. I think it's the timing belt snapped again."

"Okay, that's not fixable here. Got the number?"

"Yes, it's on my membership card."

After unlocking it, he handed her the phone. "Are you far from home? You don't sound local."

"Wales. I'm on holiday," she said, tapping in the number, which seemed odd considering the uniform she was wearing. Perhaps she was just on her way to starting her holiday, he thought?

She put the phone to her ear, and he saw her screw her eyes up and breath in sharply.

"Are you okay, love?"

"I'll be okay in a minute. Can you ask for me? Here's my card with the membership number." She held the phone to his ear. He didn't see the tiny black body that crawled around from the back of the phone. Within a second, he screamed as tiny legs pierced his inner ear with razor-sharp precision, making him writhe in agony.

He didn't understand what happened and sat rigid in the car for a few seconds. A slight trickle of blood ran down his neck, soaking and spreading out across the collar of his white shirt.

Staring ahead through the windscreen, helplessness overwhelmed him. Just an onlooker. Even when he had the urge to do something that horrified him, he couldn't resist the abhorrent urge. He stepped out, gripped her elbow, and guided the woman back to her car. She complied without resistance, a willing participant to an unspeakable act, unaware of the mortal danger she was in and was party to. After pushing her into the seat, he leaned across her to secure the safety belt, watching the belt clicking into place with a hand he was not controlling. Try as he might, he could not stop.

"Drink this," he said, reaching over and picking up the first bottle of brandy. Why he had told her to do this? A sickening ache in his gut spread upward as he realized the terrible thoughts, just a few seconds ago, were going to happen and he would have to watch.

She took several gulps before he took it back off her, emptying the rest of the contents over her head. She sat motionless, unblinking, as he poured the other two bottles from the seat over her. Why didn't she try to stop him?

With the driver and front passenger windows opened, he prayed for a miracle as he could do nothing to resist the madness. Was this a nightmare? Was he in some horrific dream that seemed ultra-real? He waited for two cars and a bus to pass and checked that the road in both directions was in darkness, then pulled a lighter from his pocket, lit a cigarette and inhaled before throwing it onto her lap. Nothing happened. Another car passed, and he waited for its tail lights to disappear over the distant hill, then lit a match. Praying for the poor woman in the car, willing himself to stop, but to no avail, he threw it at her and ran to his car. He started the engine and inched forward, about to pull off when he looked back and exhaled, pleased there were no flames visible.

The brandy ignited, glowing at first, licking blue flames spreading up her arms and torso. The green paramedics' uniform scorching and melting as the flamed rose higher. Her face was bright in the glow of the flames, expressionless and seemingly unaware of the scorching death rising upward from her chest. Then her face disappeared, obliterated by a flash, spewing orange fireballs out of the both open windows. He accelerated to the exit onto the main road, eyes locked on the rear-view mirror. Headlights from an oncoming vehicle dazzling the horror show behind. The cold-blooded murder of another human being should have left him in total shock. Instead, he was calm, with a strange emotional disconnection. No remorse filled his mind even though he knew he should beg for forgiveness at taking the woman's life and just as he began to analyze his thoughts and inhumane actions, the human side of his brain shut down.

After resolving the issues with the female, who had far too many mental issues and resistance to control, the new host put the plan right back on track. At the roundabout, he took the first exit and floored it.

TWENTY-FOUR

Merthyr Tydfil town center was, as usual, busy on market day with stalls stretching the length of the narrow high street that spurring off into the old shopping precinct. A thin, gangly youth ran across the bridge over the River Taff, from the college car park toward the first level above the shops.

Half way across, an old man toppled over, scattering shopping bags, apples and oranges rolling across the wet surface in all directions as the youth bundled past. The old man raised himself on one elbow, watching the youth taking two steps at a time down the concrete staircase into the precinct before he slipped on the last step, sprawling forward, arms flailing into a cabin selling cut keys with a resounding crash. It was just the break the police officer chasing him needed and pounced on the youth on the ground, putting him into an armlock. The youth flailed, twisted his head around, trying to bite the officer and got to his knees. A second officer caught up and between them they wrestled him back to the ground, handcuffed, and frog-marched him, kicking and screaming through the precinct to a waiting police van.

Jimmy 'Jinko' Griffiths, a regular 'guest' at the police station, made the custody sergeant shake his head in despair as they led him in.

"What have you been up to this time, Jinko?"

"Nowt, copper."

"No need for that, Jinko. My officers aren't in the habit of arresting the good people of Merthyr Tydfil for no reason."

"You deaf, copper? I ain't done nothing wrong. This is harassment."

"Pray, what has he done this time, constable?"

"Caught him breaking and entering a car in the college car park. He also resisted arrest and assaulted an elderly man on the Taff Bridge while we were in pursuit," said the arresting officer.

"Is the man okay?"

"Didn't touch the old git. He fell over," said Jinko, staring defiantly.

"Yes, sarge, the gentleman is fine. PC Williams is taking him home as we speak."

The custody sergeant cautioned and searched Jinko, after removing his handcuffs, then took and logged his belt, shoes, and belongings. "I trust the room will meet with your approval, Mr. Griffith's."

Jinko gave him the finger as the constable escorted him to cell two.

"You can't lock me up. I ain't done nothing wrong, I know my rights," he screamed as the steel door shut behind him.

"Sarge, the old man fell over because Jinko was running at him across the Taff Bridge and scared him half to death, but he doesn't want to press charges, and I wasn't close enough at that point to eyeball what happened."

"So, the little sod gets away with it?"

"Sorry, sarge, but he's like greased weasel shit. We only caught up with him as he fell into the locksmith's cabin in the precinct and dislodged the frame on one side, bloody keys all over the place. Can we could do him for criminal damage? "

"Does the owner of the cabin wants to press charges?"

"No sarge. He fixed it in a couple of minutes and said he's too busy to take it further. To be fair, I see his point. If he had to come here to make a statement, he'd lose business and his kiosk is always flat out with customers."

"Shame that. Still, you've got him for the car. Any damage to it?"

"None. Looks like an opportunist moment for Jinko. The owner hadn't locked the door. Easy to spot these days with mirrors that retract on a lot of newer models."

"Did you see Jinko inside the car?"

"No, but he was just about to climb into the driver's seat when we spotted him."

"You should have held off until he got into the car."

"Why would I let him do that?"

"You have a lot to learn, constable. He didn't get inside the car and therefore he wasn't stealing it. His brief could say that he saw the door of the car open and was being a good citizen and was about to close it for the vehicle owner to safeguard the car from theft."

"But, sarge, he was about to climb in. It was obvious, and he's always nicking cars!"

"I know that. You know that, and most of the population of Merthyr Tydfil knows what the little gobshite is like, but his past doesn't come into it in court until they have found him guilty. His brief would eat you for breakfast."

"Are you saying that all that was for nothing?"

"We'll let the little sod stew for a couple of hours, but it's a waste of time pursuing it. Don't worry. He'll be back in this custody suite before the end of the week and sooner than later he'll be off the streets."

Jinko, who had been out all night on his usual drug-supplying route, wore himself out after ten minutes of ranting and fell asleep.

In cell one, Russel Fox pushed himself up from the padded armchair his colleagues provided and lay on his back, almost touching the door. His head jerked back, and he stifled a scream as the alien moved inside his skull, extending all six razor-sharp legs through his eardrum, exiting out of his ear. Scything through his thick bushy beard, the tiny being paused on his shoulder, checking for others who may try to stop any progress.

It sampled the air and scanned the surrounding cells before dropping to the ground, dripping with blood. The legs contracted almost back to the sphere of its tiny body, allowing it to crawl into the gap under the cell door and a micro-filament extended from its body, just inside the custody suite. The custody sergeant, engrossed in writing a report at the front desk, was the only movement observed. Crawling under the door into cell two, it paused again, observing the sleeping prisoner before moving forward. Six legs extended and bent as it crouched, then jumped, landing silently next to Jinko's head. It paused, scanning Jinko's entire body, looking for defects and found none. The new host appeared to be in good health and had a well toned muscular body. It detected a small amount of a mind enhancing chemicals seeping from skin pores, and from researching the human race before the spacecraft ditched into the reservoir, the chemical was a drug obtained from inhaling smoke from a plant called cannabis. With the alien in total control of the new host, there would be no further contamination by this substance. Satisfied with the new host's physical qualities, it extended and twisted its legs together into a sharp point, making swift entry through the left ear, before Jinko awoke, clutching his ear, screaming and crying with pain.

"Shut it, Griffiths," shouted the custody sergeant. It fell silent. The sergeant walked to cell two and lifted the flap. Jinko was fast asleep on the mattress.

He laughed and closed the flap. "Nightmares. Good enough, you little scumbag!"

He opened the flap to cell one. Russel Fox was in the padded chair, staring at him.

"You okay, Russ?"

"What am I doing here?"

"Safekeeping, mate.?"

"I don't understand. Why am I in a cell?"

"I'll explain in a minute. Fancy a cuppa?"

"Yes please."

"I'll have one as well," shouted Jinko.

"I thought things were too quiet. You're not having any tea, sunshine. I'm letting you out. You can sling your hook and buy a cup in the precinct. Better still, go home, make a brew and stay out of trouble," he said, unlocking the cell door. "I don't want to see your face in here again today."

"You won't. Told you I hadn't done 'owt wrong. You lot just pick on me."

The custody sergeant laughed. "Keep up your thieving ways and we won't have to pick on you. It'll be some big butch prisoner picking on you in Cardiff, Nick."

After the formalities, Jinko stepped outside to freedom, making his way toward the town center and walked at pace up the High Street, not knowing why he needed to get warm clothes or survival gear and then find a car to steal. Hankering for a fresh pack of rolling tobacco, Jinko tried to turn into the tobacconist, but kept walking straight past. What the hell was going on? He looked over his shoulder at the shop and attempted to turn around, but couldn't. He felt driven like a guided missile towards the precinct where he had been arrested just a few hours earlier, even though he had no reason to get the unnecessary list of items. Where would this weird experience take him?

Jinko found it impossible to pull his hoodie up, which he always did before shop lifting, and was relieved to find Trespass, a store selling outdoor and survival gear and equipment, full of shoppers, making it easier for him to blend in. He gathered up the items and, to his disgust, found he could not make his hands hide them under his hoodie and pockets. Instead, he queued with other customers and paid, even asking for a bag, which cost more money, to put them in.

Anger swept through him and he tried to fight the will of the unseen force that controlled him.

Two police officers handcuffed Russel Fox to take him to University Hospital, Cardiff, where Dr. Hernandez and his team prepared to receive him. As they left, the custody sergeant checked the vacated cells before the cleaner could go in and sanitize them. Everything looked in order in cell one until he turned to leave. A small smudge of blood by the door caught his eye. A partial footprint that repeated twice into the corridor. He looked at it again and a very thin streak with tiny dots of blood around it disappeared under the door to cell two. When he opened the door, the streak stopped at a small pool with six more dots of blood spaced around it, plus another pool on the mattress near the cell door.

He went behind the desk and picked up a camera and his mobile phone, taking several images and a video following the tiny trail of blood. The station inspector was called down from the offices to view the strange phenomenon.

"Could it have been one of us going from cell to cell?"

"Not a chance. Something has scraped along the floor from one cell to the next. We've been asked to keep an eye out for anything unusual, and this looks bloody weird."

"Tape it off. Keep the cleaner out of here and tell anyone else that comes in to stay away from the cells. Is there anyone else in the cells at the moment?"

"No, guv, but a drink driver is being brought in."

"Redirect them to Ponty. I'll ring the DS at Ponty, so there's no problem."

"What about Jimmy Griffiths?"

"Who?"

"Jinko. One of our regular customers. He was in cell two, where there was also blood. I released him not long ago, without charge."

"That pain in the arse. We need to find him straight away and bring him back in. Put everyone on it."

"Russel Fox is on his way to the hospital in Cardiff. Do you want me to let them know what has been going on here?"

"No, e-mail the images up to me. I'll pass it on to the powers that be, and they will contact the hospital. Through the chain of command, otherwise, we'll end up with a bollocking. Sorry, but can you write a report out for this asap?"

"Already sharpening my pencil, guv."

TWENTY-FIVE

As the BMW rounded a leafy bend, the site at Sellafield appeared, out of character against the rural backdrop, and wasn't as large as Ben had imagined. An aging sci-fi skyline with strange towers, chimneys, and a coppery globe that was once a nuclear reactor building, looked unearthly against the surrounding fields of green and grazing livestock.

After the lengthy signing-in procedure, they followed a security van, guiding them to the lab block.

The security officer ushered them in and seated them in a small waiting room.

"The site director's assistant will be with you," he said and left.

"We're demoted to the assistant then," said Claire. "All this way and we get the director's skivvy!"

"Claire, patience is a virtue!" said Ben, who was also unimpressed with the level of contact.

They sat in silence apart from an old wooden clock that ticked with an annoying scraping sound every few seconds. Ben checked his watch several times and tapped the side of the hard plastic chair. Fifteen minutes passed, then twenty.

"Where the hell is everybody in this damned place?" hissed Ben. "Do they think we have all day? What can be so bloody important to keep us waiting?"

"You were talking about virtues?" whispered Claire.

Robyn Gates put her hand over her mouth.

A short, bald man poked his head around the door, with a nose so pointed it looked like a beak.

"Dr. Sharman. Pleased to meet you."

"Likewise," said Ben, forcing a smile. "May I Introduce DI Robyn Gates from Cumbria Police and my assistant Claire Manson? Are you the site manager's assistant?"

"No, she wasn't able to be here."

"Demoted again, are we?" said Claire under her breath.

"I'm Nigel Selleck, the site human resources manager." He shook hands with everyone, twice.

Claire shot Ben a glance. He glowered back at her as her face gave away too much.

"I apologize for not being here to greet you. Unforeseen staff issue I had to deal with. Security protocol and all that. Hope you will forgive me. It ran over, as you can see. Please, please follow me."

He hurried off at an alarming pace and the group just about kept up.

"He's like a bloody greyhound," said Claire.

"More like Roadrunner with that nose," said Ben.

Robyn Gates buried her mouth in her sleeve as they marched forward.

"You wanted to see Helen Groves' lab," he said, stopping at a huge glass screen. "Here," he said, swiping a card. A door swung open, and they stepped into a laboratory of two extremes, ultra-modern at one end, and a much older section at the other, resembling an ancient school chemistry lab.

"Helen's office is through the blue door at the back, next to the kitchen. While you are looking, ask me anything you like."

Ben walked around the lab with a great deal of interest. "What was Helen like?" he said, taking in the sharp chemical smell mixed with floor polish and something he couldn't quite put his finger on.

"Dedicated, brilliant, perfectionist, workaholic. I'd love to spend all day telling you about her attributes. In short, Helen Groves is one of our best scientists, and I don't know how to replace her if she doesn't return. We could get someone as qualified, but her knowledge and experience of this place is irreplaceable."

Ben walked around the edge of the lab, admiring the quality of the latest high spec' equipment making a mental note to get his act together and tidy up his own lab, which usually resembled a bomb site. Helen Groves either did very little lab work or kept it spic and span, and after hearing Nigel Selleck's glowing appraisal of her, he suspected it was the latter.

"What about Jeff Randle?" said Ben.

"I must confess, I don't speak to him much. Just casual chat at the security gate."

"On the night he became sick, Helen Groves returned to work after hours. Why was that?"

"Sometimes our staff finish urgent work they can't complete during normal working hours—"

"Which are?"

"Flexible. Our policy for lab technicians is eight hours between seven am and seven pm. The scientists don't have that written into their contract but more or less follow the same policy."

"Did she often work late?"

"Not really. If you think it might be important, I can send you the details since she has worked here."

"What was so important for her to return to work on this occasion?"

"Not a clue. She works autonomously most of the time. She has specific work to do, of course, but works to her own schedule. Do you want a member of her team to talk to?

"That would be helpful. Can I ask what chemicals or other substances you store in the lab?"

"I can do better than that. I'll send you the latest inventory. It's very detailed. Has to be as you would appreciate. You'll receive an in-depth inventory from me, including everything from equipment to consumables. Everything is strictly audited."

"That would be useful," said Ben, pulling out his notebook. "How frequent are the audits?"

"First of the month, or on the last working day before, if it's a weekend or bank holiday. It's company policy."

"The most recent audit occurred before the incident at the Groves' house and Jeff Randle going home sick?"

"Yes, that's correct."

"Not sure if this is significant, but would you mind arranging a fresh audit as soon as possible?"

"Sorry, I don't understand?" said Selleck, raising his eyebrows and pushing both hands into his lab coat pockets.

"I can't go into the nitty gritty of our investigation, but I just need to be clear that nothing has gone missing here."

"That would be impossible. There are strict controls on all waste going off site and checks on all staff in and out of the site."

"But you could do a new audit within a day or two?"

Nigel Selleck paused, raising his eyebrows once more. "Of course, if it is absolutely necessary," he said, exhaling. "Excuse me a minute. I'll just get a lab technician."

Claire watched the little man walked down the corridor. "Ouch! He didn't like that."

"Just covering all angles." Ben took some photos of the lab and opened Helen Groves' office door to the sight of a mass of books, scientific journals, and reports. The mahogany desk and captain's chair would appear stately if it wasn't for the heap of papers strewn across the desktop, in compete contrast to the lab.

"Claire, it could be your workstation," he said, sifting through the mess for anything of significance. Minutes of meetings, several scientific journals, and two travel brochures for Vietnam and Cambodia. A locked door behind the desk caught his eye. Ben looked for a set of keys, felt above the door, and searched through the desk drawers without success.

"Guys, is there a key cabinet or keys you can see out there?"

A soft voice made him jolt upright from the drawer. "Can I help?"

"Are you a lab technician?" said Ben.

"Not exactly." She put her hand out. "Grace Monkwell. I'm Helen's assistant."

Her hand lingered in Ben's for a bit too long for comfort. Grace was as wide as she was tall, with thick-rimmed, black glasses crowned with a wild forest of gray hair.

"Ben Sharman. Pleased to meet you."

"I know who you are, Dr. Sharman. I've read all about your recent encounter with an alien at Moreton-in-Marsh. Fascinating. Simply amazing. Much more interesting than this place."

"I am sure this is just as interesting and a lot less dangerous."

"Did you communicate with it?"

"Sorry?"

"Did you communicate when you came face to face with it underground in those caves?"

"You mean the alien?"

"Yes. Did you link up? Any verbal interaction?"

She was staring, with a slight twitch in one eye.

"The alien didn't speak, but made other verbal sounds."

"Like what?"

"Grace!" said Nigel Selleck, entering the office. "Dr. Sharman is here to ask us questions. Not the other way around!"

"Sorry, Nigel, I'm fascinated. I used to watch the stars from my back garden. I often had a telescope outside and always thought we were not alone. Looks like I was pointing the telescope in the wrong direction!"

"Grace, if you don't mind."

"Sorry, Nigel."

Ben pointed at the cupboard. "What do you keep in there?"

"That's the secure store room where Helen keeps her dodgy stuff," said Grace.

"Dodgy?"

"Isotope samples, and any toxic materials, chemicals, powders, and some of the most valuable equipment. Not a good idea to display anything like that out in the open and the main reason it's all kept in a secure, fireproof container in the cupboard. Four hours of fire resistance. Not a good idea to let some of the stuff burn on a lab shelf."

"Wouldn't you keep it in a secure store away from the building?"

"Larger quantities, yes, but these are small samples. A pain in the neck to keep everything locked up in a remote store. This is a far better way of controlling the stock."

"Can I take a look?"

Grace tried the cupboard door, which was locked. "Helen must have the keys."

Nigel Selleck tried the door, giving it a good rattle. "Staff are not supposed to take keys off site!"

"We'll locate them and bring them here," said Robyn. "But not today."

"She has a bunch of keys clipped to her hand-held radio in her lab coat. I'll go and see." Grace scurried out of the office.

"My apologies, this is not the normal way we do things here." Nigel Selleck, crimson faced, walked into the lab and a hushed argument ensued, as the keys were not to be found.

"Her lab coat's not here. She takes it home to wash now and then," said Grace, when she returned from the lab.

"Sorry about this. Do you need to look at anything else?" said Selleck.

Ben took a last scan of the lab. "No, I think we're done here."

Selleck pointed out of the window toward the main entrance. "Shall we see Mick in security now?"

"Mick?"

"He was on duty on the night shift with Jeff when it all kicked off. He's in the security gatehouse waiting for you."

"Grace, you said she may have taken her lab coat?" said Claire.

"Washing it I expect. She has a spare in the store cupboard, which is the one we can't get in."

"Helen's hand-held radio?"

"Good question. It's not in the charger where she would have put it. It must be in the cupboard with her spare lab coat or still in the pocket of the one she took home."

TWENTY-SIX

Mick Comley started to cry.

"We've been working together for the last two years. Worked together, got drunk, and played at the same golf club together. Much more of a friend than a colleague."

Ben placed his hand on the man's shoulder. "I'm sorry to go over this again, but it would help us find out why he was in South Wales."

"That's okay. Anything I can do to help," he said, pulling out a box of tissues from the desk drawer and blowing his nose. "Just makes little sense."

"Could you tell us what happened on the shift that night?"

Mick wiped his eyes with another tissue and shook his head. "Sorry. You must think I'm a right wuss?"

"Not at all. You're upset and still in shock. I'd react the same if something happened to a close friend of mine. Please, take your time."

Mick nodded and took a deep breath.

"Everything was normal until Jeff felt ill. Nothing untoward. Just don't understand why he drove all that way. He seemed to be ill before he left for home, unless he was pretending. If he was, it was a bloody good show. I have known him for a long time, and I was convinced that he was ill."

"How long was Helen Groves here for?"

"Give me a moment." He pulled the visitor's book out of the rack and thumbed through the pages.

"She logged in at twenty past nine and left at ten forty-five. She seemed okay on the way in. Full of the joys of spring but left in a bit of a hurry and didn't speak, which I suppose was odd for her as she was always so chatty."

"Where was Helen Groves while she was on site?"

"In the lab where she works. There's nothing else open at that time of night, so nowhere else for her to go.

"Is there a canteen on site open at night, or vending machines she could have visited?"

"We have vending machines, but there are so few of us working after office hours that the staff room they're in is locked for security. Anyone here after hours brings their own grub to work," he said, pointing to a lunch box and coffee flask on the desk. "Helen Groves has a kettle and a coffee machine in the lab and can make her own hot drinks."

"No Gym here?"

"Closed outside normal office hours. It used to be open all the time, which was great for us to stay in trim, but the health and safety nurds forced it to shut at night."

"So, she could only have been in the lab?"

"Yes, the lab, for certain."

"What about Jeff Randle? I understand he carried out building and perimeter checks at the time she would have been here."

"That's right. We take it in turn, checking every building is secure, and do a tour of the perimeter and access points. Hang on." He lifted another file from the desk. "Here we are. Jeff started the checks at ten and was back here at ten fifty-five, complaining of feeling unwell. I had to arrange a replacement. Company policy, because we can't be here on our own, which is a pain in the arse if you fall ill, but I can see why they made it a rule because of what we do here. A replacement arrived an hour later, and Jeff drove off site as soon as they got here. I assumed he was going straight home to bed and not to bloody Wales!"

"Jeff did his rounds when Helen Groves was in the lab," said Ben. "Would he have seen her?"

"Yes, he told me he popped into the lab to check in on her."

"Did he get on with Helen?"

"We all did. Nice woman. One of the few on site who doesn't think she is too important to speak to the likes of me. You know, like a normal human being. I didn't say this, but there are a few managers here who talk at us like they would talk to a dog, but she was, well, just normal."

"I'm sorry if this sounds a bit — I'm not sure how to put this but—"

Mick stared at him. "What?"

"Do you think—I mean, what I am trying to say is—"

Claire interrupted. "Mick. What Dr. Sharman is trying to ask you is, was Jeff was having an affair with Helen?"

Mick colored up and looked out of the window. "What sort of question is that?"

Ben glared at her. "I'm sorry we're having to ask you this, but it is important. Do you think they were seeing each other?"

Mick stared at the floor, clenching his hands together.

"I don't like speaking ill of the dead, especially my friend. All I'll say is that I'm not sure and leave it at that."

"I understand. And please forgive me, but it is important, and I had to ask, especially as you are a close friend. One other thing before we go. What system is in place for your hand-held radios?"

"Sorry?"

"Who carries hand-held radios?"

"All security staff have them and there are some allocated to each department."

"So that include Helen Groves as an official user? I know she has one."

"Yes, all section heads have one. It's a large site and if there's a problem, communication is vital between security and managers."

"Can I see one?"

"Sure." Mick passed his own radio across the desk.

"How does it work?"

Mick tilted the device. "Power switch here, channels one to nine here, and press to talk. Quite simple."

"Does it work off a base unit or are the radios independent?"

"Think they're all independent." He swung around and looked at the radio charger unit. "Pretty certain there is no base unit, just this multi charger, and each user has their own individual charger."

"So, you could talk to another security guard anywhere on the site?"

"Yes, but there are limits. A few black spots on site. They are only good for about a mile."

"Do you each have your own?"

"No, the security lodge has a pool of eight units which we use between us."

"Any of them ever go missing?"

"If we get problems with any of the hand sets we replace them, but no, none missing. Sorry. I forgot. There was one that got thrown out in the scrap my mistake about six months ago."

"Who did that belong to?"

"It was the labs general hand set. They have a spare. She said it went missing in the lab when they had a clear out and thinks it was thrown out with a pile of old lab equipment by mistake. I thought it was a bit bloody careless at the time but she's a senior member of staff and there was no reason to doubt what she said so I didn't question it and replaced the lab with a new set."

"Thank you, Mick. You've been so helpful and I'm sorry you lost your friend."

After they had said their farewells to Robyn, it was a somber ride back to the hotel. Once they were clear of the site, Ben made the other two almost leap out of their seats as he thumped the steering wheel. "Why did you have to be so bloody casual with him, Claire? What was your degree in—tact?"

"I was helping you out. Dithering around what you wanted to ask."

"Next time I dither, keep your nose out."

It took a mile of silence before Ron broke the ice.

"I bet that hand set didn't go missing and Helen Grove gave it to Jeff Randle. That's how they were able to communicate without any trace."

Ben nodded but didn't respond.

"Are we staying tonight?" Said Ron.

"Yes," said Ben, having regained his composure, "It's been a long old day, and I'm knackered. We'll rest up at the hotel and head off early tomorrow."

"You sure about that?" said Claire with her head buried in her mobile. "Just had a text from Robyn. The car we saw screaming away from the hotel has turned up. Green Fiesta, with the matching number plate, burned out in a lay-by a few miles from the hotel."

"Some little scrote, trying to pinch a better car I expect," said Ben.

"No. It's a woman called Sue Dean. Found dead in the car."

"This is getting weirder!" said Ron, leaning over the back to look at the at the screen.

"And listen to this," said Claire. "She's a paramedic from Monmouth. I take it we won't be leaving first thing in the morning?"

"Bloody hell! said Ben and braked hard before stopping on the verge. He killed the engine.

"Text Robyn. Tell her I'll ring when I get back to the hotel. This nasty little jigsaw is slotting into place. They've all been in close contact."

"Weirds not the word," said Ron

Ben nodded. "Peter Jenkins meets Dr. Richard Parker, then almost dies of an overdose. Richard Parker drives to Whitehaven to the house on Elmwood Drive then jumps off a cliff. Helen Groves shoots her husband and tries to top herself. Then, her lover drives to South Wales and tragically dies in an accident. A paramedic from Monmouth who may have broken into my car ends up dead up here."

"You don't know for sure if Jeff Randle was her boyfriend and you don't have evidence that Sue Dean broke into your car," said Claire.

"That security guard we just spoke to... Mick whatshisname."

"Comley," said Ron.

"Mick Comley was as good as saying his friend and colleague was having an affair with Helen Groves without spelling it out. I think we can take that as read, and I would put money on that the woman in the burned-out car having either been at the scene of the accident near Monmouth or wherever they took Jeff Randle's body."

"Or both?" said Ron.

"You're forgetting something," said Claire. "The Polish guy who tried to resuscitate Jeff. They took him to hospital."

"You're right. Are we in agreement that it looks as if something transfers from person to person?"

"Yes," said Ron, "I'll go with that."

Claire didn't answer straight away, staring ahead.

"Claire?"

"Sorry. Yes, I'm already on board. I'm wondering why Sue Dean broke into your car, assuming it was her?"

Ron leaned over the seat again. "Perhaps she planted something in the car?"

Claire cracked the window open to get rid of the aroma of stale cigarettes wafting from Ron's breath.

"I'll come back to that," said Ben, pulling into the hotel car park.

"I suspect something is transferring between each person involved and they are, for want of a better term, 'possessed'.

"Possessed for what reason?" said Ron

"To do tasks for whatever landed in that reservoir. I am more convinced now that there is an alien spacecraft at the bottom of that reservoir and it is using human victims. They need something, and I'm pretty sure I know what it is, but it's why they need it that's gnawing at me."

TWENTY-SEVEN

"Welcome to Divisional HQ," said Robyn. "If you would like to follow me I have a conference room at our disposal. You'll find this interesting."

She led them through a series of corridors to reach a vast room with a huge black conference table meant for many more attendees. "Sorry about the barn! It's the only one I could get. They booked all the other smaller rooms for meetings and morning briefings." She laughed. "It's always the same here, with the force seeming to believe it can run smoothly on never ending meetings. There's tea and coffee on the small table in the corner. Don't be shy and help yourselves, otherwise it will go to waste."

Claire stirred her coffee, watching Ron tucking into a plate full of biscuits biscuits, wondering how he could possibly eat any more after the enormous meal at the pub?

"Have you identified the other vehicle you mentioned last night?" said Ben.

"Yes, and I know who the owner is. Take a seat, everyone, and shuffle down to the front, otherwise I'm going to have to shout!"

A screen lowered down from the ceiling and lit up. "Are we all comfortable?"

Ben nodded

"Here's a view from the traffic camera which is located facing toward the lay-by from the roundabout on the A595 at Howgate. This section of video starts just before the dark colored Fiesta, driven by Sue Dean, pulls into the lay-by."

The monochrome scene is of an empty lay-by, separated from the main road by a thin grass verge and footpath, with several cars passing in both directions. A small dark-colored car approaching the camera signals to pull in and stops halfway in the lay-by. Sue Dean gets out of the car and walks up the carriageway on the verge, just before the entrance to the lay-by, and waves at passing cars. This goes on for several minutes before she returns to her car and stands next to it.

"She kept waving at passing cars until this one pulls in. It's difficult to identify face on this camera because of poor street lighting in the lay-by and passing headlights are the only source of illumination. It will switch to a second traffic camera in a few second which is better."

They watch a second car which pulls in front of the Fiesta. Sue Dean approaches the passenger side of the other car and talks to the driver.

"She passes him two objects through the window. We can't tell what the first is, but the second," she said, pausing the video, and zooming in, "is a mobile phone."

Ben stood up and walked closer to the screen. "You're right. I can make out a square of light in her hand from the phone screen."

"I'll run it on," said Robyn.

Sue Dean pushes the phone into the car for a few seconds, then pulls her arm back out and steps back with the phone.

"Robyn, can you stop it there?" said Ben. "Is it possible to wind it back frame by frame?"

"What do you want to look at specifically?"

"Sue dean's arm going in and out of the car window."

Robyn reversed the video and ran it forward in slow motion. "Best I can do," she said.

The man lurches around inside the car, stops for a few seconds, and gets out. He takes the woman's arm and escorts her to her car, opening the driver's door and pushes her into the seat. Both their faces are quite clear as the second traffic camera is looking directly at the front of the Fiesta and a street light is just the camera side of the car of the car. The man passes her an object through the open window.

"This was one of the three bottles of brandy that we found in the vehicle. All empty."

She drinks from the bottle before the man takes it off her and lifts it higher.

"We can't make out the bottle because of the camera angle, but we believe he is tipping brandy over her head. She was drenched in it."

The man leans into the Fiesta again and lifts out two objects, which he holds inside the car out of camera view.

"They are the other bottles of brandy which again, he tips over her head."

They sat mesmerized at the horrific events unfolding. Robyn was impassive, as she had already overdosed on the footage during the investigation.

"I'll stop it there. Questions?"

"Did you find out who she was calling on the phone?"

"She wasn't calling anyone. I'll come to that in a moment. Before I resume the video, I must warn you that the rest is not pleasant," said Robyn, looking at Claire.

"We're all big and ugly enough to watch," said Claire. She looked around, and Ron didn't give her any confidence to back up her statement. Sweat beaded on his forehead. His Adam's apple bounced up and down as he swallowed several times.

"Okay." said Robyn. "The man lights a cigarette and throws it into the car, which does not ignite the brandy. Then he strikes a match and throws it in. I would have expected the car to go up like a torch at that point. The fire investigation team has seen this and think there was so much brandy vapor inside the car that it wouldn't ignite spontaneously. If there's too much fuel and not enough oxygen, ignition can't take place. There was enough on her lap to keep the match going. I think that when he got back into his car and pulled away, enough oxygen had got in through the open window for combustion of the brandy fumes to occur, probably the breeze forcing air into the car."

The small flicker spread and suddenly exploded into a bright fireball, bursting out of the driver's open window.

The door slammed behind them as Ron left the room.

Robyn stopped the video.

"Excuse Ron, he'll be okay. Something he ate," said Ben, rolling his eyes at Claire. "Please carry on. We'll fill him in with the details later."

"The fire inside the car is so intense that you can barely see the poor woman inside. He drives off and, for some strange reason, she doesn't appear to make any effort to struggle and get out. Just sits there and lets herself burn to death."

"You said you've identified the man?" said Claire.

"Not yet, and what makes this even more bizarre is the number plate. It's registered to a Sheila Carey with an address in Gowerton, near Swansea in South Wales."

"Blimey! All roads lead to Wales," said Ben. "This is getting complicated."

"Claire, pull up Google maps. Where's Gowerton in relation to the reservoir in the Brecon Beacons?"

"Give me a second." She checks the location and searches Google. "Gowerton is forty miles from Cantref Reservoir. About an hour in the car, so not that far."

"The police in South Wales are paying her a visit as we speak." Robyn checked her laptop. "They are on the ball. There's a message from Swansea police. Sheila Carey is in France on a walking holiday until the end of next week, but a neighbor says she part exchanged the car a month ago. They're on it, so we'll wait to find out who the current owner is. Looks like whoever has bought the car hasn't registered it under their name yet."

"How long before you get the name?" asked Ben.

"Top priority, so I would expect a result today or tomorrow at the latest. Depends on what resources they've got available. All forces are short-staffed with all the cutbacks. We'll have to be patient."

Ben sat back in his chair. "In the meantime, another victim, another killer on the loose, and we don't know who they are."

TWENTY-EIGHT

He peered around the open door of St. Gervans' church before looking back at her and nodding. A thin mouse of a girl side stepped through the door, her eyes wide, almost fearful. She fidgeted with her hair with one hand and gripped him so tight with the other that he lost all feeling in his fingers.

"Michael and Jennifer?"

"Yes," whispered the young man. The girl nodded.

"Please. If you would like to follow me," said the vicar, ushering them to a side door toward the back of the church.

They shuffled forward and smiled at each other as they entered the vestry.

"Have a seat and make yourselves at home. And don't worry. You're not on trial here. I won't bite!" said the vicar, who saw the girl fidgeting, unable to look him in the eye.

He opened an ornate, glass-fronted cabinet, took out the register, and thumbed through the yellowing pages. Jennifer clung to her fiancé, looking around the cold room.

"The Banns will have to be read out on three consecutive Sundays before the wedding date, which we have already agreed upon. Both of you must attend at least two of the three consecutive Sundays when the Banns will be read out before our agreed wedding date. I will read them out at every service, and it would be great if you could come for all three readings, as it is an important part of marriage."

She looked at her fiancé, frowned, and shrugged her shoulders.

"Ah! Forgive me. I sometimes take things for granted. The Banns are a public announcement that you intend to enter into holy matrimony."

Her eyes widened.

"Don't worry, my dear. You won't have to make a speech or anything like that." Jennifer tried to smile and gripped Michael's numb hand even harder.

"Now, what time would you like the wedding ceremony to start.? The only time that is not available is in the evening at six o'clock."

"What time do you reckon, babe?" said Michael, smiling at his fiancée.

His neck flushed. "I—I—don't know. I mean—I don't mind. What do you think?"

Michael smiled and squeezed her hand back. "Is one o'clock alright for you, vicar?"

The vicar pointed to them with both hands. "It isn't whether I mind. It is what would suit you both. Does one o'clock fit in with all your other arrangements on the day?"

Michael looked blank and looked at Jennifer.

"What I mean is, will one o'clock give Jennifer enough time to get ready for the wedding? Hair, makeup and all the other things a beautiful bride needs to do, and what about the reception after? I assume you are having a reception?"

"We've booked nowhere yet," said Michael. "Jennifer's dad says we can book some posh place overlooking Lake Windermere, but we haven't been to look yet."

"That sounds delightful," said the vicar. "Such a romantic venue. You'll get some fantastic wedding photos there. Shall we say one o'clock provisionally, and if you would confirm in the next week?"

"Provisionally?" said Jennifer.

Michael shrugged his shoulders.

The vicar sighed. "It means I will hold the wedding time of one o'clock for you until you confirm a definite time, after you have been to see the wedding venue."

Michael nodded. "One o'clock should be okay. What do you reckon, babe?" She stared for a moment, then nodded.

"One o'clock it is," he said, writing the date in the register, taking their details, and then snapping it shut. "Let me know by this time next week if you need to change the time, otherwise I'll fix that time in the diary."

He discussed the format of the service and asked them to consider hymns and other music and readings for the service.

"I think that will do us for now unless you have any other questions?" The couple stared at him, blank faced, saying nothing. "Okay. I'll be in touch shortly, and good luck."

As they walked away hand in hand, he watched and waited till they had closed the door before sending the host's mind into stasis once more.

The couple was too young and naïve. He needed someone who could get closer to the scientist and would need to be a person from outside the area that wouldn't arouse suspicion. Intelligent and trustworthy. If he was lucky, someone that Ben Sharman knew personally.

He lit several candles for the evening Mass and locked the church from the inside, seeking silence to plan. The steady stream of engagements was a hindrance. An inspection by social services to approve the church hall for a creche, the weekly coffee morning, plus services and appointments for two funerals and a christening. Everything was pointing toward getting a new host, but that increased the risk of failing the mission. If the church were to be abandoned, there would be too many interested parties who would know, and the police would be looking for him.

An interim host needed to be found before Sharman left the area. Or would Sharman have to be pursued to another part of this wretched island?

In the service later that day, during a monotone reading of Ephesians 5 from the New Testament by a guest reader, the reverend surveyed his meager flock.

Most were too old or too young. There were only two or three who might make a suitable host. As the reader sat down, he asked the congregation to stand for the hymn. He sang, but in a nondescript mumbling, such was his attention to the three candidates. After noting her glass eye, he discounted the first candidate, a tall goose of a woman. The second, a man in a smart suit, was a front runner, while the third, a lady in her late forties, early fifties, looked quite alert and bright.

When it got to the final refrain, the door of the church eased open and an elfin figure crept in, standing with her back to the front wall of the church. Tracy Doone, a homeless girl who helped in the church, often ghosted in after the service started, and more often than not disappeared before it ended. A flash of inspiration came to the reverend. Tracy lived on the streets, sleeping rough, giving her a valid reason to be anywhere and apart from her attendance at the church, Tracy was virtually invisible in Whitehaven and wasn't a local from the town.

The congregation was leaving as he made his move, walking to the front of the church before the final hymn was through the first verse. He asked Tracy if she would like to stay and help prepare for the morning service. A slight figure at just over five feet tall, Tracy was quite frail in appearance. He watched her collect the orders of service and stack them on the racks at the back of the chapel. While she was in the vestry store cupboard collecting new candles, he locked the front door.

"How many candles should I put out, reverend?"

"Two dozen. What do you think?"

"Two dozen sounds pretty good to me," she said, placing each one carefully. When they were all in place, she turned and looked at him for approval.

"Great job Tracy. Stand back and look at your handy work."

She turned back to the candles and took several paces back. He put his hands on her shoulders.

"Move back and you can get a better view of the whole candle display."

As she took another step back, he bent his head and pulled her back toward him, about to line his ear with hers.

His world inverted as the wood lined arched ceiling slid under his feet, and he crashed to the floor in one swift movement. On his back, he looked up at the diminutive figure, stunned.

"What the hell are you playing at?" she said with his hand twisted in a wrist lock.

He tried to struggle, but she put on more pressure, pinning his shoulder down with her Doc Marten boot. Pain lanced up through his wrist and elbow.

"I only wanted you to help me," he gasped

"No. Try again." She cried and released his arm.

The alien was in turmoil, panicked and reactivated its host's mind.

Sat on a pew, with head bowed, she sobbed. "I trusted you. Why would you want to do something nasty? You're supposed to be good."

"Please Tracy. You can trust me." He went to put a hand on her shoulder, then thought better of it.

"What were you going to do to me?" she said.

"Nothing. I swear I wouldn't do anything bad to you."

"Vicars are supposed to tell the truth. Now what are you up to and don't lie to me?" she said, her eyes tearful and blazing.

"I don't know what came over me."

The host was becoming more aware and attempting to regain control of their own mind. The alien bore down and focused on control, and the inner turmoil receded.

"You were going to hurt me."

"No, no, I promise I would never do that to you. You are special, and I really like you."

"I thought you wanted to hurt me."

"No, never!"

She stopped crying and stared deep into his eyes.

"Why would you like me? I'm a nobody."

He got up and sat at the other end of the pew. She was giving him an opportunity he could exploit. He could feel her tension ebbing away.

"I have watched you helping here so often. You are such a kind person. Please forgive me for what I did. I just wanted to hold you in my arms. You are beautiful. I wanted you to stay behind so I could talk to you."

"Funny way of showing it."

"I just wanted to tell you how much you mean to me."

"If you meant that, you should have just said it. Not pawed at me like that."

"Yes. It was stupid, and I just wanted to hold you and it came out all wrong."

"Men! You are all the same, stupid. Sorry, reverend, that was harsh."

"No, I'm the one who's been harsh and ridiculous. Can you forgive me?"

She stood and paced around him, staring at the floor, wiping tears away.

"Isn't that what this place is all about?"

"So, you will forgive me?"

She looked at him sideways as she walked past. "I believe I just did."

"Can I ask you a question?" he said. "Well, two, actually."

"Yes." She stopped pacing and sat next to him.

"Where did you learn how to throw vicar's over your shoulder?"

They both laughed.

"I'm a martial arts instructor, or at least I was. Black belt in two disciplines."

"You were?"

"Long story. I used my martial arts skills when I shouldn't have and put someone in hospital."

"Oh, dear."

"Oh, dear, indeed. Lost my job, and my flat. Couldn't get work anywhere with a prison record."

"There is so much more to you than meets the eye."

"All people are deceptive in some ways. And your other question?"

"Are you hungry?"

"I'm always hungry. Why?"

"Can I take you out for something to eat?"

"Are you asking me out on a date?"

"Would that be weird? A thirty-eight-year-old vicar you have thrown to the ground asking his teenage assailant out for lunch?"

"Yes, it would be if it were true."

"But you just—"

She laughed. "I'm thirty-one and I'm starving. But this is dinner, not a date. Let me take this weirdness in first."

Thirty minutes later, the Vicar of St. Gervans' shared poppadoms, mango chutney, and mint sauce with a convicted female vagrant.

TWENTY-NINE

The welcome warmth from the flames cut through the cold as Jinko Griffiths started to undress and throw his clothes through the car window. An assortment of thermal clothing and hiking boots could have been a better fit, but seemed adequate. Such a pity to watch the car burn with only five thousand miles on the clock and a dream to drive. The perfect vehicle for torching and with its high proportion of plastic bodywork there wouldn't be much of the car left after the flames destroyed it, considering Trefil Quarry was at least four miles from civilization, and out of sight from anyone who would call the fire service. He'd dumped and burned several cars there before, and most were never discovered until they rusted and fell apart.

With a well-stocked rucksack to last at least three days, he set off into the dark wilderness toward the Brecon Beacons, knowing a difficult trek lay ahead. Difficult in daylight but almost impossible for any human in the dark; an interesting journey. The alien in control of Jinko Griffiths enjoyed guiding his host even more than steering the ship. Admittedly, it required full attention and was far more difficult than negotiating a vessel through open space, but the alien's highly developed sensors saw everything ahead in multiple layers. Heat, radiation levels, altitude, and a dozen more readings that made walking across the treacherous route of wet grass and slopes of loose scree easy.

Jinko's consciousness shut down after the car fire. The alien appreciated the resourceful individual with exceptional skill and experience in deception, but the risk of letting him steal everything it needed for the mission was too great and it became a pitched battle to override Jinko's inherent need to thieve. Illogical to stop him from stealing the car, as it had to be sourced immediately and involved minimal risk. Now Jinko's mind no longer provided any benefit walking across open moorland, as the alien's own skill proved competent enough to navigate nine miles to the reservoir with no local knowledge.

Thoughts drifted to the other volunteer who left the ship inside the first host. Several earth days had passed since the departure and although there had been frequent reports; it was not the same as being at the location. A pang of jealousy had crept in at the thought of controlling so many humans before the commander chose a second volunteer to control the second host. This, hopefully, would not be the last mission for that volunteer.

The mountain paths, forged by hill sheep, dipped, winding down to the first reservoir. There were more hills to negotiate before reaching the landing site.

Foxes and badgers foraged through the base of the thick pine woodlands, skirting the edge of the long stretch of water called Ponsticill by the humans. It had been difficult to decipher the language and writing, but time spent in research before reaching the planet proved useful and the learning center of the current host's brain contained a configuration of two languages. One common to the entire island and the other, an ancient language spoken in this smaller district. Humans had so many varied languages and dialects, which the alien found illogical and was relieved its own race only had only one way to communicate.

It took over three hours to reach the ultimate peak, which

provided the welcome view of the landing site. Through binoculars, the alien could make out a small glow that pulsed in the middle of the black body of water far below, signaling acknowledgement to the new host's controller on the mountainside, over a thousand feet above.

Jinko looked up into the sky, then down at the dark outline of the reservoir and the events leading up to the forced landing came to the aliens mind. The commander steered the ship a mile above the planet's surface to scan for minerals. When the time came to leave, no one realized the fuel supply had run out save for a small emergency backup meant only for cruising in open space. The battle against Earth's gravitational pull would never be successful, and a simple malfunction had not allowed a warning of the short circuit to the low radiation converter of the main thrusters to reach the ship's bridge. Skillful flying by the commander, and evasive maneuvers kept the craft from a fatal impact. The commander, forced to shed the outer cloaking shields because of a lack of power, performed a controlled touchdown in the large body of water with almost perfect precision, saving the ship and the lives of the entire crew.

Following impact and descent to the bed of the reservoir, one of many automated survival plans kicked in when, by sheer chance, a human life form entered the water. After capture, they kept the man subdued in a specimen capsule alongside the ship for further study and allowed the intrusive entry of the first volunteer to control the captured host. The first volunteer guided the man out of the water five days later, and two humans discovered him on the road next to the reservoir, picking him up and taking him to the heart of the capital city of the region, another fortunate turn of events.

More humans were expected to arrive at the reservoir to look for the missing man and search for the celestial body entering the water. After performing a complicated maneuver made in haste, they captured a second human who was searching the bed of the reservoir. The alien, selected as the second volunteer to possess the man's mind and body, transferred to its current host at the police station.

The new host fascinated the alien. Intelligent but misguided, the human had the potential to do great things, but his feral upbringing and a dubious social circle pushed his mental skills along the wrong course, turning him into a skillful and resourceful thief. A pity his upbringing hadn't been better, as this human was far too clever to be a simple stealing machine. An interesting thought but, when the ship could fly again, there would be no future for this human or any other once the collective learned of this amazing planet and either enslaved them or wiped them all out of existence.

Guided down the mountain path and across the A470, Jinko Griffiths reached the pebbled shoreline of Cantref Reservoir. He stripped naked, hiding everything in a rucksack under a patch of ferns on the bank before wading into the icy water up to his neck. Difficult to balance on the fist sized pebbles, he lifted both feet off the bottom, treading water while a light skimmed below the surface, an unnatural ripple snaking its way toward him from the center of the reservoir.

The alien watched in anticipation as the ribbed metal retriever surfaced, rising in the air a yard in front. Jinko lowered both feet and took a step forward, raising both arms out to his sides and allowed the retriever to slide and wrap around his torso twice. It contracted, gripped and lifted him above the water, keeping him bolt upright, a few inches above the water's surface. He sped off, like a water skier with no following wake, before plunging into the depths of the middle of the reservoir.

Thirty minutes later, bubbles popped on the surface and a torrent of water spray burst upward from beneath. An upstretched hand, holding a metal object broke the surface, and Jinko, like a naked Statue of Liberty without the crown, rose slowly above the surface, turned a hundred and eighty degrees and flew back across the reservoir, entwined in the metal serpent. Released from its grip, he waded out, pulled the rucksack from the ferns, towel dried, dressed and jogged up the bank, across the main road, disappearing into the forestry overlooking the reservoir to the rendezvous point high above.

Ben Sharman looked in amazement at the police video footage of a naked man flying upright just above the surface of the reservoir. The man, identified as Jimmy Griffiths, had been in custody earlier in the day next to the cell containing Russel Fox. If two mind-controlling aliens existed, why couldn't there be three, four, or even an entire army, and how many more innocent people's lives would they destroy? It was now a matter of life and death to find both Jimmy Griffiths and whoever murdered Sue Dean.

THIRTY

Ben hoped that the story of Sue Dean's murder, along with video footage of her murderer, would make it to the local news. It delighted him when it not only appeared on the local news channel but also made national news headlines on all channels and Sky News. The video of the assailant made an interesting story and a result from national coverage was swift.

Several crank calls and many others who thought the man in the video looked like someone they knew provided nothing, with an alleged sighting from a man who said he had seen the same man in New York on the same day that Sue Dean had burned to death. It was the call from Betty Webber that brought the appeal to its conclusion.

Robyn replayed the call received at police headquarters to Ben.

"You're through to the Cumbria Police witness appeal. Can I have your name, please?"

"Betty, sorry, Elizabeth Webber, but everyone calls me Betty."

"Just to confirm. You understand that this is the call center for the appeal for information on the incident in the lay-by on the A595 near Howgate roundabout?"

"Yes, that's why I rang."

"I have your telephone number on the screen. Can you confirm your address?"

"Yes, it's 34 Chapel Crescent, Howgate."

"Have you some information to help with the inquiry?"

"My brother is the person you are looking for."

"Okay. What is your brother's name?"

"Colin. Colin Leech."

"So, when you said your brother is the person we are looking for, do you mean your brother is the man in the video that was shown in the appeal?"

"Yes, it's him, without a doubt. I know my own brother and it is definitely his car."

"His car?"

"Yes. It's his new car. He bought it just over a week ago."

"Do you know who he bought it from?

"No, sorry. He just said he got a fantastic deal on it."

"What is your brother's address, please?"

"He lives with me."

"Is he there now?"

"No, he's in hospital. He's not very well at all."

"Do you mind telling me which hospital?"

"He's in Cumberland Infirmary in Carlisle. They think he's had a stroke. It was on the same night as that lady died in the car. He came in late, which wasn't like him. Sat down and closed his eyes. He hasn't opened them since—"

Robyn stopped the recording.

"Everything checks out. Substantial evidence in his car, on his clothes with traces of brandy, and the video footage matches him and the car. Many other people have called in and identified the man in the video as Colin Leech. Work colleagues, friends of his at the social club in Howgate he goes to, parishioners in the chapel he attends, and a couple of other family members. Every one of the callers, without exception, said they could not believe he would do such a thing."

"Why wasn't the car registered in his name?" asked Ron

"He hadn't sent the registration documents off and neither had the seller."

"Any chance of a blood sample and a brain scan?" said Ben. "And if this man recovers enough to talk, could you arrange for me to talk to him?"

"Yes. If he recovers," said Robyn, "but his condition isn't looking too clever at the moment. It may be some time before we know if he will recover enough to be interviewed."

"Wouldn't it be far better to have him quarantined away from anyone else as a precaution?" said Claire. "He might still be infected and try to kill someone or pass it on to yet another host."

Ben agreed, "Good point, Claire. You should lock him up and under supervision."

"I can't see that happening any time soon," said Robyn. "Our chief isn't on board with this, although he said he would give as much assistance as possible—"

Claire was about to respond when Ben held his palm up to her.

"I understand, Robyn. It is way off the normal charts and I can see why your chief in sceptical. But knowing what we have to contend with, can you put a larger watch detail on him? At least until a scan confirms it one way or the other?"

"I have one police officer sat outside his room. The chief would go ape if I asked for another. Sorry, but that's all I can offer at the moment. I totally agree with you and if I had my way, I would put Colin Leech in a straight jacket under armed guard."

"Okay, can you do anything to speed up the scan?"

"He's already had one to check out the brain for damage."

"Can we see a copy?"

"I'll ask his sister for permission. I can't order it myself. Patient confidentiality and all that jazz."

"Today?"

"I'll ring her immediately."

Two hours later, the scan arrived and confirmed that no additional life form was present within the brain cavity or in any other part of Colin Leech's body. The blood test showed traces of the unique chemical found in previous victims.

"Where the hell do we go from here?" said Ben, studying the hematology test report. "We appear to be chasing a ghost."

"Perhaps you need to stop chasing and let the ghost come to you," suggested Ron, looking queasy again.

Ben looked at him and nodded. "Great idea Ron, you might just be onto something there. If it's infected anyone in this hospital, we wouldn't be able to tell without strapping them all down onto the MRI table and looking inside their heads."

"What are you thinking, Ron?" said Robyn.

They all looked at Ron, who was not looking his best. He'd lost even more color that his usual ghostly pallor.

"You okay, Ron?" said Claire. "You're looking a bit peaky."

"I'll be fine when I'm out of here. I just hate any hospital stuff. Only got to mention it to make me feel sick."

He pulled out a hanky and spent the next minute blowing his nose. Claire grimaced and stared out of the window, beginning to feel nauseous herself.

"I have a theory," said Ron, ramming the hanky up his sleeve. "This alien. Yes, let's not pussy foot about. It has to be an alien, is looking for something, and when it's got its hands on, it will return to Cantref Reservoir."

"We should all go to the reservoir and wait for the alien to arrive?" said Ben. "Is that what you're suggesting we do?"

"Yes and no."

Claire rolled her eyes. "Good answer, Ron. Shall we start with the yes?"

"Okay, just hear me out. Some of us should focus on finding the other alien's host that's on the loose at the reservoir, and to be there in case the one from up here goes back and—"

Claire butted in. "And I suppose that would be a job for you?"

"I didn't say that. Some of us should try to track the current host up here. It broke into Ben's car once and took nothing. Which begs the question, Ben. What have you got in your car that it wants enough to kill for?"

"Has to be something from the crash site at Monmouth!" said Ben, slapping his hands on the desk. "I took evidence for analysis. A small silver flask and a magazine."

"I picked up a cup, a windscreen ice scraper, a comb, and a service book for the car," said Claire.

Ron raised a finger. "What was in the flask Ben, tea?"

"I didn't look and just assumed it was tea or coffee. Bagged and sealed. Didn't open it."

"Did you send all the swabs and samples for test that I've taken up here and from the Monmouth crash site?" said Claire.

"Yes. Everything we've collected."

"Where are they now? said Robyn. This could be crucial."

"They are in a safe place at the hotel and they'll be arriving by courier at the lab at Moreton in the morning. I'll send it by special delivery this afternoon. I'll call Roger and tell him to put everything in the safe till we get there."

"Are we going back to Moreton?"

"You and Ron are. Ron, can you hire a car and send me the bill? Do you mind dropping Claire off at the lab? And, Ron, you liaise with the police in Merthyr Tydfil and the reservoir. Face-to-face is key here. Emails and texts never give the full picture or get the right response. We need to get a better handle on this."

"Why don't I take the samples with me?" said Claire. "Makes no sense to mail them when I am going to the lab, anyway?"

"It may seem ridiculous to put therm in the post, but I want those samples and items we retrieved from the car at Monmouth somewhere other than with you and Ron. It would be very difficult for the aliens to track them down in the good old British postal service."

"You're not coming with us then?" said Claire, dreading four hours in the car with Ron and his abundant, used tissues.

"There are a few loose ends that need tying up here and a visit to our friend on the ward if he ever wakes up. I'll get a taxi back to the hotel," he said, throwing Ron the keys. "Take my car back to the hotel and leave the keys in reception."

"Sounds good to me," said Ron, whose pocked cheeks were glistening with sweat. "Claire, can we get the hell out of here away from all this medical talk before I end up in a ward bed?"

THIRTY-ONE

Ben looked past the constable sat in the corridor, through the side ward door at Betty Webber, seated at her brother's bedside with a book in her lap but not reading it, and noticed the striking resemblance, mousy hair, fair skin, and the same upturned, pointed nose. He put Colin Beech at around mid to late forties with the slightest hint of gray hair. A regular guy, plain ordinary and not like someone he would identify as being callous enough to burn someone to death. But then, some of history's mass murderers looked as if butter wouldn't melt in their mouth. A not guilty verdict at the inevitable trial would be impossible to prove if an alien was responsible for his actions, assuming he was lucky enough to recover, and Ben doubted that this was a straightforward stroke condition.

"Robyn, would it be okay to chat with Betty Webber?"

"Not with her brother within earshot. We can't be sure if he can hear us."

"I doubt that!" said Ben, staring at Colin Beech's deathly white face.

"I'll ask her to come with us to the canteen. You get the tea and biscuits in and I'll talk to her."

Betty's haunted stare in the dim lights of the hospital canteen as she clutched at the styrene cup of hot chocolate made Ben's heart sink.

"I don't understand why," she said. "He isn't capable of murder. He couldn't have done those terrible things they said he did."

"Could you tell me when he came home that night?" said Ben.

Seeing her eyes brimming with tears. Robyn passed her a tissue.

"If you don't feel up to this, we can come again when you are feeling better," said Robyn.

"No, I'll be okay. I just want to know if it is true, and if so, why he would have done it? He came in well after midnight. He never stays out late and I was about to call the police when he turned up. I know it might sound silly to worry about a man of his age, but Colin has a few mental issues and is easily influenced. So, I thought someone might have taken advantage of him because he is so kind and trusting. I was so worried." She blew her nose into the handful of tissues.

"Did he say anything when he came home?" said Ben.

"That was the strange thing. He said he had been out for a ride in the car after work. My brother works in our uncle's carpentry business. Sweeps up, does odd jobs, that sort of thing. After our parents passed away, my uncle took him under his wing and gave him a job because he would never have held a job down anywhere else."

"Did he say where he had driven?"

"No. Colin kept saying he had been for a drive over and over. Just wasn't making any sense. When he repeats himself, I can always snap him out of it, but this time he wouldn't stop. He must have rambled on for half an hour, then stopped and fell fast asleep. It was odd because he fell asleep in mid-sentence and I knew something was terribly wrong when one side of his face went wonky."

"In what way?"

"The skin. It drooped below his eye and cheek for a minute and then was back to normal. My father had a stroke when I was still at home. I was there when it happened and saw his face go wonky, just like Colin's and my father was only fifty-one. He died the next day, so when Colin's face did the same thing and he wouldn't wake up—" She started crying. Robyn put her arm around her and shook her head at Ben.

"Come on. I'll take you back up to your brother."

Robyn returned to the canteen. "I spoke to the doctor treating Colin. He said he's stable and hasn't had a stroke, so you could be right. Looks like our extra-terrestrial friend has been at it again."

"Okay. If the alien has transferred to another new host, it must have been after he torched the car. We need to find out where Colin drove to when he left that lay-by. He must have met someone else who is now infected. We need to find out where."

"Perhaps we've already met the new host," said Robyn.

"Who?"

"His sister."

"Hell, I hadn't thought of that."

When they returned to the side ward and looked in, Betty Webber sat stroking her brother's hair, murmuring softly to him.

"That doesn't seem like someone possessed by an alien," said Ben. "She wouldn't be hanging around if it was controlling her. Looking at this through a logical eye, what benefit would it have to use her and sit here doing nothing for days? We're wasting time even considering it."

"Can't discount it, though," said Robyn. "Tell you what. I'll ask the doctor to do the test on her and tell the constable watching him to watch them both."

They returned to the canteen and ordered more coffee.

"Can't stick around here all day," said Ben. "We have to assume that a new host is out there somewhere."

Robyn's mobile rang.

"I better take this outside. Be back in a minute."

Ben pushed a half-eaten biscuit around the plate. Why would the aliens need to hitch a lift to get around by taking control of anyone that took their fancy? That the team had something they wanted seemed to gain more significance. What was in the flask, or was it something else the team had picked up from the crash site? Perhaps the aliens thought the team had something they needed. His inner conviction held that the spacecraft was still at the bottom of Cantref Reservoir and hadn't moved. The fact that one of the latest alien hosts, caught on video, floated across the surface of Cantref Reservoir, reinforced that conviction. Were they abandoning ship and moving into the human world using a symbiotic relationship? Or hitching a human ride to get something else?

"Penny for your thoughts," said Robyn.

"Sorry?"

"Miles away Ben. You're brainstorming. I can tell."

"Always the detective, eh?"

"It was obvious you were in deep thought. Are you going to finish that biscuit before you turn it into crumbs?"

He stopped and pushed the remains of the custard cream aside and laughed.

"Received more information on Sue Dean. She was on the first response to the crash site and accompanied the lorry driver, Jakub Lipska, to the hospital. Medical reports show that both Jakub and Sue Dean share the same strange injuries to their ears. Something has punctured the inner ear of both of them. They also show the same trace of the chemical detected in all victims so far."

"Is that the call you just took?"

"Yes. It's transferring from one host to another. Quite risky, but successful so far. The enemy is in plain sight. Quite a brilliant strategy. That must be how the other alien made the transfer from police diver Russel Fox to Jimmy Griffiths in the next cell at Merthyr police station. The photos taken by the custody sergeant are pin sharp and bear that out."

Ben nodded. "Whatever moved from one cell to the other must have several legs. The alien in the first victim's MRI scan in Cardiff fits the bill apart from the size. The one in the cell at Merthyr Police Station was much smaller."

"Different versions?"

"Maybe. Or the ability to change shape, which, after our last incident with an alien that could change shape at will, in the caves under Moreton-in-Marsh a few months ago, makes it a possibility."

"What do you suggest? Ask everyone in Cumbria to wear cast iron ear plugs?"

"A brilliant strategy, Robyn!" said Ben.

"I was joking," she said and laughed. "The next host could prove tricky to find, although I have just been told that our friend Colin Beech, on the ward upstairs, also attended church that night. St. Gervans, close to here."

"What?"

"He wanted to pray. Looks like he had a lot to pray for."

"That may be where we find the next host."

"A needle in a haystack. If the alien wants something that you've got, then why not put it in the public domain and draw it out?"

"All the items we gathered should arrive by courier at the lab in the morning, two hundred miles away from here at Moreton-in-Marsh."

"The alien doesn't know that."

Ben slapped his forehead. "Robyn, you're a genius!"

"You are so observant," she said with a smile. "I'll arrange a press conference and drop the hint that you are still here with your team and even slip in that you've collected significant evidence. I'll get the hotel staked out and see who crawls out of the woodwork. In the meantime, I'm sending plain-clothed officers to the chapel. Would you advise they wear spider-proof earplugs?"

"I would rather we go there ourselves and case the joint, as they say, in your line of business."

"Okay. Makes sense. Shall we?" she said, pointing at the exit.

Tracy Doone raised herself and turned with only her eyes above the back of the seating, observing them leave the hospital canteen. She stretched an arm to the table behind and instinctively grabbed the half-eaten custard cream.

Allowing two minutes, she walked to the car, climbed into the passenger seat, and shuffled across. As Tracy's head moved closer to his, fine black, needle-sharp legs emerged from her right ear, and a small trickle of blood soaked into the chintz pattern of her blouse collar. The legs moved outward, wrapping around his ear lobe before crawling into the Reverend James Lee's left ear. He winced in agony, leaned over, fixed her seatbelt, and as the car pulled away, Tracy Doone's eyes were open and her mind closed.

THIRTY-TWO

The telephone at Moreton Scientific Investigation rang non-stop from the minute they arrived at work. Kath O'Brian did her utmost to confuse every journalist that asked to speak to Dr. Ben Sharman and succeeded.

"I didn't think we would get that much publicity out of this," said Claire, as she took the phone from Kath, placing it off the hook. "Bloody press. Can't they leave us alone to get on with our job? Anyone would swear that someone parked a spaceship on the roof!"

"You better see this," said Roger, handing Claire a newspaper.

Her eyes widened as the headline sank in.

'Police and Bungling Scientist Fail to Protect British Citizens from Alien Attack.'

"The ungrateful bitch," said Claire, noting the all too familiar name of the author of the story. "Has she no scruples?"

"Clever bitch. All crap, but very well-written crap," said Roger, peering over her shoulder. "She may be a nasty piece of work, but you have to give it to her getting her article on the front page of the Daily Express!"

"Does Ben know about this yet? He'll blow a bloody gasket."

"If he had seen this, he would have been ranting down the phone from Cumbria already."

"You're right. I better ring him and give him the bad news. Why did that cheeky cow pull a stunt like that with her husband being the first victim?"

"Say what you mean, Claire," quipped Roger, but he could see she wasn't in the mood for banter.

"Look at this! 'Dr. Benjamin Sharman, the top scientist leading the investigation into alien contact in South Wales, has been driving around the country on a wild goose chase. A source from the police force says they have made no progress trying to locate a person infected by parasitic aliens'—"

Claire's mobile phone started buzzing on the lab bench.

"Source from the police, my arse. All bullshit that she's concocted. She should stick to writing fiction novels."

"Are you going to answer this?" said Roger, handing her the phone.

"And this bit takes the biscuit—'Sharman, who is on a substantial retainer from the government...' That is so unfair. He has to battle to get paid on time, and it's never worth the effort he puts in." She snatched the mobile from the bench.

"HELLO!"

"Crikey, Claire, did Roger piss you off that much?" said Ben.

"Sorry Ben, I've just been reading Jill Jenkins' fake news. That woman is disgusting" "

"Ah, that."

"You've seen it? Total crap. She'd kept quiet for too long. I expected you to rant."

"No. Robyn already put me in the picture and told me to chill. I must admit, I blew a fuse when I first read it. She must have made a bundle out of the story to get it into the Express."

"Can't believe how well you are taking this pile of crap so well."

"Robyn said the police are always getting roasted in the press and to take it on the chin. The papers will soon move on to the next shiny new thing they can twist a knife into, and she's right. We'll get a result in the end just you wait and see. Anyway, how is it down there?"

"Like a zoo on fire, we're under siege. The press is camped outside in the Street. The phone hasn't stopped, but we have a secret weapon."

"Oh?" said Ben, puzzled.

"Our new switchboard operator."

"What are you talking about? We don't have a switchboard operator?"

"Kath. She's been taking the million calls we've had so far this morning. The press must think they rang the wrong number via a time warp and got connected to a Victorian asylum, with one of the inmates answering. She says ' Hello, Cotswold Home for the deranged and bewildered Kath speaking. How may I hinder you today?' then dives straight into a monologue about her Patrick's bad back and his gambling and drinking addiction. So far, every caller has put the phone down on her."

Ben started to laugh and couldn't speak for almost a minute. "Just hope she hasn't spoken like that to any of my clients."

"No. I've rung all our main clients and suppliers and told them to use my mobile until this nonsense is over."

"Well, be prepared for a siege today and it could go on for a while. You should get my parcel this morning. Don't open it till I get back as a precaution and keep it to yourself. Don't tell anyone. Not Roger or anyone else in the lab."

"Hang on a second, Ben."

Claire walked out of the lab and into the ladies' restroom.

"Sorry about that. Roger was in the lab and might have been able to hear you."

"Did he catch anything of what I said?"

"No, only me talking. Okay, this sounds serious."

"Something we collected from the crash site is valuable to the alien. Could be anything, but my money is on the silver flask I found wedged down in the back seat of Jeff Randle's car. Robyn is making a statement to the media later today and drop a few hints that we are still collecting evidence and analyzing everything up here."

"Why?"

"Because it might draw out the person who is being manipulated by the alien."

"And you're the bait, I suppose?"

"Not really. I'm just the front to make it appear as if the thing it needs is still here."

"Bit of a long shot."

"I agree, but I am getting nowhere fast with this. At least her idea is a plan of sorts."

"When this parcel arrives, shall I put it in the safe?"

"No. That's the first place anyone would look, and who knows what technology the aliens have for breaking in?"

"Shall I take the parcel home with me and hide it in the attic?"

"Absolutely not. I don't want to make this too complicated, and with the press hanging around, they might see or photograph you. Besides, would you want the parcel in your flat when this alien is still on the rampage?"

"Point taken."

"You need to go to the depot at Evesham to pick it up, as the courier is sending it there. They will not be delivering it to the center. Place the parcel in a shopping bag when you come back to the lab. Tell everyone you're popping out to the shops."

"Bloody hell, Ben, you should be into espionage, not science!"

"Just being ultra-careful. We have to find out what the alien wants, and why, before they make their next move. I'll forward the text from the courier when you can collect."

"When will you be back?"

"Depends how long this entrapment scheme of Robyn's takes. She's arranged for a load of cops to watch the hotel round the clock. They will be trailing me as well, so don't worry, I'll be fine. Amy's going to monitor the lab, so you'll see one of the local cops hovering around outside.

"Amy? Hope she's not coming here. Your other half is scary enough without being a cop."

Ben sniggered. "Don't let anyone into the building for the next couple of days, and I mean no one. The man who walks on water is still on the loose, and he's not that far from Moreton-in-Marsh."

"Thanks for reminding me. Shall I shut all the windows in case he flies in?"

"Actually, that's a good idea. We know the alien can travel under its own steam, so yes, keep the windows closed."

"Ben, I've had a brainwave. I know the very place to hide the parcel."

"Go on?"

"Above the false ceiling in the store cupboard, where you hid a microphone on our last case."

"Brilliant! Do it! Lock the door to the cupboard and hide the keys."

By lunchtime, the full media circus, ensconced in Church Street, crowded around Roger, asking for comments. Several local police officers marshaled press vans that blocked the road, creating complete chaos.

"Dr. Sharman is continuing his investigations in Cumbria, working closely with local police. And for the record, he does not receive a substantial retainer from the Government as misreported in the Express today and is far from being on a wild goose chase. Moreton Scientific Investigation will send more technicians and staff to work alongside Dr. Sharman. We will relocate to Cumbria for a while." A multitude of questions followed the statement, but Roger ignored them and stepped back inside.

"Kath, did Claire get away okay?" said Roger.

"Yes, your press briefing worked a treat. Got to get her back in without those bloody vultures getting at her. I don't blame Ben for not wanting her put under the spotlight. She's just a young lass."

"Odd that she gave me that statement to give them. Would be nice to go to Cumbria. I've never been."

"You haven't lived, lad. Next to Cork, it's one of the most beautiful places on earth. All those great big mountains and lakes. Me and my Patrick, we must have walked every hill and dale, a hundred miles or more." Roger wished he hadn't mentioned Cumbria. She was still talking of her walks across Helvellyn and Snaefell Pike when Claire's text came through.

"Sorry, Kath. Must dash. Claire's back from her shopping trip. The press awaits!"

Roger delivered another short, prepared statement as Claire returned through the back entrance and locked herself in the store cupboard, hiding the parcel above the ceiling tiles before returning to the lab.

"Thanks, Roger. How did it go?"

"Scary as hell. Please don't ask me to do it again."

"We'll soon tell how scared you were being in front of all those cameras," said Claire, laughing.

"I feel sick. I don't want to watch the news."

"Don't be so bloody soft. Are you a man or a mouse?"

"Pass the cheese."

"I bet you were brilliant!"

"I was dying, but do you know what?"

"What?"

"I was born for TV."

"Get out of it! Next time, we'll send Kath out. That will give them something to report. Can you imagine? They'll be passing the razor blades to each other by the time she's finished with them."

Roger peeped through the Venetian blinds. "There're loads of them and plenty of police to sort them out. Bit of illegal parking, but doesn't justify so many coppers. You bet your life you wouldn't have that many cops turn up if the telly people weren't here."

Claire, grateful the police turned up mob-handed, didn't care if more officers were monitoring the building.

"What did you buy then, Claire, anything for us to eat?" said Kath with a hopeful smile.

"Sorry, no, just some more paper and pens to pick up for the office," said Claire, hoping Kath's eye for a lie wasn't on duty.

"Oh well," said Kath. "It'll soon be tea time. My darling husband said he was taking me out tonight. Can you believe that? We usually have a fish supper from the Mermaid Fish Bar, but for some weird reason he's taking me out." Claire didn't reply and just shook her head. A trick she'd learned from Roger. Don't engage in small talk, and Kath will leave you alone. It worked and Kath turned and sauntered off, whistling to herself.

Two hundred and sixty miles away at the Vicarage of St. Gervans, The Reverend James Lee was on the telephone.

"No, no. On the same policy. Same standard of cover. No motoring convictions and none pending. Yes, I will pay by debit card. Yes, the added driver, Miss Tracy Doone, that's D-O-O-N-E. How soon can you amend my policy, please?"

THIRTY-THREE

On the first calm night since the craft ditched into the water, stars above the reservoir reflected in perfect clarity. Silent apart from the occasional call of a lone tawny owl, hunting deep in the surrounding conifers with its mournful hoot, and the slight, swirling ripple developing in the center of the dark water as three entwined black rods broke the surface. Concentric rings of disturbed water radiating outward from the emerging rods, making the reflected stars shimmer and dance. Extending upward, five meters above the water, the tips of each rod peeled back, spiraling out, exposing a web of black unfurling ribbons. The rods bent ninety degrees to the surface as the ribbons expanded, creating a huge gelatinous circle, like a spider's web of dark kelp. When the water settled, the sharp reflection of the Milky Way returned.

At sunrise, the webbed pad lifted on one side, tracking the endless source of radiation from the rays of the sun, now risen above the distant peaks of the Brecon Beacons. A large solar flare boosted the ship's secondary fuel system with a surge of energy, collected by the pad, streaming electrical current downward into the deepest part of the reservoir, converting to plasma energy, and refueling the reactor for the secondary engine.

Claire's hand searched for her mobile phone, ringing for the third time in a row. It wasn't there. With one eye open, she could see her partner, Dave, standing at the bedroom door in his running kit.

"Good morning," he said, offering her the phone.

"What's the time, Dave?" she said, opening the other eye.

"Five past six."

"Who the hell is ringing at five past six? Take a look at the screen for me. I can't focus my eyes yet."

"It's Ben."

She sat upright and snatched the phone off him.

"Thanks, Dave. Make me a cuppa, there's a love, and make us a bacon sarnie, lightly toasted."

"Yes, boss." He laughed, threw her a salute, and disappeared downstairs.

She checked the call log. Three missed calls from Ben and half a dozen from the local police.

"Claire. Sorry to wake you. Something's happening at Cantref Reservoir. I had a half-baked message from the police coordinator. A large round object has surfaced and is floating on the surface, right in the middle, where that thing landed. They were supposed to contact you, not me, while I'm up here."

"Sorry Ben, I missed their calls because I was exhausted and didn't hear my phone. Dave would have heard it, but he's been out on an early run. I'll get it checked out and get back with some details."

"Don't you go there. I need you to look at all the stuff we collected from the crash scene. Ask Ron and Roger to go if you think you need to. Oh, and if Roger goes, don't book him into that posh hotel."

"Understood. Have you had any joy flushing out the alien's latest host?"

"Not exactly, but I believe I've narrowed it down to a church where Colin Beech went after murdering Sue Dean. I'm going to a service tonight with Robyn to do some ferreting."

"Spending quality time with Robyn, eh?"

"Cut it out. It's a professional investigation."

"Sure Amy would see it that way? You snuggled up nice and cozy with a good-looking copper on a pew!"

"Never mind your entertaining but inaccurate theories. Get yourself dressed and find out what's going on."

Claire was at her desk half an hour later, looking at the strange photos and video clips the police had sent from Cantref Reservoir. She forwarded them to Ben and sat back in the chair with a notion she hadn't experienced since Ben had given her the dream job. Ben trusted her enough to run the lab while he was away. It was a surreal moment and, for all her scientific skills, it overwhelmed her with insecurity. How could she, a twenty-five-year-old who had been working there for such a short time, start telling the rest of the small team what to do? While she contemplated the task, Kath O'Brian forced the door open with the vacuum cleaner.

"Sling your hook. Your office is on my list today, my lovely girl."

Kath had blown her assumed authority out of the window and Claire burst out laughing.

"Jeez, did I say something hilarious?"

"No, Kath. Just being yourself. You are a little gem, do you know that?" She walked out, leaving Kath O'Brian with vacuum cleaner in hand, and for once, lost for words.

The situation at the reservoir became interesting enough to warrant a visit and, as instructed, Roger left to meet up with Ron Logan, which pleased Roger no end, to be given something to do offsite, using his own initiative. Claire booked him into the next best accommodation to the Lodge Hotel. Ben Sharman was a great boss, but expecting staff to sleep in fleapits wasn't acceptable to her, especially when Roger was fully aware she chose and booked the accommodation. She would argue with Ben about the cost of the extortionate hotel another time.

With Roger out of the way and Kath off for the afternoon, it left two other technicians in the building and not a lot of work to do. She took the executive decision and gave them the rest of the afternoon off, with the option to recall them if anything important required their attention. The shock on their faces at being told to go home with no catch made her smile.

Laid out on the lab worktop the items retrieved from the crash site included several containers with swabs and samples, a small silver flask, a driver's license, a windscreen scraper, a magazine, a car service book, a cardboard coffee cup, and a well-used comb.

Claire worked through the sealed samples, first cataloging each before running blood and substance analysis and a multitude of other tests. Next, the comb, which provided little information other than it probably contained hairs belonging to Jeff Randle, which she was confident would be the case after further tests. The car service manual proved uninspiring with evidence that Jeff Randle had held it, and at least one other person. From the last service, only a week before the accident, she assumed that whoever did the service, or someone in the garage's admin department or both, had also handled the book.

Claire failed to open the flask expecting a twist-off lid and contents of cold tea or coffee. On closer examination, the lid, sealed solid, wouldn't open, and there did not appear to be a mechanism to open it. She lifted the flask and turned it upside down. No sound of any liquid moving inside. It seemed empty, but felt weighty for such a small flask. The etching on the base of the flask gave the answer; a trefoil radiation sign etched into the metal base. She checked the outer container with the survey meter but could detect just a small reading over and above normal background radiation.

Claire logged, examined, and tested everything before calling Ben a few times, leaving a message to ring her, guessing he was with

Robyn, hunting for the alien's latest host. The only outstanding issue was the flask which she failed to open. She turned it over and over in her hands, looking for clues, wondering if it had some weird lock that required special deactivation like a security door fob, or maybe through an app? With all the samples re-sealed and placed back in the void above the false ceiling in the store cupboard, she decided to give herself a few hours off and left.

Three hours later, after the burglar alarm activated and the security receiving station alerted her. Claire met Inspector Amy James at the front door.

"Hello, Amy, I didn't realize you were back at work."

"Can't keep me away for long. Just started back full-time today. Shall we go in?"

Claire reset the alarm and they walked around the building together.

"The window's broken in the rear prep room. I can see it from here," said Claire as they walked through the main corridor.

"Okay, don't go in or touch anything, just check it out through the window. I'll get scenes of crime here. Ben spoke to me and said it's important to find out who is behind the break-in as soon as possible. Did he expect it?"

It surprised Claire, but she didn't want to get embroiled in what Ben had discussed with Amy.

"We're in the middle of an intense case and this break-in may well be connected, as it's too much of a coincidence to be random."

"Diplomatically put, Claire. There's more to this than you are letting on, but I commend your loyalty and discretion. I wish some of the nerds I work with were the same."

Claire blushed and decided not to comment.

The SOCO team arrived and began their examination inside with Amy after Claire was asked to step outside. After twenty minutes, Amy emerged, pulled down her face mask and threw Claire a set of keys.

"Here. Back seat of my car. Plastic box with a spare suit, mask, gloves and shoe protectors. Make sure you put them on before you come inside. SOCO wants to know if anything is missing."

Amy turned and walked back into reception.

'Rude', thought Claire, pulling the white suit out of its packaging. What did her boss see in this woman who treats people with such indifference?

Claire checked both floors and waited till she was alone and out of sight before entering the stationery store cupboard, locking herself inside to check above the false ceiling. Everything was in its place. In the lab, a hurried search by the burglar was clear, but nothing appeared to be missing. The feeling that the flask was the logical target and whoever wanted it would return was stronger than ever.

THIRTY-FOUR

A crowd gathered outside the locked chapel door.

"Good job it's not raining, otherwise I'd be heading home," said a man leaning against the chapel door.

"It's not like him to be late," said a young woman, "and I've never known him not to open up the church well before the service."

Robyn interrupted. "Excuse me. What time does the service start?"

"Supposed to start in about a minute, but the vicar's late, and even if he turns up now, it'll start late and I haven't got my keys."

"He's usually on time?"

"Always punctual. Best vicar we've ever had. Great fella. First one for a long time that makes you want to come to church. Remember that Reverend Naesby we used to have?"

The man grunted. "Horrible man. Used to shout and scream hell-fire and brimstone at us in his sermons. He made out you were evil, and we were all going to roast in hell. Couldn't stand him."

"Where is the vicar coming from? Is there a vicarage? Does he live locally?" said Robyn.

The young woman pointed to a house behind the church. "That's St. Gervans' vicarage."

Robyn knocked on the door of the rambling old house and turned to Ben. "I should have remembered this. I came here years ago when I was a sergeant after local thieves stripped lead flashing from the church roof. The vicar, the lady just referred to, was called Naesby and yes, he was rather abrupt, as I remember. Quite a miserable character who gave me the impression that he didn't have time to be questioned and I should just get on and catch whoever nicked the lead."

Ben took several paces back to admire the ornate stonework of the old vicarage. "I'm not into religion myself, but most vicars I've come across have been quite pleasant and being miserable can't encourage people to join your flock. Not a job I would relish, but there are some perks you get as a vicar. What a house! I bet it would cost a fortune to buy if it was on the open market. Heading towards the million pound mark?"

The large Edwardian vicarage stood in almost a third of an acre, with mature gardens and vast lawns sweeping around the house. A monkey puzzle tree stood on the front lawn, a dark green, spikey giant, towering a good twelve feet higher than the house.

"You're comparing Cotswold prices. Cheaper up here, so half a million plus, I reckon. Big house for one person to be rattling around in, assuming he's a single vicar."

"Looks like he's not in," said Ben. "Shall we take a stroll around the back?"

"No, we're supposed to be incognito," said Robyn, her eyes flickering left toward the church. "Give it five minutes, then we'll start snooping. Besides, there are lots of of eyes watching us."

Ben turned. Several parishioners stared in their direction at the other end of the vicarage drive.

"We'll go back and wait."

"Nobody in then?" asked the young woman.

"No. Perhaps he's popped out and got delayed," said the man.

"Perhaps he's with that little girl that's been hanging around. Bit weird if you ask me," said another woman with a small child in a pushchair.

"Who's that then?" said the young woman.

"Lives on the streets. She's been helping out in the church and visiting the vicarage for the last day or two."

"That's that kid Tracy," said the young woman, frowning. "The vicar is just being his usual kind self. He always looks out for waifs and strays."

"She looks too cozy with the vicar for my liking," said the other woman with a smirk.

The young woman raised her voice. "She's been living rough in the area for about three months. The vicar's doing what any decent Christian would do. She isn't from these parts, and probably scared and lonely being so far from her family."

The other woman shook her head, still grinning, and walked off with the pushchair.

After twenty minutes, everyone except Robyn and Ben had gone.

"First impressions of the small congregation?" said Robyn

"None seemed alien, although some looked as if they were from a different planet. The woman with the baby enjoyed twisting the knife into the vicar as if he was having an affair with one of his flock. Nothing jumped out at me, not that I would know someone carrying an alien joy rider in their head."

"Same here. Shall we take another peek at the vicarage?" said Robyn, looking all around for anyone watching.

They walked back toward the grand stone house and, after several attempts to get an answer, they walked around the back of the property.

"Wowser, this is one hell of a vicarage. The conservatory is huge," said Ben, enjoying the sheer beauty of the house and grounds. "Looks in better shape than the church!"

After looking through every window, Robyn put a neoprene glove on and tried the back door. It was open.

"Aren't you supposed to need a warrant?"

"Did you hear that?"

"What?"

"That distant cry, coming from inside."

"Oh, I get it," said Ben, smiling.

"No. There really is something making a noise inside. Can't you hear it?"

A faint, low moan came from inside the house.

"Come on, let's go in and touch nothing."

"What you up to?" said a voice from behind that startled them both. It was a young woman from the congregation. "I wondered why you stayed behind. I've called the police."

"Who you are?" said Robyn

"Janet Lewis. Church warden for St. Gervans," she said, frowning. "More to the point. Who are you?"

"Thank you for calling the police. Saved me doing it myself," said Robyn, raising her ID card. "Miss Lewis—"

"Mrs., she said, correcting Robyn.

"Mrs. Lewis, would you mind waiting at the gate and showing the officers where I am when they arrive?"

She stood for a moment like a goldfish, mouthing, but unable to speak.

"Mrs. Lewis?"

"Sorry. Yes, of course. What's the problem here?"

"Not sure yet, but step away now and go to the gate, please —now."

It was said firmly enough that she took the hint and hurried away.

Robyn moved into the kitchen. A whimper came from upstairs. As she trod on the first step, the noise stopped. Ben followed her as she made her way up the wide wooden staircase.

A golden Labrador lay on the landing, sat up, and started wagging its tail.

"Hello, boy, was that you whining?" said Ben, patting the dog's head, its tail thumping on the carpet.

"Ben. I said touch nothing. That includes the dog."

"Oops, sorry."

Heavy oak doors surrounded the head of the stairs. Robyn pushed open the first door to an empty bathroom. Next, a study with hundreds of books clinging to every wall, and a single bedroom with a stripped bed covered in a layer of gray dust which also coated the carpet. She eased open the last door, which creaked loudly. The dog pushed past, tail wagging furiously. Robyn stepped into a sparse master bedroom with a double bed and dressing table. In a chair facing the dressing table sat the Reverend James Lee staring at himself in the mirror, oblivious that they were there. The dog licked his hand and started to whine and paw at his arm, which swung limply.

"Mr. Lee," said Robyn

There was no reaction.

"Mr. Lee, I'm Detective Inspector Gates from Cumbria Constabulary."

Reverend Lee didn't respond, and continued to stare into the mirror.

Ben walked over and was about to lift his hand.

"Careful, Ben. You know what it did with the others."

"I don't think it's here. He's alive alright. breathing looks normal." He lifted the vicar's wrist. "Pulse steady."

"Police!" came the cry from downstairs.

"Up here" shouted Robyn.

An officer appeared.

"Oh, it's you, ma'am!"

"Handcuff this man. I want him taken to Carlisle Police Station in a van, in the cage. I don't want anyone near him. Put him in a cell with no other prisoner in any adjacent cell and keep a watch over him. In fact, move all other prisoners and tell the duty sergeant to relocate them to the next available station that can take them. Ask a doctor to attend but not to examine him till I get there. I'll follow you soon to the station. Is that understood?"

"Yes, ma'am," said the constable, looking perplexed.

"I want to speak to the crew taking him before we leave, okay?"

"Will do, ma'am."

"Not worth taking any more chances, but I agree with you this doesn't seem like an alien-infested victim, but better safe than sorry."

Janet Lewis, the church warden, was still at the gate.

"Thanks for doing that," said Robyn, shaking her hand. "That was brave, and forgive me for saying this, but a little foolish to come looking for us. We could have been burglars, carrying weapons. But all the same, I appreciate your initiative. Most people these days would do an about-turn and walk the other way."

The woman reddened. "Jeff always says I jump in at the deep end."

"Jeff?"

"Sorry, my husband. Says I should step back a bit and not dive in head first sometimes."

"No harm done. You were talking about a girl called Tracy when we were waiting by the chapel door. Can you describe her?"

"Tracy Doone. She's boyish. About five foot two or three. Short, mousy hair and always in a hoodie and jeans, the only clothes she possesses, I would imagine. She's not local, a bit like me, except my accents from Derbyshire, while hers is a lot further south. London I would guess."

"Derbyshire. Which part? I started my career with Derbyshire Police?"

"Glossop."

"Small world. That was my first posting after training school at the old brick station on Ellison Street. Many happy memories and a great place to live just outside Manchester."

Ben coughed.

"Sorry. I'm drifting down memory lane. We were discussing Tracey Doone. How old would you say she is?"

Janet stared at the floor for a second. "Difficult to say. She looks quite young."

"Age range?"

"Huh! you can't tell these days. If I had to guess, I suppose I would put her at between sixteen and twenty. She could be older, but to me, she looks in her late teens."

"What sort of build?"

"Easy one that. Thin, like a stick."

"What about skin and eye color?"

"Not sure about eyes, blue, or are they hazel? No doubt about skin color, though. She's white. In fact, she always looks like a ghost."

"Anything else that might make her stand out? Tattoos, piercings?"

Janet shook her head. "Can't say. Hoodie covers up her arms. Can only see her face. She even keeps the hood up during the services."

"Is she a regular attender?"

"She comes in the evenings. Always creeps in after the service starts and the first to leave, until a couple of days ago when she stopped behind to help Reverend Lee pack up, which was annoying and not the done thing."

"Why would that be?"

"Because it's my job. I always do that and he shouldn't have asked her." Robyn saw the glint of resentment in her eyes.

"The vicar asked her to stay behind. Are you sure about that?

"Oh yes. He even locked the door after he told me to go. He was very nice about it, but I wasn't happy.

"How do you know he locked the door?"

"I returned to insist that I also help and found it locked, which was odd, as he always leaves the door open for anyone until he leaves.

Robyn scrolled through her mobile and turned the screen. "Do you recognize this man?"

"I ought to. It's Colin, Colin Beech. He's been coming here longer than I have. Lovely man. Can't believe he had something to do with that murder at Howgate, and if you don't mind me saying, you've got the wrong person. Just can't imagine him doing those awful things."

"When did you last see him here?"

"The night before, that woman was murdered in the fire."

"You weren't here the night the woman died in the car?"

"No, I was helping a friend out babysitting, but I know Colin was here that night."

"You seem certain about that?"

"It's been the talk of the village."

"How do you know that for sure, if you weren't there yourself?"

"I was told by the nosey one you met earlier. Jodie Small gossip for the whole chapel. She lives in the house across the road," said Janet, pointed to a terraced house opposite the entrance to the vicarage.

"Jodie said she saw Colin visit the vicarage late at night."

"You have been a great help," said Robyn. "Here's my card. If you see Tracey Doone, can you call me straight away, day or night? It's very important."

"Do you want me to look after George while the vicar's not here?" said Janet.

"Whose George?" said Robyn, worried they had overlooked another person in the vicarage.

She pointed at the labrador she was now stroking. "My kids love him. Don't worry, we'll feed and walk him. I always wanted a dog but my Jeff wouldn't have one, but he won't mind if it's just for a while."

Robyn agreed and took Janet's contact details. They stood at the vicarage door, watching Janet Lewis fussing over the dog, leading it back to her house. "Good job she mentioned the dog," said Robyn. "It slipped my mind. The poor sod would have been locked in and starving until I'd remembered."

"This Tracy Doone. How are we going to find her?" said Ben. "If this alien keeps jumping from person to person, we'll never keep up with it. I'm beginning to think Ron was right. We ought to wait for it to turn up at the reservoir down in Wales."

"Don't discount the Reverend Lee. It might still be inside his head."

"I don't think so. I just get the feeling it's jumped ship into this young girl's head. It makes me wonder how it selects its hosts?"

"There must be some logic. Tracey sounds young, probably fit and street wise if she's living rough. Maybe it saw it as an advantage to be in a host who can blend in. Let's be fair, a vicar is pretty high profile in a small place like Whitehaven."

The police van arrived to collect the reverend Lee and, after Robyn gave strict instructions to the officers escorting him, they followed the police van to Carlisle.

THIRTY-FIVE

The ribbons retracted into the black rods, staying upright for several minutes before submerging into the depths without a ripple. Roger had the full account on video from the police RIB, which circled the same spot. With the motor cut, it slewed forward over the point where the rods submerged, allowing Roger to lean over, scooping up water samples in several plastic tubes, sealing each one and while filling the last tube, he noticed a pulsing light deep below the surface.

"Look down there!"

Ron and the police diver peered over the side at the flickering white light.

"That has to be the sphere that Jane and Russ spotted," said the diver.

Roger aimed the video at the light source deep below the surface, hoping it could pick out the detail through the reflection of the sky and water movement caused by the RIB.

A distinct whining rumble made the RIB judder. The water's surface around the boat also vibrated in a large circle. The glow from the depths split into three distinct lights shining upward, growing in intensity.

"What do you reckon it is, Ron?" said Roger, watching the light glowing brighter.

"Dunno, but I think we should get the flock out of here," said Ron.

The RIB's powerful outboard motor screamed into action, pulling them away at full throttle. A circle of bubbles appeared, popping through the surface. The surface bulged, followed by a spout of water bursting upward a hundred feet. Shale, stones, and thousands of gallons of water rained down, drenching the crew as they sped away.

Roger kept filming as best he could as the boat approached the jetty. With a deafening screech, a brilliant white orb, two meters across, surfaced and rose above the water, beginning to revolve, picking up momentum, spinning faster till it became a blur. Everyone in the RIB had to cover their eyes, such was the intensity of the light. The screeching of the orb grew. The pitch rose in a painful crescendo. There was a loud crack as the orb sped up, accelerating away over the dam wall and was gone in an instant, advancing far in front of the sonic boom it left behind. The thrust shock wave hit the surface of the water, almost parting the reservoir in two, drenching everyone again as another deluge cascaded from the sky.

Roger wiped the camera and himself dry. Ron stood motionless, still looking at the dam wall.

"Everybody okay?" said the crew leader.

Nobody answered. Roger could hardly hear anything above the buzzing in his ears.

The boat rocked as waves spread in several directions.

"That was impressive," said Ron, searching for his glasses.

After getting out of the RIB and drying themselves off, Roger rang Claire. She already knew. It was on Sky News from its mobile unit camped out on the road next to the reservoir. An immediate breaking news story with footage of the whole thing.

"Where has it gone? Do they know?"

"No," said Claire. "It was moving fast."

"Keep me updated. I'm going to ring Ben. Best I do it in case he has questions."

Before he could redial the brilliant white orb flew back over the reservoir, sending everyone diving for cover, and disappeared, in an instant, over the top of the mountain toward the peak of Pen y Fan mountain.

Jinko stared at the skyline from the cover of a huge spruce at the edge of the forest. After walking over ten miles to reach the spot, well off the Beacons' trail routes in a secluded ravine, he waited. An instruction came that the ship had sourced enough solar energy to move and relocate. Too much attention from humans at the current position made the risk of remaining too high. The white orb appeared from nowhere and stopped dead in front of the tree. Its spinning motion slowed to a halt, revealing the metallic silver hull of the dazzling, spherical scout ship hovering a few feet above the moorland grass. Jinko listened. Silence apart from the bleating of terrified sheep, bolting in all directions.

He screwed his eyes shut, held both sides of his head and screamed as the alien began moving inside his skull. Its folded black legs pierced through his inner ear canal. He dropped his arms to his side as it forced its way out of his ear and slid onto his shoulder, dripping blood. As he walked forward toward the ship, the alien crawled down his outstretched arm onto the palm of his hand. Blood trailed behind, soaking and spreading outward into the fabric of Jinko's sleeve.

The ship moved closer. He felt the sudden urge to move his arm nearer and took another step forward, not aware of how far the ship was in front through the intense glow until he touched the surface with his fingers. Jinko didn't register any pain on the super heated metal. Nerve signals masked and blanked out by a subliminal suggestion from within his skull allowed skin on his fingertips to blister with no pain. A tiny hatch appeared above his hand and he had to rip his fingers away, now welded to the metal surface to reach it. Skin, from his fingertips, stuck to the ship, sizzled, blackened and flaked away in the breeze. The alien's legs retracted. Its body shrinking to a tenth its original size, and passed through the opening into the shimmering craft. He pulled his hand back as the hatch closed, steam rising from fingers, cooked up to the first knuckle. Jinko turned to his left and walked up the mountain.

The orb revolved, picking up speed until it spun so fast it became a featureless, glowing orb once more. It screeched and accelerated away with a deafening crack as it broke the sound barrier once more, disappearing due east over the black mountains, skimming the Malvern Hills, reaching its destination in under four minutes, keeping low to the ground, favoring isolated terrain. Many reported a 'shooting star' streaking across the sky but couldn't see what was flying a hundred feet above them. Because of its immense speed, witnesses could only say they had seen a split second of blurred streaking light.

It took Josie and Karen over two hours to reach the top.

"Jose, I've got to sit down before I fall down. My legs have had it and we've got to walk back and all."

"Come on, you lazy cow. The more you park your arse in the grass, the less you'll want to do it. Come on. Grit your teeth, girl."

The well-trodden track up the mountain had been deceptive, and they were unfit and under-prepared to take on the strenuous trek. Friends who climbed Pen y Fan said it was a stroll, more like a hill that a mountain. Josie, never having walked farther than the bus stop or the local Chinese takeaway, was experiencing a world of pain.

"We're almost there. I can see the top," said Karen, waiting for her exhausted friend to catch up. "Think of the selfies at the top and a live video feed on Facebook. That'll shut everyone up that said we wouldn't be able to do it."

Josie burst out laughing and pointed. "Are you kidding me? Have you seen the state of your hair, Karen? You look like Einstein's cat!"

"We can sit down for half an hour and have a drink and food first. Sort my hair and face out, then do the video."

The two girls stopped when they reached the top of what they thought was the peak, which revealed the real peak in the distance up another steep incline.

"Sod it Josie. I've got to sit down."

They collapsed next to the stone path and lay in the grass. Karen pulled a packet of marsh mallows from her rucksack and offered them to Josie.

"I really shouldn't," she said, forcing her hand deep into the bag, "but I need a sugar fix to get to the top. It's still bloody miles away."

A couple of hikers walked past and waved. "It's worth it when you get up there," one of them said, smiling.

Josie forced a smile. "All right for them. they're going down. No wonder they're so bloody happy."

Karen hauled herself up. "Come on, you fat bloater, let's get a move on. No pain, no gain and all that crap."

Thirty minutes later, after a lot of swearing and sweating, they reached the stone cairn at the summit of Pen y Fan. Josie's mouth widened into the first genuine smile since setting foot on the mountain slope. The magnificent view had been worth the huge effort.

They were about to celebrate reaching the top when they found Jimmy Griffiths, sitting with his back to the National Trust summit post on top of the stone peak cairn, eyes wide open.

"Alright, mate," said Karen. But he didn't respond and carried on staring out at the panoramic view.

"Let's move away from him from him till he goes," said Josie in disgust and loud enough for him to hear.

The two girls ate sandwiches and crisps and downed two Prosecco miniatures they had brought to celebrate reaching the summit.

"He's still not budging." Josie got up and sauntered over to the stone cairn.

"Excuse me mate, but would you mind moving for a while so me and Karen can take some photos?"

Karen stood beside her. "Is he okay?"

Josie walked up to him and shook his shoulder. His eyes remained wide open as he keeled over onto his side.

"Oh my god, Jose, I think he might be dead!"

Josie stepped back. "What are we going to do?"

"Hang on, his chest is moving. He's breathing. Can you see him breathing?"

Karen pulled him upright. "How do you check for a pulse, Jose?"

"Search me. We need to get help. He's staring like my uncle did when he had his stroke. Oh my God," she said with one hand over her mouth, pointing at his burned fingers. "That looks really nasty."

"Perhaps he's high on something?"

"I've never rung the emergency people before. I don't know if I can."

"Don't be such a bloody wuss. Give me your mobile."

"Shit, only one bar on the phone. I'd better keep still. You keep your eye on him, Jose. Make sure he keeps breathing."

After Karen made the call, both girls pulled Jinko upright, leaning him back against the stone cairn.

They didn't speak and sat in the strong cool breeze watching him.

A distant thud, thud, thud of rotor blades heralded the arrival of the search and rescue helicopter.

"Bloody weird day this has turned out to be," said Josie, looking out at the speck approaching from the distance.

"Isn't it strange?" said Karen. "We're all the way up here looking down at a helicopter."

The Leonardo AW139 from RAF St Athan was approaching lower than the peak of Pen y Fan, and rose rapidly till it leveled out almost parallel with the stone cairn and lifted slowly, glistening red and white in the sunlight as the flight crew checked out the landing site. Jinko made no movement and didn't even blink when it hovered overhead, sending clouds of grit and dust flying in all directions.

With eyes screwed shut, both girls huddled together, hands over ears as the downdraft blasted them until the chopper gently lowered and settled on the large flat area next to the cairn. With the rotors slowing, the girls dared to look up at a man and a woman in orange flight suits striding toward them, carrying a stretcher case and large holdall.

"Are you okay girls?" said the woman, unpacking the stretcher.

"We are, but he's not," said Josie. "He's been sitting and staring like that since we got here and he's burned his hand."

"Are you with him?"

"No, said Josie, "never seen him before. We got to the top of the mountain and he was there, where he is now. Do you think he'll be alright?"

The woman smiled. "He's breathing, pulse is steady. his fingers are pretty badly burned, but as far as I can make out, he should be okay when we get him to hospital."

"Can we come with you," said Karen. "I'm bloody knackered."

The woman laughed. "Sorry, no passengers on this occasion."

Within twenty minutes, they had secured him on a stretcher and airlifted him off the mountain.

Jose and Karen stared up and waved as the helicopter climbed nose down, turned, and flew off.

"You would have thought they'd have given us a lift?"

"Jeez, Karen, you're a cheeky bitch. Did you see 'taxi' written on the side of that chopper? And even if they had given us a lift, we would have ended up at some bloody hospital miles away."

"I hadn't thought of that." Then she stopped laughing. "I hope he's okay,"

"Don't worry, Karen. Those helicopter ambulance people are brilliant. He'll be fine."

"Should have taken a selfie with the chopper in the background."

"Never mind. I felt guilty that we sat there scoffing and slugging back the prosecco, calling him rotten while he was half dead against that post."

They both started laughing.

"Right, are we having that selfie video or what?" said Josie.

"Shit, Josie. You won't believe this. My batteries gone flat with that 999 phone call."

Satisfied with the new location and certain that there had been no electronic tracking to the current site thirty feet below the surface of a murky gravel pit pond, the commander considered the next move. Water had become a useful barrier to keep the humans away. Now they would have more time to complete the mission in a location much nearer to the energy source they so desperately needed. Time was running out, but at least the mission was back on track.

THIRTY-SIX

Ben arrived back in Moreton at lunchtime following a grueling five-hour drive from Whitehaven after he established that the Reverend James Lee had traces of the mind-controlling drug in his blood, left by the alien and news arrived of the break in at the lab, making it pointless to stay in Cumbria.

"We need to expand the incident board to include the flight path of the alien craft," said Ben, looking remarkably fresh after the long non-stop stint behind the wheel. "I checked the witness reports and marked each sighting on the wall map with red pins, starting at Cantref Reservoir."

The pins stretched from the Brecon Beacons over the Black Mountains and Abergavenny, skirting north of Monmouth and Ross on Wye toward the Malvern Hills. Next sightings were at Strensham Services on the M5 motorway, as it passed overhead, then Snowshill in the Cotswolds, where the last witness reported the strange shooting star, just six and a half miles from Moreton-in-Marsh and the lab.

Ben added some yellow pins in a straight line from the last two sightings and continued it beyond for another ten miles. The line passed straight through Moreton.

"Surprise, surprise," said Claire. "It's headed straight here!"

"Looks that way," said Ben, tapping his finger on Moreton. "My guess is that it will either be in dense cover. Plenty of trees here in the Cotswolds or in water again."

"Water's logical, more difficult to detect anything underwater," said Roger, "and pretty damned difficult to get at them, as we've seen."

Roger ran the video of his and Ron's encounter at Cantref Reservoir.

Ben wrote two words in large capitals on the board—FUEL and WEAPONS.

"So, which one?" said Claire.

Ben pinned up photos taken from the reservoir. "This black pad that the alien craft constructed on the water's surface is a communications device or a good, old-fashioned battery charger. My best guess is they had a fuel shortage and a backup means of propulsion using solar power."

Claire nodded. "Logical, wherever you are in space. There are always stars to draw energy from."

Roger laughed. "Intergalactic charging points!"

"Exactly." Ben drew a smiling sun on the board. "Solar power is sufficient, but unlikely to be any good for great distances, unless they can convert it to some other type of energy that we haven't discovered yet. It makes sense the primary power source might come from radioactive materials like plutonium, but this is only an assumption based on known propulsion systems. Or maybe a temporary solution until they source another fuel we are not yet familiar with, whatever that may be. We have seen from our previous encounter with extra-terrestrial life that they may have something up their little green sleeves we haven't seen on Earth yet."

"Could well be," said Ron. "It doesn't seem plausible to travel across galaxies on any conventional fuel known to man."

"Now, let's consider the unthinkable. What if they want plutonium, which is weapons-grade? Is it for that specific purpose, weapons? I already checked with Sellafield. The sample in the flask is weapons-grade. But no need to panic. You'll also be relieved to know its poses minimal risk to us, even out of the container."

Claire was unconvinced. "If they wanted raw materials for weaponry, it doesn't sit with what's happened. Crash landing in a reservoir, re-powering up with solar energy? They could have infiltrated a site storing weapons grade plutonium and hidden much closer than the Brecon Beacons. There is nothing for them to source plutonium in the immediate area of Cantref Reservoir. It doesn't add up."

"I agree," said Ben, "but let's leave the theory on the table that this is for something more sinister."

"I've another map to track the victims." Ben pinned a large map of the British Isles with red and blue circles drawn on it. "It's strange that two people have been murdered, one person has survived an attempted murder, and the rest are alive. I assume the aliens took control of each victim in the locations marked with blue circles on the map, and the places where the victims were found are represented by the red circles. Any theories?"

"Why would they come to Morton-in-Marsh? I mean, there's no plutonium here at the lab," said Roger.

Ben gave Claire a knowing sideways glance. "Anything from you, Claire?"

"What I don't understand is why the alien murdered Sue Dean and Paul Groves in such a horrific way, and then let Jimmy Griffiths, Helen Groves, Colin Beech, and the Reverend Lee go unharmed, albeit in a vegetative state?"

"Don't forget Richard Parker," said Ben, pointing at his photo on the victims' section of the board. "I don't believe for one moment he intended to take his own life. Seems like a total diversion to throw everyone off the scent."

"But why Sue Dean?" said Claire.

"It was a half-botched attempt at making it appear to be suicide and a lot of evidence lost with a total burnout," said Ben.

"But what was the point? They obviously have control over the victims after they finish with them, so why not just let her go back to Monmouth? Or just left sitting in the car?"

"Perhaps the circumstances at the time dictated the outcome, or something wasn't right with that host. Maybe they are a vindictive bunch and Sue Dean pissed them off. Who knows?"

"I hadn't thought of that. I've done more tests on this chemical that helps them overcome their victims and it might be the way to unlock this."

"What do you mean, Claire?"

"They have introduced this enzyme into the victims' bodies that remains in the blood, allowing them to control them even after they have vacated the host's body. What if we could block its effect or remove the enzyme? The simplest way might be through a blood transfusion."

"Great in theory, but transfusions are supplements, not total replacement."

"What about multiple transfusions?"

"Might work, but there is the risk of complications with too much iron being introduced, causing heart and other problems."

"Worth trying a single transfusion to dilute the influencing enzyme?"

Ben nodded. "I'll contact Robyn and see if they can do anything with James Lee. I don't know what the legalities would be, so I'll let her sort that one out, but in the meantime, I'll speak to Dr. Hernandez in Cardiff. He may have pull with the medical team looking after Jimmy Griffiths. He's the best chance of finding out what the aliens are planning."

"Shall we assume that a water hideout of your two theories is the right one?" said Roger. "As I agree with you on that. I'll track down potential sites in the area, say, a fifty-mile radius of Moreton, excluding areas already covered in its flight path."

"Please Roger, and can we add an aerial view of each potential site to each mapped location? This might turn into a huge operation if every one needs to be assessed on the ground."

Kath O'Brian appeared at the door. "Would you all like a brew? I know I do. And would you mind switching the heating off? Central heating shouldn't be on in the summer. It's bad for you and costs a fortune."

"You mean this central heating?" said Ben pointed to the air conditioning unit in the ceiling.

"Yes. Pumping out loads of air. Bad for you."

"Kath, it's air conditioning. Cool air is being circulated. And, yes, we would love a brew."

"Air conduction or whatever. Makes you as dry as a bone. I'm drinking water like a bloody camel and can't stay out of the little girl's room. Goes straight through me like an express train going down a cliff, so it does."

"Spare us the sordid details, Kath," said Ben. "I'll turn it down a bit, but I'm not roasting myself for anyone."

"And your better half rang about an hour ago; says it's urgent."

"Oh, thanks for telling me straight away, Kath!"

"You're welcome," she said with a forced smile and was gone.

Ben rang Amy and took a very brief message.

"There's been an incident. A neighbor saw a girl watching my house and called it in, not knowing Amy was at home. When the police arrived, the girl jumped in her car to get away. The police caught her before she drove off. She got out, flattened both of them, and escaped. One officer had to be admitted to the hospital with concussion. They said she overpowered them with some kind of martial arts."

"Are you thinking what I'm thinking?" said Claire.

"Amy only gave a brief description. Young girl, in a hoodie and very thin. The neighbor got the number plate while the fight was going on and guess what? It belongs to the Reverend James Lee. It has to be the girl that was mentioned when I visited the church." He pulled out his notebook. "Tracy Doone, who lives rough in Whitehaven."

"It shouldn't take long to find the car around here?" said Claire

"Claire, we live in a sleepy hollow. Apart from Amy and her desk sergeant, those two coppers were the only police officers on duty today, from here to Evesham!"

"Doesn't this girl realize that the plutonium they're after is miles away?" said Roger.

Claire looked at Ben and he gave an almost imperceptible shake of his head. Roger saw it.

"You've got it here, haven't you?" said Roger.

"This Tracy must have followed me here," said Ben, but couldn't look Roger in the eye.

Claire stepped in. "We're wasting valuable time here. Roger, check out all those water locations you mentioned. I'll liaise with Dr. Hernandez and Ben. You need to talk to Amy about this girl, Tracy.

"Okay, I'll call Amy back," said Ben. "Let's get busy."

"Ben," said Claire, pointing at him. "Watch yourself when you are out and about. It could be inside someone else's head by now!"

THIRTY-SEVEN

Smoke surged up into the trees on the edge of the forestry track, swirling through the upper branches, heading skywards in thick black plumes and with only a slight breeze in the air the cloud rose high above the green canopy, mushrooming upward, growing in volume, and visible for miles. Watching Doctor Sharman's house had been a disaster and her poor judgment made the car a liability, no longer of any use.

She walked away from the crackling of the lower branches of pine, amazed how a small flame from a cigarette lighter could develop so fast into an inferno. The temptation to get away from the fire as fast as possible was overwhelming, but if she did and someone saw her, they would remember her running away from the fire. No need to rush. It would take time for someone to ring this in and the fire service wouldn't be here for ages.

Self control stayed with her until she took another look over her shoulder at the mesmerizing sight of fire crowning through the tree-tops. She stopped and stared and her stomach lurched, knowing that everyone for miles would see the flames and smoke. Her heart pounded as she broke into a jog to attack the track, climbing upward through a section of cultivated Douglas firs and vaulted over a stile into a section of year old, planted pines. Flames on the hillside below spread, engulfing a large swathe of trees. She smiled, realizing the scale of the fire would keep the emergency services busy for a long time before the police identified the car, by which time she would be well away.

The substantial amount of cash withdrawn from Reverend James Lee's account, before leaving Cumbria, allowed her to leave no trail. Tracy needed a different approach to infiltrate the lab building at Moreton, as she didn't find the flask even after searching every inch of every room and even with the aliens sensors on maximum power, there was no sign of it. Dr. Sharman or one of his team needed to be infiltrated to find the container's location.

In a high clearing where recent logging created a break, she watched the fire develop far below, engulfing more conifers, flames leaping from one tree to another. A satisfying result as the car would be toast and identification of the car's registered owner wouldn't be happening this side of tomorrow.

Tracy stayed out of sight until dusk before putting the next stage of her plan into action. The distant sirens signaled the cue to move, and she walked over the top of the hill, reaching a bridleway that would take her to another vantage point overlooking the town. By the time the fire service brought the hectare of burning trees under control, darkness would arrive. Their only hope of vehicle identification would be a visual comparison of the metal shell remaining. The vehicle identification number from all three locations on the car was easy to remove before torching the car, a skill she learned from an inmate at HMP Bronzefield in Surrey and one of many skills she gained while being locked up for nine months for grievous bodily harm.

Exhaustion crept over Claire when she arrived at her flat. It had been an intense day with a lot to do and process. She unlocked the door and the familiar greeting of the annoying beep welcomed her home. Stepping inside, she tapped the four-digit code to deactivate the burglar alarm. Total silence. She gave Ben and Roger, parked outside, the thumbs up, watching them pull away, and closed the door to her inner sanctum.

Home was a welcome break to step away from the current madness of work, even though it was a job she wouldn't swap for the world. It worried her she often overstepped the mark with flippant and sometimes suggestive remarks, but Ben didn't seem to mind the banter and, so far, had given her as good as she'd dished out. So refreshing to find someone unshackled from modern ways, where you could say something without someone queueing up to be offended by a trivial remark that the politically correct brigade always seemed to view as offensive. She thought of the individual members of the team and laughed to herself when Kath O'Brian's often shocking remarks, never meant to be offensive, would have the PC do-gooders rushing to find the nearest lawyer. Everyone in the lab was level-headed and never tried to bring anyone down who had an opinion they didn't agree with. And it was nice to be allowed to have a firm opinion. "Bloody hell, what is this stupid world coming to?" she said out loud and laughed again.

Hunger pangs hit as the fridge revealed a bottle of milk and a yogurt, both past their sell-by dates. If Dave had been here, the fridge would have been full to bursting and supper would appear as if by magic. Only cereals and pasta sat on the food cupboard shelf. A take-away from the Mermaid Fish and chippy or an Indian beckoned.

She ran the bath and stretched out on the sofa, reading the local Indian menu before placing the order to be delivered ready for her in an hour, long enough to take a bath, dry her hair, and get herself sorted out.

Tracy Doone's restyle neared completion. The rechargeable shaver she took from the vicarage made quick work of her mousy hair, now lying on the grass. An almost perfect number two reflected from the mirror. She scooped up the hair and dropped it into a nettle-filled ditch with the mirror and shaver. She stripped, changing into jeans, trainers, and a Pokémon tee shirt. Her discarded clothes joined her hair. She hurled the rucksack deep into dense ferns, then stepped into the ferns and treaded it in deeper, hoping it would no longer be needed.

The strains of 'Crocodile Rock' being sung badly drifted out of the pub into the dark, empty side street. Tracy pulled out the set of keys taken from a security box in a lab drawer and found the one with the yellow tab.

She chuckled at the absurdity of the unlocked metal security box containing the keys and the only one on the bunch inside the box that fitted a Yale lock. Stupid to mark it 'Home - Spare', with the flat's address on the tab. She'd completed the successful test run earlier to establish the location of the door that 'Home-Spare' fitted.

The alien wanted to place Tracy's mind into dormancy, but needed her martial arts skills if a problem arose. It scanned from outside, disabling the intruder alarm before turning the key. Tracy switched the dim hallway light off as she turned the latch to close the front door behind her. It didn't make a sound, but she already knew that. The new lightweight running shoes acted perfectly, silent on the wooden flooring with just a slight creak now and then as her weight pressed down. The staircase bent to her left in total darkness and with arm and fingertips outstretched, Tracy touched the cool, painted wall, taking one slow step at a time. Stopping at the head of the stairs, she heard a noise. Just a faint splash of water. A tap dripped into a full bathtub. She put her ear to the first of three other doors on the landing. The door felt warm to the touch and she could hear the faint sound of water pipes inside. Boiler cupboard. The next door gave no clues. silence inside. It had to be the last door. Crouching, she felt for the handle and lowered it, making sure she pulled on the door with the handle, fully engaged to prevent any sudden click of the door cam.

It made only the slightest brush of carpet under the door as she pushed it open. Street light through mesh curtains revealed a single bed and wardrobe, and no one asleep in the room.

She backtracked to the second door. The handle proved silent, but the door groaned as she pushed it open. She held her breath, waiting for someone to wake up. Not a sound. She pushed it wide enough to let her through. Crawling forward in the darkness, fingertips stroking the carpet and touching walls and furniture, she reached the side of a double bed and paused, preparing herself to grab the new host.

It would depend on how they slept. On their back could cause problems, but the element of surprise would take care of that. On their front would make it much easier. A simple arm lock and it would all be over and done with in a couple of seconds. On their side would make it easy.

Tracy rose slowly, holding her breath till she reached full height before pulling the powerful torch from her belt. Rocking back and forward, she counted to three in her head, about to jump onto the sleeping host. On three, she leaped, flicked the torch as her feet left the floor and landed on an empty bed in an empty house.

She took a sharp breath and stepped onto the landing, shut the bedroom door, reset the alarm, and ran up the stairs into the single back bedroom, waiting for the new host to return. No point in going out to look. She was still waiting the next morning when Dave arrived home, just as she flushed the upstairs toilet.

"Morning, Claire, I'm back," he shouted up the stairs while deactivating the intruder alarm. "I thought you would have been at work this morning?"

Tracy froze. There was no lock on the bathroom door. He walked up the stairs and knocked on the bathroom door.

Tracy took a deep breath, then opened the door, drying her face with a towel.

Dave stepped back. "Who the hell are you?"

"Just about to ask you the same," said Tracy. "I'm John, Claire's nephew. Who are you?"

"I didn't know we had visitors."

"You must be Claire's boyfriend. Pleased to meet you," said Tracy, stretching her hand out.

He shook it.

"Sorry if I sound rude, but Claire didn't mention a visitor."

"I only just got here this morning. My mother and Claire popped out. I have to meet them in a minute."

"Sorry, I'm Claire's boyfriend, Dave."

He shook Tracy's hand again.

"You're her nephew? I didn't think Amy had brothers or sisters?"

"My mother is Claire's half-sister. You didn't know?"

"No, Claire never told me she had a sister?"

"My mother isn't a true sister. Claire's mum. Sorry, my Nan adopted her for a while."

"I see—"

"Better catch up with them. I might be late already."

"Can you tell her I'm home, John? She thinks I'm home tomorrow. Hang on, I tell you what, I'll come with you and tell her myself."

"No need for that," said Tracy. "I'll be leaving with my mother and won't be coming back here, anyway."

"Nonsense, I'll just change my shirt, swill my face and I'll be with you in a second. I want to meet your mother. Wow, I'll be damned, Claire has a sister!"

By the time Dave came down the stairs, Tracy, alias John, had disappeared.

THIRTY-EIGHT

"His parents said we can do what the hell we like with him," said Dr. Hernandez.

"Could you repeat that please?" said Ben. "Did you say we can do what the hell we like with him? Are we talking about Jimmy Griffiths?"

"I filtered what they actually said, as it was obscene. Mr. and Mrs. Griffiths are not too fond of their son. I fact they gave me the distinct impression that hate him. His father said he is the 'Scum of the Earth', not exactly an endearing term you would use for your son. I told them an exchange transfusion was a straightforward procedure. But they said they didn't care. I made sure I got a letter of consent drafted by our legal section for them to sign as nothing like something going wrong with a medical procedure can turn indifferent parents into 'caring parents', screaming for compensation."

"Unbelievable," said Claire. "What type of parents would say that about their son, no matter what they had done?"

Ben shrugged his shoulders. "We live in a weird world. I wouldn't be too harsh. You don't know the circumstances."

Hernandez tapped Ben on the shoulder. "We won't be able to use the antidote you have been working on, Dr. Sharman. I'm sure you realize it would be unethical without extensive medical trials and official approval, and as such, my legal advisers have told me it would be illegal to prescribe it."

"Don't worry, I didn't bring it and I never intended to. When will the transfusion begin?"

"Already has. That's why I asked to meet you here."

"Brilliant! Any signs of a recovery?"

"Yes. follow me."

He led them to an operating theater.

"We don't normally carry out the procedure in a full-scale operating theater, but we are not talking about a normal situation here. Let me qualify blood transfusion. This is an exchange transfusion."

"Sorry, can you explain the difference?" said Ben. "I have heard of an exchange transfusion, but refresh my memory."

Hernandez explained. "Putting it simply, a blood transfusion is where the patient is hooked up to a bag of blood which flows into their body to supplement their existing blood. In an exchange transfusion, the medical staff withdraw small amounts of blood and replace it with fresh blood. We do this in little steps of around 20ml at a time."

"Will it take long—20ml at a time?

"Each step is quick, so over time, a lot can be done. I'm going to run the exchange for four hours if all goes well."

"How long has he been undergoing the procedure?"

"Two and a half hours. He's showing signs of coming out of this strange comatose state that he's in, and he has said a few words."

"Can we speak to him at some point?" said Claire.

"Yes. It would be a good time for you to go in and observe. But you will have to scrub and gown up with full PPE. I appreciate it may seem over the top, but I'm doing everything with belt and braces, as this is so far off the charts."

Once they had been through the rigmarole of pre-entry, Claire and Ben walked into the theater with Dr. Hernandez. Jinko's eyes were open, and he appeared to be alert.

"He sees us," said Claire, who waved at him.

He blinked. She waved again, and he blinked.

"Can you hear me?" said Dr. Hernandez. He blinked again and tried to move his mouth, but had trouble opening it.

Claire stepped up to the bed. "Jimmy. My name's Claire and I'm here to help you and we also need your help. If you understand, blink once." He blinked.

"We are aware of what has been going on and how you have been manipulated by an alien using you to do tasks for it." We are simply trying to find out what these aliens are doing here and what they want. Are you okay with answering a few questions to help us?"

There was no hesitation. Jimmy blinked once.

Claire took his hand and squeezed it. "Thank you Jimmy."

She looked across at Ben and he signaled for her to go on.

"Are the aliens looking for fuel?" He blinked once again.

"Is the fuel in a silver flask we found in a field at Monmouth?" Yes, was the response.

"Is the spacecraft underwater?"

He answered yes again.

"Is it near Moreton?" He didn't blink.

"Okay, is it close to where the aliens believe the fuel is?"

He blinked once.

"Very close?"

He didn't blink.

"Far away?"

He didn't blink.

"It doesn't know where it is, Ben."

He blinked once again.

"Do they intend to harm us when they get the fuel?"

He blinked once and then twice.

"Yes and no?" said Ben.

"Hang on," said Claire. "Let me ask a different way. Jimmy, have they got a purpose for us?"

He blinked once.

"Are they going to use us for something?"

He blinked once, and almost inaudibly, said, "Yes."

"You're doing great, Jimmy."

"If they leave Earth, are they going to come back?"

"Yes. Danger."

"We're in danger?"

"Yes, everyone."

The heart monitor skyrocketed, and his eyes rolled back in his head. He opened his eyes and his heart rate slowed to normal. He stared ahead and was again unresponsive.

"It looks as if they regained control of him, but how?" said Ben.

They tried for a further twenty minutes until Dr. Hernandez decided enough was enough and stopped the exchange transfusion.

"I have to care for my patient. This is important to you, but any more of this could harm him."

"Would it be possible to run another MRI scan on his brain? There may be something still inside that is controlling him," said Ben.

"I'm going to rest him for a few hours and we'll do another scan."

Halfway across the hospital car park, Claire grabbed Ben's arm.

"I've just had a text from Dave asking where I am and is my nephew with me. This is weird. Let me ring him. I'll catch you up."

Ben watched her from the car and she looked rattled. She hung up and walked to the car.

"What's up?"

"A young lad was in my house this morning when Dave arrived. He spun some yarn about being my nephew. Dave said it seemed odd, but went along with it. This has to be another victim looking for me."

"Hell, this is serious. Good job I made you all camp out at the lab last night, otherwise you would have been in the same state as Jimmy Griffiths, or worse. I'd better check if our other staff are okay.

"I tell you what, Ben, you ring Amy and update her. They need to find this lad. I'll ring the troops and make sure they're okay."

"No, don't do that. If it has got at any of them, how could you tell?"

"Good point. This is horrible, Ben."

"That antidote we've developed, what are the risks?"

"None, it should be safe."

"Should?"

"It's harmless to us."

"Will It prevent them from taking over our minds?"

"Like a vaccine?"

"Yes. Perhaps more like an insurance policy."

"I'm not sure, but I'm going to give it a go anyway, knowing it's after me."

"Are you sure this lad wasn't a burgler.You know, a break-in?

"Dave said there was no sign of a break-in and how the hell would a kid breaking in disable the alarm and reset it without the code?

"He was sure it was a boy?"

"Oh, God! I didn't consider that. It's that Tracy girl, isn't it?"

"A strong possibility. I'll ring Amy now and see if she can get scenes of crime to give your flat the once over. Can you give Dave a ring and ask him to call Amy to let her in and tell him to stay out of the flat till they have done their magic?"

"I feel ill. That thing was in my flat. Glad you made us all stay in the lab overnight. You were right. I owe you—big time!"

"Yes, you can buy me fish and chips on the way back!"

The bus ride to Evesham was frustrating. The alien was furious that another attempt had failed, and the host's new disguise was no longer a reliable cover. It considered changing the host, but soon discarded the idea since Tracy Doone had too many valuable assets. The way her thought patterns and experience came into play to manipulate and lie were impressive. The disguise needed to be altered to allow her to find the flask.

New hair, glasses, a dress, heels, and a handbag from several charity shops created a new persona that not even Tracy's mother would recognize.

THIRTY-NINE

Claire pointed at various points on a large local Ordnance Survey map of the Cotswolds pinned to the wall.

"Thanks to Roger's hard work, we've plotted the projected flight path of the alien spacecraft from its last sighting as it passed over Strensham Service station on the motorway and he located nine lakes, five ponds, and a gravel pit within a mile of either side of the flight path. When you stray off the flight path by just five miles, either side, that total goes up to over sixty-five and exponentially increases the wider the search area, which would be a logistical nightmare if this spacecraft has veered off the assumed flight path."

"A needle in a wet haystack," said Ben. "I've some good news on that front. The guys at Cambridge are liaising with the RAF and the army and are doing some detailed searches of all potential sites within a twenty-five-mile radius of here. Ron has been busy."

"Bloody hell, he has some use then," said Claire.

"More than you assume," said Ben, attaching a large copy of a hospital brain scan on the whiteboard. "Jimmy Griffiths has still not recovered and something interesting has come up on his scan. A microscopic anomaly at the top of the brain in the same spot where the alien's body was in the scan of the first victim, Peter Jenkins. A tiny organic sphere that wasn't picked up before or perhaps wasn't there before. Strange as it has appeared from nowhere, as if it has grown since the alien vacated and appeared after an all clear scan. I have my own ideas on this, but would like to hear your thoughts?"

"An egg?" said Roger. "The alien lays it before moving on to the next host?"

"It might be an implant that had grown from something the alien left behind, so small it couldn't be detected on a scan," said Claire. "An implant that can be controlled remotely."

Ben nodded. "Both are very plausible. Here's the way I see it. It's unlikely to be some form of reproduction, as that would be far too slow. But, I'm not discounting it as we don't know how quickly these aliens take to replicate, so you may well be right, Roger. I think the more plausible theory is Claire's implant and the reason I believe it's on the right track is because of the assumed timescale for reproduction. Maintaining control of the host after the alien leaves the person's body, stimulating the brain or producing the enzyme itself or perhaps both is the more logical theory taking everything into account. I just can't see how reproduction on such a small scale benefits the aliens at this point."

"But controlled from where?" said Roger.

"That's a good question," said Ben. "I assumed it would be controlled by the alien leaving the brain. But what if each victim is being controlled by the alien ship?"

"Or not remotely controlled at all," interrupted Claire.

"Expand on that?" said Ben.

"What if the implant is pre-programmed before the alien leaves the host's body? Preset functions, tasks: a mission to do something, like jumping off a cliff at Beachy Head, or shutting down to a vegetative state?"

"Jimmy Griffiths disproves that. When we began to get information out of him with the exchange transfusion, he mysteriously shut down again."

"Doesn't this prove rather than disprove the theory?" Said Roger.

"Hang on, Ben, that could be part of the pre-programming. If the ex-host does something off kilter to the alien's preset plan, there might be corrective mechanisms in place," said Claire jabbing a finger at the tiny gray dot on the brain scan, "such as a swift dose of the controlling enzyme to shut Jimmy up. He will know things they want to be kept quiet."

Ben paced the front of the lab. "Okay, there is one common denominator. If this is a 'control unit' inside the brain, it needs to be removed or deactivated."

Claire shook her head. "Wouldn't it be too risky for the host?"

"On balance, which is the greater risk? A medical procedure which, in terms of brain surgery, I would say is straightforward, as it is resting on top of the brain and does not appear to have embedded itself. Or take the risk of not knowing what the aliens' plans are for us. Remember what Jimmy said 'They will return, and everyone is in great danger.' That more than tips the balance for me."

"So, what are you saying? That a surgeon opens up Jimmy's skull and takes it out?"

"He's the obvious candidate. Young, fit as a butcher's dog and consent from his wonderful, caring parents to do whatever the surgeon pleases. All the advantages plus time. If permission had to be gained for any of the others, it might take too long. There is also the recovery time from a brain op to consider before we can talk to him. This needs to be dealt with as soon as we can arrange it. Removing the unknown threat from the aliens Jimmy described must be our priority."

"There is a procedure that can shortcut the recovery time," said Roger, firing up his laptop. "Awake craniotomy. A procedure which is just as it sounds. The surgeon exposes the area of the brain concerned during the surgery, while the patient stays awake. As soon as the implant or egg is out and not controlling the host, they can talk straight away. Just think about it. Jimmy can dig the dirt on the aliens as soon as the surgeons have operated and before they close him up!"

Claire walked up to the scan. "We haven't pinned down what this anomaly is yet, have we?"

"No, but it shouldn't be there, whatever it is, and removal seems to be the most logical step. Dr. Hernandez is doing a detailed scan of that precise area. He will update me with more information in the next hour and I'm going to put my neck on the line and advise him to arrange for it to be removed from Jimmy's brain, subject to the outcome of the new scan."

"You're right," said Claire. "If they've got the power to kill some hosts, then they might do the same to the others."

"My sentiments exactly," said Ben. "We'll take a quick break, and I'm going to call Dr. Hernandez for any new information. Roger, can you check with Amy to see if there has been any progress locating the lad who appears to be the latest host?"

Kath O'Brian clattered through the lab door, spilling several biscuits off a heavily laden tray. "Wish you would fix that bloody door, Ben," she shouted, laying the tray down on the lab bench. "Hanging off its hinges; nearly took my thumb off last week. Do you eggheads do health and safety? Like I said to my Patrick, scientists can solve the mysteries of the universe, but do you think they could mend a bloody hinge? Tea, everyone," she said, with a beaming smile.

FORTY

The farmer watched the armored personnel carrier making slow progress along the potholed approach to the farmhouse. That morning, the farmer did not receive the telephone message well and responded colorfully to a request to access and assess all water sources on the farm.

A crack shot with his beloved Rizzini twelve-gauge shotgun and with a temper to scare the devil himself, he had the sense not to tempt fate and put the gun back in the cabinet. He would love to feel the beautifully engraved, guilty pleasure in his hands, but he knew the limits of his temper might reach boiling point. A pheasant, yes, but pointing a lethal weapon at armed soldiers didn't seem a good idea, so he would have to bear the intrusion.

Two special forces teams using a range of high-tech equipment, including a submersible and aerial drones, targeted static water sources south east of Morton-in-Marsh. So far, nothing of significance had turned up. Hurley's farm, outside Chipping Norton, with two open water sources had to be checked. A large lake at the front of the barn and a gravel pit on a hill, a mile beyond the back of the farmhouse.

The personnel carrier pulled up and the officer in charge stepped forward and offered his hand. The farmer did not reciprocate.

"I am sorry for the intrusion, Mr. Hurley,"

"Sure you are," he said, stone-faced.

"No. I mean it, Mr. Hurley. I would hate a bunch of squaddies turning up at my house."

Roly Hurley chewed the long stem of ryegrass and stared into the distance.

"We will be careful not to disturb anything. I need to access the pond and the gravel pit. Is that okay?"

He shrugged his shoulders, turned, and stalked back to the farmhouse. "Come on, Jet, leave 'em to it," he said gruffly to his blue merle sheepdog. He turned and shouted at the officer. "Don't forget to shut the bloody gates behind you."

The soldiers spent over an hour setting up drones and the submersible, analyzing all the images and data from the pond in front of the barn. Like the previous results throughout the day, this also drew a blank.

"We could be searching forever, sarge," said a young corporal.

"We could be. Unless you want to be doing something else on the drill ground or maybe a nice cross-country run lad. Would that be more appealing?"

"I only meant that this thing we are looking for could be in any of the hundreds of watering holes around here."

"True, but we have our orders and, if I am not mistaken, that's what we do—follow orders."

"But what if this thing isn't in the water? What if it's gone or stuck up a tree or hiding in a building like a barn?"

"Too many 'what ifs,' corporal. Here's a 'what if' you need to pay attention to. What if you just get on with it?"

The steep track to the gravel pit tested the four-by-four, built for the roughest of terrains.

"This is going to be fun," said the sergeant, peering over the edge of the steep slope, almost encircling the deep, round, gravel pit pond below. "Pity we can't get the wagon around the other side. Beats me how this farm operates. It's like a bleeding death trap!"

The driver walked back from the vehicle. "Reversing out will be interesting. Absolutely blind with the slope and those bends."

"It'll be good for you lad, character building," said the sergeant, looking down the horrendous track they had just negotiated.

With the drone airborne, they watched the monitor with a pitch-black hole in the ground filled with murky water filling the screen.

"Smith, are you ready with that submersible?"

"Yes, sarge."

"Launch the submersible, Smith, and use the controls from down there. Too dodgy up here, right on the edge."

The sergeant watched the monitor as the submersible propelled itself into the middle of the pit before it sank below the surface, disappearing from the aerial view. The sergeant switched to a dual view with the drone's view of the gravel pit on one side and the view from the onboard camera of the submersible on the other. As Corporal Smith adjusted the lights, the bed of the murky pit became clearer. At only sixty feet across, it appeared to be a straightforward task.

The submersible negotiated the pit, cruising a yard above the heavily littered bed.

"Another dead end, by the look of it," said the sergeant. "Keep going Smith. Do a sweep of the perimeter. There doesn't seem to be anything of interest down there from what I can make out." A few seconds later, the view of the pit bed jolted and froze.

"What's going on, Smith?"

"The sub's caught on something."

"Try reverse."

"Tried that. Stuck fast."

"Can you move the camera, so we can see what's it's caught on?"

"Moving the camera now, sarge."

"What the hell is that, Smith?"

"Dead cow. The sub is stuck on one of its horns. Undercarriage strut caught in the tip of a horn. I think I can get it free."

"Carry on, Smith, and hurry. We need as much daylight as possible to get out of this hellhole of a farm!"

After several attempts, the submersible broke free. Corporal Smith raised the small surveillance craft above the remains of the cow, which proved vital to avoid getting snagged on other livestock skeletons that had built up over the years.

The submersible followed the rest of the perimeter, before criss-crossing the pit with nothing significant found.

"Okay, chaps, let's wrap this up."

"Smith, bring it up. We're going."

The drone landed on the nearest piece of flat ground, and was boxed and stowed back on the personnel carrier.

"Sarge, the sub's gone."

"What do you mean gone?" said the sergeant, walking over to the monitor.

"Was about to surface when the control unit and the screen went dead."

"Smith, do you know how much that sub cost? God help you if you've lost it! I'm coming down."

The sergeant climbed gingerly down to the side of the pit, where Corporal Smith was pressing buttons on the control unit.

"Here, Smith," he said, pulling the control unit away from the corporal. "You were supposed to fully charge it before we got here," he said. "Did the low battery alert go off?"

"No, sarge."

"Hang on. If the sub power fails, the automatic float mode kicks in. Why isn't that happening?"

A glimmer of pulsing light showed deep below the surface.

"Can't have lost all power, Smith. I can see its light shining. Let's put the control unit back on charge for ten minutes. That might kick start it."

Twenty minutes later, they were sliding down the bank.

"Look, sarge!" said Smith, pointing at the middle of the pit.

The submersible was floating on the surface.

"Bloody strange, Smith, the auto float mode must have been delayed. Anyway, we need to get that truck off the farm before it gets pitch dark. Get the damned sub out of the water and pack it away. Fast as you can, lad." He stormed off up the banking, cursing to himself.

Corporal Smith turned on the control unit, and the sub skimmed across the water. He lifted it out and began drying the bodywork. Everything looked intact, apart from a small panel on the back plate that was missing. The eight tiny metal screws that held it in place had also gone. The back plate had been there, he was certain. It didn't add up that a dead cow horn had removed it with no visible damage. He decided to not mention it to the sergeant straight away, as he was obviously in no mood for more bad news and it was getting dark.

At the bottom of the gravel pit, the commander of the ship was in more than a bad mood. The crew member, sent to investigate the humans' submersible craft, had finished the task but hadn't re-attached the plate. Would the humans suspect?

Corporal Smith had his ear chewed off back at the barracks, and a new panel was quickly scavenged from a scrap sub to avoid reams of reports before they made more searches of the next three lakes, scheduled for the following day.

FORTY-ONE

The sight of the first cut into Jimmy's scalp made Ben wince. He wasn't squeamish until cold steel cutting into flesh came into play and looked away at the floor as an icy tingle shuddered between both shoulder blades.

"Not enjoying this, are we?" said the surgeon.

"Not exactly a spectator sport," said Ben, still looking at the floor.

"Let me enlighten you with some explanation. I am now drilling burr holes around the area of the skull where we will create a flap. After that, I use a craniotome to connect the burr holes and cut a section of skull bone out to expose the dura underneath."

"Dura?"

"The leathery membrane covering the brain, the outer layer of the connective tissues making up the meninges. Are you following?"

"Yes," said Ben. The icy shudder drew inwards from his shoulder blades once more.

"Good. I use this beautiful instrument, which is basically a handheld bone cutter, except far more intricate. A craniotome, named for obvious reasons. Diamond tipped and rather expensive."

"Out of interest, how expensive?" said Ben.

"Not sure. Big bucks. I just use and abuse the devices they give us to play with, but hazarding a guess, I would say a thousand to two thousand, maybe more. Who knows and who cares as long as I can use one!"

"Pretty expensive tool kit in here," said Ben, admiring the pristine operating theater.

"The skull flap will detach, hopefully, without tearing the dura. "

Ben glanced at the screen. With the scalp peeled back and secured, the surgeon bored three holes into Jimmy's skull and the back of his neck tingled as he watched, making him shudder once more. He wanted to look away, but, like a moth, attracted irresistibly to a porch lantern, he couldn't. It was fascinating to see how the skill of the surgeon made light work of what seemed an incredibly risky operation.

"Ah, good. The skull flap has separated without coaxing."

Once the surgeon moved the protective layers out of the way, he exposed the top of Jimmy's brain.

Jimmy looked ahead, expressionless, as the surgeon pulled the scope down for a closer look.

"I can see what we're looking for. The size of a pinhead. On screen now, Dr. Sharman."

At first, Ben noticed nothing other than the brain's glistening surface. Then a tiny dark speck came into focus on the screen, in bold contrast to the pinkish gray surface of the brain.

"Can you make it out, resting in a sulcus on the cerebral cortex?"

"Sulcus?"

"Sorry, Dr. Sharman, talking technical stuff here. Force of habit. Ridges and depressions, almost-like valleys on the surface of the cerebral cortex. The valleys are called sulci."

"The question is, can you take it out?"

"Why not? From Dr. Hernandez's scans, I can detect no form of bonding to the cerebral cortex. Shall we try?"

The surgeon, selecting a delicate pair of forceps, attempted to secure the tiny black object between the tips, but as the forceps touched the object's surface, it disappeared, sinking into one of the valleys the surgeon had just described.

"Good Lord!" he said, stepping back.

"What happened?" said Ben

"Unbelievable," said the surgeon.

"What?"

"It moved. The damned thing moved."

"It's alive?"

"Hang on, it's reappeared. There has to be a logical explanation."

"Did you disturb it and push it further in?"

Two eyes flashed in disgust above the face mask.

"No, I'm certain I didn't do that, but it's the only way it could have moved. Unless this object is alive."

He moved closer again and steadied the forceps. Even before he got close, the tiny object disappeared again.

The room filled with noise as several monitor alarms sounded.

"He's arresting," shouted a nurse.

Ben watched the medical team default to life-saving mode. The lead surgeon moved out of the way and, as quickly as the emergency had occurred, normality returned.

"Pulse and breathing normal," said the nurse on the monitors.

Resuming his position at the back of Jimmy's head, the surgeon leaned forward, and the alarm sounded again.

"He's arresting again."

The surgeon moved away once more, and Jimmy's vital signs returned to normal.

"It's protecting itself and doesn't want the patient awake," said Ben.

Every time the surgeon tried anything near Jimmy's scalp, he went into cardiac arrest.

"Fascinating," said the surgeon. "I think we'll have to leave it there as it doesn't want me to touch it and I'm not prepared to go any further with this. Okay, let's replace the flap and close him up, if it will let me!"

As he approached to carry out the procedure to re-secure the skull flap with titanium plates and screws, there was no adverse reaction.

"The damned thing knows what you are doing," said Ben, shaking his head in awe at the resourcefulness of the aliens' technology.

After they wheeled Jimmy out to the recovery ward, Dr. Hernandez ushered Ben into a consultation room.

The operation had been a waste of time in many respects, but at least the consequences of removing the implant were clear. Hernandez turned on a large light box in the consultation room. A high-resolution image of the top of Jimmy Griffiths' brain.

"What do you make of it?" said Ben.

"I don't know what to say about this other than this implant may be mechanical rather than a living organism."

"What gives you that idea? All I can see is a black bean shape."

"Observe," he said, swapping the image for a highly magnified version.

"Wowser, you're right." The surface of the implant appeared to be machine-like, with small holes, vents, and strange markings.

"The symbols on the lower half of the image are what you would expect on the surface of some kind of construction or machine, not a life form. Unless they are the weirdest tattoos I have ever seen!"

"Must be non-metal?" said Ben.

"Why do you say that?"

"MRI scanner. An implant like this would cause a problem?"

"Human implants such as pacemakers and cochlea implants, yes. Some metals are okay during scanning, but who knows what this thing is constructed of, or what's inside it?"

"This is a nightmare," said Ben. "Pre-programmed, working autonomously or controlled externally."

Ben contemplated the enormity of the problem as he drove back to Moreton-in Marsh. They had to stop the alien craft from getting its hands on the plutonium. But with its location still unknown, Tracy

Doone, still unaccounted for, and the inability to get information from the hosts, the outlook was far from promising.

To add to the frustration, the gantry lights ahead flashed the warning that the M50 motorway was closed. Ben pulled off to follow the diversion, got fed up with the heavy traffic, and plotted a route across-country. He slowed down, enjoying the emptiness of the rural roads, lined with hedges, and fields filled with cows and sheep. After a series of bends, the road straightened out and an image in a field caught his eye. A giant advert. 'Stop the Mast' emblazoned above a giant telecom mast with a red cross over the top. Ben pulled over and stood on the grass verge, staring over the hedge at the huge protest sign. Not a professional job, made with odd pieces of wood and old scaffolding poles, but it certainly grabbed attention and drove home a powerful message. Ben smiled and sat back in the car, mentally thanking the locals for constructing the monstrous protest, which provided the seed of an idea. A second and third sign with the same slogan flashed by in the hedgerows, and the seed grew into a plan as Ben pulled over and rang Ron.

"What's new, Ben? Good news?"

"No, nothing to celebrate. Just been with that kid from Merthyr, having the top of his head lifted off in surgery to get that implant out. The bloody thing moved every time the surgeon got close. He couldn't extract it."

"You're kidding me?"

"No. An implant left by the alien which at first, I thought, was pre-programmed, but I'm pretty sure an external source controls each of these alien implants. I have an idea how to disable it. Can you or anyone you know get hold of a signal-jamming device? I'm no expert, but I've heard you can cancel any signal with the right kit.

"I can do one better than that. We've just developed a room in our building that even the pentagon or MI5 combined couldn't breach. The only problem is it's here in Cambridge and your victim is in Wales."

"I wasn't considering Jimmy Griffiths. He's in no fit state. I was thinking more of Tracy Doone if we can catch her."

"What about the vicar in Cumbria?"

"Good idea Ron. I hadn't thought of our friend the Reverend Lee, but he's way back in the chain of events now."

"If we can bring him out of their control, he might know something useful."

Ben considered the idea. "Perhaps it wouldn't be so difficult if I could cut all the red tape through in record time. I'll ask Robyn Gates to pull a few strings. The only thing is that once he's in the room and if the jamming system works, he won't be able to come back out of it until this is all over."

"You're right. It'll have to be done carefully," said Ron. "I'll make sure that everything is in place for a lengthy stay."

"He'll have to be under lock and key. If Lee gets out, they might kill him. Anything's possible. We've got to anticipate the worst scenario."

Ron chuckled. "I'll tie the rev up myself if I have to."

FORTY-TWO

The message from the ship's commander left the alien in no doubt of what had to be done and the urgency of the task, with time running out.

The mother ship, still out of contact, would soon leave this quadrant of the galaxy and with main ship-to-ship communications offline, it would assume them missing unless they could return before its departure. Strict protocols in place dictated the outcome for a missing scout craft; abandonment and automated destruction. If they didn't return before its departure, they would be assumed missing and face abandonment and automated destruction, unless they could reach the mother ship.

Success would bring great wealth to the commander with the discovery of Earth's vast resources and the potential for billions of human slaves. Control of humans would be easy, as they had proved during their brief visit to the planet. With several trillion of their own kind, they could dominate all humans and plunder Earth. If they decided to eliminate all human life on Earth, mass parasitic control with termination implants would ensure that Earth became theirs to do with as they pleased. Other life on the planet could be dealt with after assessing its potential. Failure meant dishonor and certain death.

With the information gathered by Tracy Doone, data for every employee at Moreton Scientific Investigation was now known. There were five staff members working for Dr. Ben Sharman, and all that was needed was access to the building while the key players were present. One individual, in particular, stood out as the perfect host—an individual with access to the entire building. The address was quite close to the lab, and the employee had been seen going home and not working that afternoon.

The commander relayed the instructions to Tracy. She pulled on the blonde wig, adjusted the necklace, and walked toward Moreton town center.

The meeting with the army and navy representatives proved fruitless. No sightings or indications of the missing spacecraft reported. After each service's representative gave their update, Ben switched the laptop to his presentation and, after guiding them through the history of events, he switched off the projector.

"Ladies and gentlemen. We've reached a critical stage in which this alien presence may be about to vacate the planet. I believe this could prove very costly for all of us.

"There is evidence that they are trying to obtain weapons-grade plutonium. If correct, you can see the problem. It may just be for fuel, but we cannot discount that it's for weapons capability.

"I would urge each one of you to look at everything you are investigating and re-examine everything you have already investigated. Any anomaly, no matter how small. Even the slightest notion of something out of the ordinary may be just the breakthrough we need to discover the craft's location."

Sergeant Bradbury, who just wanted to get back to the parade ground, contemplated the incident with the missing plate on the submersible at Hurley's Farm. It wasn't normal for an access plate to fall off with eight screws holding it in place. He dismissed it as incompetence by Private Smith, who had simply forgotten to secure it. He listened with disinterest, wondering what the mess manager back at the barracks, would rustle up for them, and struggled to keep his eyes open.

"I would ask you once again to be vigilant and pass this down to all personnel under your command. If we can't find this craft, it may come back to haunt us all."

Ben thanked them all as they left.

"Do you want me to clear up all this crap, Ben?" said Kath, staring at a mountain of cups and saucers. "Only I was going to the bank before going home to do the ironing and prepare Patrick's tea, but I don't mind."

"Please, Kath. I appreciate it and make sure you take the time back."

"Oh, you can rest assured about that," she said, clattering the plates and shuffling the saucers.

"Just be back here by eight tonight and it's your turn to bring a cake, Kath."

Ben watched as she burst into her own innovative version of Danny Boy, when the phone rang.

"Do you want the good news or the even better news?"

"Go on, Ron, thrill me with both!"

"Spoke to our head-honcho. You can have full use of the signal-blocking room."

"That's great, Ron. Robyn has already had the go-ahead to move the Reverend Lee down to Cambridge."

"Hang fire, there's better news. The room is mobile."

"What do you mean, mobile? I thought you said it was in a room at your Cambridge site?"

"It's now in a large van and we can set up the equipment just about anywhere."

"That's fantastic. There is one issue. Would the kit be compatible in a hospital?"

"Already sorted, Ben. I've spoken to Dr. Hernandez, and there is an empty isolation ward available. We can set it up at the hospital in Abergavenny and the isolation ward is big enough to accommodate all the host victims we know of if needed."

"Great stuff, Ron. How long before you can arrange it?"

"Don't shout at me, but I knew you were in that meeting with the services this morning. I've taken the liberty of putting the transfer of the kit into action. We are on our way now. Should reach Abergavenny in just under an hour with the blocking function up and running a couple of hours after that."

"That's fantastic Ron. I can't thank you enough."

"Hey! No need for that. We're all in this together. I'll give you a shout when its all ready, so you can get here to talk to Jimmy Griffiths."

Tracy Doone stared out of the charity shop window.

"Anything I can help you with," said the sales assistant, following her around the shop.

"No thanks, I'm browsing," she said, trying to peer over the woman's shoulder.

"Okay, I'll be over there, behind the counter, if you need me."

"Thanks," she said, wishing the assistant would go away and stop hounding her.

The main street in Moreton was so quiet it would be easy to spot the next host. As they would have to walk this way from the lab to go home. Tracy checked the time confirming they were now late, was half tempted to walk over to the lab and follow from there, but it would be far too risky as the police might be looking out for anyone suspicious and the disguise she had chosen was, to her regret, way over the top. A smidge too tarty for a sleepy Cotswold village. A middle-aged dowdy appearance would have been much better to blend in with the locals.

Tracy walked out of the shop after the assistant sidled up to her again, turned and peered back at the window from outside. She stared at the reflection, and after a couple of minutes, the target host walked past. She pushed her sunglasses onto the bridge of her nose, turned, and followed. Glancing sideways at her reflection in the window of a bookstore, she checked herself and toned down the swagger and almost laughed. It was far too obvious. Maintaining the same pace and distance, they both crossed the road and turned into Corders Lane. About halfway down, she stopped, pretending to go through her handbag for something, and when she looked up, the target stepped through a door into a house. Tracy followed and knocked on the door.

FORTY-THREE

With plenty of time to get there, Ben took the scenic route to Abergavenny, a longer rural journey, without the boredom of the motorway and heavy traffic, providing the opportunity to think clearly. By the time he reached the Welsh border, the strange events whirled in his head on a loop. Ben wondered if the good doctor would spare him a couple of tablets as he lowered both front windows, savoring the noisy, cold air buffeting his ears. Without a way through the never-ending maze of dead-ends inside his head, he gave up looking for a solution and admired the view instead.

Dr. Hernandez instructed his staff to say nothing to their special guest. The less Jimmy Griffiths knew, the less the aliens would know of any development that could give them an unwanted advantage.

As instructed, Ben drove through the rear entrance and parked as close as he could to the distinctive black personnel carrier belonging to the Cambridge Scientific Team. He swung his legs out and winced as the headache stabbing the front of his head made him pinch his eyes shut. He was about to sit back inside the car for a few more minutes until the throbbing pain subsided when someone shouted.

"Over here."

Ben found it hard to focus in the voice's direction, but the familiar figure soon came into focus.

Ron, taking yet another cigarette break, stood half inside the building hanging out the door, waving a raised an arm, beckoning him over.

Ben locked the car, and holding his hand over his eyes, walked toward the open door.

"You look like crap, Ben,"

"Many thanks for your kind and uplifting observation. Quite rich, coming from a picture of health," said Ben, trying to laugh. "So, what's the score, Ron?"

"The lads and lasses are doing a test run inside, and it's all looking good. The shielding device works perfectly."

"Fabulous. If we can get him to talk, we might find out where these little green bastards are hiding."

"Yep. Fingers and toes crossed," said Ron, flicking the cigarette end into a bush. Ben watched the small spiral of smoke drifting out of the dry leaves, wondering how Ron hadn't burned his own house to the ground.

"When Jimmy's moved in, can we test the shielding device again with no one present from your team, Ron?"

"Already thought of that. It's all done from outside. Follow me."

They turned the corner to a large white panel van, parked on its own at the back of the isolation block.

"We're on the ground floor on the other side of the wall next to our wagon."

A spaghetti trail of cables led from a locker in the back of the vehicle through a plant room door into the building.

"There's an access hatch between the hospital's electric intake room and the internal services room. We've taken the hatch out and run cables straight through a sub-corridor into the ward. Took some doing as the hatch has never been removed since they built the place, but our guys are very good," said Ron, fishing out a half-smoked dog-end from his top pocket and lighting up. "Jimmy won't see anything. The guys have done a great job of hiding all the equipment, and we can see and hear everything from the van."

"Seems like you have a plan."

"Yes," said Ron, stepping back to the entrance door. "But don't give me any credit. The team is superb at what they do. I just followed their guidance. Well, I told them what we wanted, and they got on with it."

"Can I take a look inside?"

"Sure," said Ron, taking a lungful of smoke and stubbing out the cigarette on a 'No litter' sign before tossing it into the same bush. Ben shook his head, crouched, looked under the small bush, and stepped on each cigarette end in turn.

"Ron, why don't you give up smoking, or at least try not to kill everyone else?" said Ben, but Ron was already out of earshot, stepping through a side entrance door.

The ward reeked of disinfectant. Dr. Hernandez had thrown the whole resources of the cleaning staff at the wing to drag it from disused and dusty to within a shining and sanitized inch of its life.

"We've had to install a fair number of dummy screens to get all the kit in place. Not just in here, but upstairs as well. It's all working tickety-boo," said Ron.

"I'm impressed," said Ben, looking at miles of snaking cables, connectors, junction boxes hidden by a jungle of hospital screens on wheels.

Dr. Hernandez walked in with a nurse.

"We're ready to move the patient, Dr. Sharman," he said. "Anything, in particular, you would like us to do?"

"I want you to ask him medical questions as you would normally do on your rounds. Keep an eye out for any response from him. Once I see he has regained control of his own mind, I'll be straight in and take over."

"Shall I fetch him now?" said Hernandez.

"That would be good. Remember, while you are moving him, please assume they can hear everything you say and do. He may be out of it, but our alien friends will be listening."

"No panic. I've instructed everyone to say nothing apart from myself and Nurse Blake here." She smiled. "We already concocted a script that we are moving him to an isolation ward in case he is carrying any 'infectious disease'."

Ben nodded his approval. "Well, ladies and gentlemen. Shall we begin?"

From ward three of the main block, the porter pushed Jimmy's bed into the lift.

"Have you checked the staff rotas, Nurse Blake?"

"We've organized overtime and assigned one agency staff member per shift until we move Mr. Griffiths out of isolation."

"I didn't want to move him, but the governors overruled my decision."

"Politics, Doctor. There is always politics in this place."

"He'll get the same treatment as he would on the ward. Just hope the poor lad wakes up soon."

The lift door opened, and they carried on the rehearsed discussion until they reached the doors to the isolation room. As soon as they were inside, Jimmy moved his arms and one eye opened.

In the back of the white paneled van, Ben watched the monitor as Jimmy sat up, awake.

"I think your shielding device works, Ron. The aliens kept him out of it until the shield cut them off."

"I told you my guys were good," said Ron, flicking the top of his Zippo lighter open and shut. Ben took it off him. "Keep focused, Ron. You can smoke like a kipper afterward."

"Where am I?" said Jimmy, swinging his legs over the side of the bed.

"You're in Nevill Hall Hospital," said Dr. Hernandez. "You had a minor operation on your head. Feeling better?"

"Feeling good, mate," said Jimmy. "My head hurts," he said feeling the thick bandages circling the top of his head with his uninjured hand, "and my finger tips are throbbing like hell on this hand," he said holding it up.

"If the pain gets worse I can give you something for it."

"It's not so bad at the moment apart from my fingers, and I can think clearly again."

"Clearly?"

"Weird."

"What weird feeling, Jimmy?"

"So strange."

"What was so strange, Jimmy?" said Hernandez, in a calm voice.

"Like I was watching myself from inside. Like I was in a dream, but it was real. So weird."

Hernandez nodded at a hidden camera.

Ben was already through the door. He pulled up a chair and stood behind it, both hands gripping the backrest.

"This is Dr. Sharman, who helps us here at the hospital. He wants to help by asking a few simple questions. Are you okay with that, Jimmy?"

"He's not a cop, is he?"

Hernandez smiled. "No, he's not a cop. He's a scientist, and like I said, he's here to help."

Jimmy nodded, and Ben moved around the chair and sat down, leaning forward.

"Jimmy. I'm Ben Sharman."

"But I don't understand. Why am I here? How long have I been here?"

"You've been through a traumatic experience. Can you remember being in Merthyr Police Station in the cell?"

"Yes, but what happened? Those dreams?"

"Just take your time. It's bound to be a shock."

"Strange dreams. So vivid."

"Can you remember anything about a spacecraft?"

He looked shocked at the question and remained silent. His eyes were wide and his mouth open as he took in where he had been.

"The spacecraft. It was spinning. It was round, and hot," he said looking at his bandaged hand. "Spinning so fast."

"There were aliens in the spacecraft. Did they speak to you?"

"No, that's absurd. It was a dream."

"Did they make you walk over the mountain to the reservoir?"

"How do you know that?"

"Jimmy. Tell me about the dream."

The startled expression remained on his face.

"Take your time, Jimmy. This is all going to seem strange, but it's really important."

"But it was a dream."

"If I can understand your dream, it will be useful, and I can help you."

"I tried to do things and I couldn't. I was watching. They made me walk for miles. But it was all a dream."

"Jimmy, you're doing great."

"Why are they doing this?"

"What do they want?" said Ben.

Without hesitation, Jimmy looked into Ben's eyes. "The flask."

"Why do they want the flask, Jimmy? This is important."

"The dream must have stopped. I can't sense them in my head anymore."

"That's right, Jimmy, we sent them away. Do you know what they want with the flask?"

"They had to land in water."

"Why did they land in the reservoir, Jimmy?"

"The Kreeg messed up again."

"What is The Kreeg, Jimmy?"

"The Kreeg built the ship. It all went wrong. No fuel left. Had to land in water."

"When they leave, will they ever come back?"

Jimmy's eyes were wide. "Yes, they will do this to everyone." Jimmy's breathing became rapid. Hernandez checked the monitors and nodded to Ben to proceed.

"Okay, you're doing fine, Jimmy. Where they are now?"

"The aliens?"

"Yes, the aliens. Where have they gone?"

"I don't know where it is. Only see it like the other place. I was down there—" He started crying. "They will call us."

"What do you mean, they will call you Jimmy?"

"When it is time for them to leave, they will call us. We will have to go to them."

"When they leave?"

"Ben, I'm switching the signal off. We've got a problem," said Ron through Ben's earpiece.

Jimmy slumped back in the bed and resumed the blank expression, staring straight ahead.

"You can't switch it off!" screamed Ben. "They might kill him!"

"I had to. Come out to the wagon and I'll show you why."

Ben ran through the doors, pushing them so hard they crashed against the wall and leaped up the steps into the back of the white van.

"Why, Ron?"

"Something jammed us. Everything on board overheated. I had to close it down. I've never seen anything like it."

"Shit. It has to be them."

"That's the bad news. I hope they don't do anything to the hosts."

"Is there any good news?"

"I tracked the source. We have a rough fix on their location."

"Where is it?"

"On the flight path you tracked and in an area the army has

already looked at. I think they need to look again. Just past Moreton, about five miles east."

"Jimmy said like the other place. He was down there. He means the reservoir. It has to be in another body of water."

"There are two farms in the area with six ponds and a gravel pit."

"Excellent stuff, Ron. They need to be taken out as fast as possible."

FORTY-FOUR

"I see you brought the cake. What type is it? Can I see?" said Claire, lifting the tin lid.

"Get your paws off," said Kath, wagging her finger at Claire, and almost slamming the cake tin lid on her fingers. "You'll find out soon enough when we have tea and coffee in about ten minutes. One of my best, If I say so myself," she said pushing the tin out of Claire's reach.

Ben strolled in carrying a large cardboard box. "I hope everyone likes Chinese takeaway. I got a meal for six, which should be plenty for seven of us."

"Didn't they do a meal for seven or maybe eight?" said Claire, examining the contents of the box and grabbing a handful of prawn crackers.

"Nope, they never do a seven and the meal for eight would burst your ribs."

"Make sure you leave enough room to eat my cake," said Kath. "And don't leave all those filthy tin foil trays all over the place. I've scrubbed your bench. Call yourself scientists. It's a breeding ground for the plague in here with all the mess you lazy sods leave lying around. God knows what we would have caught if I didn't scrub the place from top to bottom."

Ben stripped off the foil lids and placed them into the cardboard box, turned and curtseyed to Kath. "Are we all here yet?"

"Kerry and Jen are in the kitchen, but Roger hasn't shown up yet," said Claire. "It's not quite eight though, so he'll not be late for the next five minutes."

"He'll end up with the scraps if he's not careful," said Ben, loading his plate with special fried rice and sticky ribs. "It's always the same with Chinese food. I don't feel hungry and don't fancy it until I smell it. Now I'm bloody starving."

"Roger said he would be ten minutes late," said Kath. "He's gone to the off-license for a few cold ones. I told him to get some of that fizzy stuff for us girls."

"Prosecco?" said Claire, hopefully.

"Aye, that fizzy pop stuff that posh people drink."

"I think that's champagne. I can't see Roger buying that for us, not on the wages Ben pays us," said Claire.

"What was that?" said Roger, appearing at the door with a carrier bag.

"The champagne you bought us?"

"Yeh! Right!" he said, placing packs of beer and half a dozen bottles of cheap sparkling wine on the bench.

They sat around the bench like a pack of wolves, silent apart from the sounds of cutlery on plates. The entire team had worked hard and not eaten since lunchtime and ate in silence for five minutes while the food hit the spot. Another long night sleeping on the job, but it was still a novelty, and a chance to get to know each other.

"Sorry about the enforced curfew," said Ben. "I appreciate the sacrifice from each of you, away from your homes and families, but it is for the best."

"Such a blessing," said Kath, going back for seconds. "I can get a decent night's kip here. Patrick is like a bloody wildebeest when he snores and it lasts for hours, even if I kick the crap out of him, he doesn't stop for long. No, Ben, this is no sacrifice. In fact, I could get quite used to this. If you would like to put a cleaner's flat in the building, I won't be objecting."

Ben raised an eyebrow. "Hopefully, you won't have to, once this is all over."

"How is this going to end, Ben?" said Kerry.

"Should be soon. The army has a better idea of where the spacecraft is now. They'll be out looking at first light."

"What will they do when they find it?"

"Hopefully, disable and destroy the damned thing."

"What happens if they don't?"

"Let's not go there," said Ben. "Be positive. I believe the army will make sure they get it."

War of the Worlds was the Netflix film of choice for the evening, during which Kath talked all the way through. After they drained every can and bottle, exhaustion set in. Roger had a mattress on the floor of the lab. Ben slept in his office, Claire in her office, and the other three girls were in the smaller research lab.

Claire closed her office blinds, changed into her PJs and set her alarm when Jen knocked at the door.

"Can I ask a massive favor? Would you mind if I slept in here with you? Only Kath kept me awake last night, snoring, and I cannot stick it?"

"Sorry Jen, I don't think I've enough room in here with the desk and boxes. It's a bit of a squeeze with me on my own."

"Please, I don't want to sleep in the store. It's so bloody creepy in there."

"I tell you what. Why don't you have my office and I'll sleep in the store? Doesn't bother me either way. I've seen enough creepy things over the last few months to last me a lifetime. I'm sure a cupboard won't bother me."

"You don't have to do that," she said, starting to retreat through the office door. "I'll go back."

Claire looked at her. Although only a year younger, Jen was

much younger in her ways. She looked so tired and no wonder with Kath O'Brian's nocturnal bellowing, enough to keep the dead awake.

"Get your bedding. I'll clear a space for you. But you better not snore, or I'll kick you out!"

Jen crept away and was soon back and tucked into her sleeping bag, with Kath O'Brian's distant roars in the distance vibrating throughout the building.

The alien waited until all human voices stopped, then shut down its current host's mind. Squeezing through the tympanic membrane, it crawled out of the ear and once outside adjusted its legs, growing, extending, and expanding the abdomen. After scanning the other person sleeping on the other side of the room, it skittered across the floor, leaving a thin trail of bloodied pinpricks on the tiled surface.

Even with legs and abdomen retracted, the underside of the door was too tight. It expanded once more and surveyed the walls and ceiling, finding no obvious breach to crawl through. Its two antennae extended upward, picking up slow-moving air and traced the source, a half-open window.

Once outside, it scaled the rough surface of the red brick wall with ease, before pulling itself over the plastic lip of the guttering. After walking halfway across the length of the building, an air vent, just below the eaves, gave it access into the attic and the roof voids above several rooms. It scanned for life forms, detecting one male in the main room, one male in the small room, an older female with another woman, and two females in another. Female humans had been far more receptive but would be risky with two in the same room. Claire Manson was the optimum target from everything learned from the previous host Kerry Bailey. Claire Manson should know where the flask was located and if not, Ben Sharman would be the next target.

A light fitting in a panel of the false ceiling provided the route from the attic into the room below. Moving across the underside of the false ceiling, while scanning everything below for movement, it came to a sudden halt, stuck fast in sticky strands. A large house spider ran out from a crack in the wall and seized the alien in its jaws, trying and failing to inject poison. The alien dealt with the spider, ripping off three legs and sending the spider floating downwards. It spiraled through the air before landing on Jen's face. She woke as the spider, with its five remaining legs, tried to escape across her cheek and forehead. Claire leaped out of her sleeping bag, awoken by Jen's screaming, and flicked the lights on.

Brushing her hand across her head, Jen wouldn't stop screeching and within a few seconds, everyone was awake and peering through the door.

"Jen, you're okay. You're having a nightmare."

"No, something crawled across my face."

Ben stepped in and dragged them both out, slamming the door.

"Was it the alien?" said Claire.

"I don't know, but I'm not taking any chances. All move back from the door."

Jen screamed again as the disabled spider crawled up the sleeve of her pajamas.

"Bloody hell, Jen. It's a tiny spider," said Ben, cupping the spider in his hands and throwing it out of the window.

"We have those little sods in our house. Bloody sight bigger than that. So big you could put a saddle on the little feckers," said Kath, who was in an emerald-green dressing gown, curlers, and had no teeth.

Ben looked at Claire. They started laughing until everyone was in hysterics. Even Kath O'Brian giggled when she realized her false teeth were in her dressing gown pocket.

"Where's Kerry," said Claire. "She couldn't have slept through Jen's theatrics?"

"She did," said Kath.

"Lucky her. Now, shall we try to get some sleep, please? It's almost three o'clock," said Ben.

"No way I can get back to sleep yet," said Claire, stifling a yawn. "Anyone for a cuppa?"

Everyone except Ben sat in the lab chatting until tiredness dragged them away one by one. Last to go were Claire and Jen.

"Do you want me to check my office for spiders?"

"No, you're okay. Sorry, Claire. I didn't mean to wake everybody up. Such a horrible shock to have that land on my face."

"Don't worry. Try to get some sleep."

Jen stared up at the ceiling and couldn't drift off, squirming at the thought of the spider's legs crawling across her forehead. Her imagination ran riot, and she swore she could still feel the spider's legs on her face.

Remaining into the attic void had been the only choice. The alien stayed motionless, waiting for the females to fall asleep for at least an hour before making its next move.

FORTY-FIVE

Perfectly still in the attic above the office, it waited for both women to fall asleep. However, with one of them still wide awake, the opportunity to use a new host diminished. It faced a decision: should it remain in place, hoping for a chance to arise, or return to the previous host?

As it moved toward the vent, its antennae detected a faint tingling sensation as it passed the top of a dividing wall. The sensation grew stronger, prompting it to change direction toward the source. It crawled into a package resting on a ceiling tile and discovered a flask hidden inside, lined with lead to shield radiation. Although out of sight, the flask emitted enough radiation to be detectable and after processing the information and determining the flask's precise location in the building; it made its way through the ventilation block, descended the external red brick wall, and entered the small lab through the half-open window.

The older female, making a terrible noise, provided a welcome distraction. The rasping sound echoed around the room, allowing the alien to move without making any discernible noise. It re-entered through the same ear it had exited earlier with the fresh puncture wound, making it easy to pass through once it compressed its body and bunched all its legs into a fine, needle-like point. Inside Kerry's brain cavity, it re-established connections, maintaining control over the host's conscious thoughts, and ingested a small quantity of cerebrospinal fluid to refuel its body.

At 5:30 am, Kerry Bailey woke, unaware that she was being manipulated by the parasitic alien inside her head.

Seventy-six miles away, in the isolation ward of Nevill Hall Hospital, Jimmy Griffiths sat up, his gaze fixed on the unadorned magnolia walls. He followed the instructions, rising from the bed, retrieving his clothes from the nearby locker, and dressed in silence. With care, he nudged the side ward door ajar, positioning himself against the door frame. Around the corner, he surveyed the dimly lit corridor where two night-shift nurses conversed in hushed tones at the central workstation. Shadows cloaked his end of the corridor, offering him the safety of obscurity.

He watched with a sense of relief as the nurses remained deep in their conversation, oblivious to his presence. This boosted his confidence, and, moving with stealth akin to a cat, he navigated the corridor until he reached a set of automatic doors. The doors slid open as he approached and the sudden motion caught the attention of the nurses. One of them leaped up, her gaze fixed down the corridor, alert and wary.

"Must be the hospital ghost again. Nobody there," she said to her colleague. "Either that or a moth flew in front of the sensors. Those doors will open if you so much as fart!"

"I haven't seen the ghost myself, but Sandra Jones, off the day shift, reckons it's a patient from fifty years ago when it used to be a fever hospital. Some old man, wandering about lost, wearing a long white nightgown."

"You don't believe in ghosts, do you?"

"Jury's out on that. I think there's a lot we can't explain. Quite a few people reckon they have seen the old fella, which makes you wonder if it's true when so many people have seen him. They can't all be making it up, can they?"

"I just hope he doesn't come bothering us. The patients give us enough to worry about without some poltergeist wandering the corridors."

Jimmy sought refuge in an alcove on the opposite side of the double doors. He waited for them to close, willing the two nurses to return to their paranormal conversation. He relaxed, allowing them to converse for a while before making his move, then crept, pressed against the wall, tracing its cool, smooth, painted contours, maintaining a safe distance from the automatic doors, which remained closed, until he reached the exit onto the staircase.

The nurses' chatter faded into the background as Jimmy eased the door open, descended the stairs, eventually reaching an emergency push bar door. He prayed it wasn't fitted with an alarm as he cautiously pushed down on the bar, hearing the distinct click as the two bolts disengaged. He paused, straining his ears for any signs of movement from the floor above, but there was nothing. Holding his breath, he opened the door with just a faint click as it reached its limit. With no alarm blaring, a rush of cold air swept across his face, making the strands of his fringe flutter over his eyes. He exhaled and stepped out into the car park, remaining alert with his eyes darting in every direction.

Rows of empty parking spaces with no visitors arriving for several hours didn't bode well. The early morning air made the wound on his head throb as Jimmy, looking in dismay at the empty parking lot, considered his options. The hospital must be near the center of Abergavenny, which he remembered wasn't a big town. There would be plenty of opportunities to find and break into a car in the surrounding streets, as the hospital wouldn't be the best place to steal a car. An alarm going off in the hospital grounds at this time of the morning with CCTV everywhere was not going to happen.

Jimmy checked the signs along the internal ring road encircling the building, searching for the exit, and just when he needed a stroke of luck, it materialized as a small, unmarked van turned the corner of the service entrance. He prayed that the driver would step out, leaving the van unattended for a moment, making it a straightforward task for him to break in. Given the van's dated appearance, he hoped it lacked an alarm system and would be easy to hot-wire.

The rising sun's reflection glinted off the bald head of the burly van driver, who left the vehicle, with its engine running. It seemed too good to be true. Jimmy observed the man's carefree stroll across the car park, whistling, without a care in the world, and then walking into an old brick outbuilding, through a door marked 'Laundry,' presumably delivering or collecting items.

Jimmy waited a couple of seconds, making sure he didn't return straight away. The driver would be occupied, chatting with laundry staff or a hospital porter. He sprinted across the car park, leaped into the driver's seat, and discovered his guess was correct. On the passenger seat lay a clipboard with the day's delivery schedule, and on the back seat sat a dozen white linen sacks. At the top of the printed schedule, he read the first delivery of the day, 06:00 am - Nevill Hall. The driver was early, about to enjoy a cup of tea or coffee. What a gift! The stupid idiot had forgotten to attach a sign on the roof of the van that read 'Please Steal Me,' but had left everything else unguarded; the van door open, keys in the ignition, and the engine running.

Jimmy's face lit up with satisfaction as he glanced at the fuel gauge. Full to the brim! The van, filled with the familiar scents of aged leather and rubber mats, reminded him of his father's old Ford Transit; a vehicle he had driven many times when his father had forgotten to hide the keys. The controls, gears, and dashboard felt like the welcoming presence of an old friend. Jimmy shifted the gearstick into reverse, gliding backward across the car park before making his way toward the rear service road's exit.

In less than a minute, the van cruised along the main road outside the hospital. It proved to be the easiest carjack of Jimmy's career, and it only came to light when the rightful driver returned to his vehicle to retrieve his newspaper at 5:45 am. By that time, Jimmy was already accelerating away on the outskirts of Abergavenny, heading toward Monmouth.

Tracy Doone remained seated in a chair inside the Corders Lane house for a solid twelve hours, rising at precisely 5:30 am. The small house yielded a pair of size five running shoes in the upstairs wardrobe. They were almost the right fit, just a half size too big, but with the laces drawn tight, they would do.

She opened the front door to a dull, drizzling morning, then looked behind the door at the coat rack, and found no coats. She retraced her steps to Kerry's bedroom, recalling a gray hoodie hanging on the back of a chair. Even though the weather was mild, she wore it to remain inconspicuous.

Tracy adjusted the blonde wig in the hallway mirror and pulled the hood forward, tugging the drawstrings to conceal most of her face, with only the tip of her nose protruding. She found a small telescopic umbrella in the hallway, cracked the front door open a couple of inches, and peered outside. With no signs of sound or movement in the lane, she ventured out, opening the umbrella, and gently closed the door behind her. Mist settled over the town as Tracy began her walk toward Chipping Norton at a leisurely pace, not to draw attention. Once she passed the outskirts of Moreton, she hurled the umbrella over a hedge and quickened her steps.

Peter Jenkins phoned his wife before heading to the hospital's parking lot and waited there. He wasn't sure why he had called her at such an unusual hour, but he knew he needed her to pick him up and retrieve some clothes before they embarked on an urgent journey. Though he couldn't pinpoint the destination, he had an undeniable sense of purpose.

It astounded his wife that he was alert and no longer in a zombie-like state, and she hurried to the hospital. She was desperate to have him back home, but she also understood that the specialist, who she had spoken to a few hours earlier, insisted on more analysis of his vegetative state. The specialist had even informed her he would have to remain in the hospital for at least another week.

Despite her efforts to persuade him otherwise, Peter pushed her back into the car and was determined to go home. She reluctantly gave in, intending to call the specialist later that morning. Upon returning to the house, he went straight upstairs to change his clothes, while she continued to argue and plead with him. He forcefully took the car keys from her grasp, and despite her protests, Peter got back in the car. As he pulled out of the driveway, the clock read 5:48 am, and she watched anxiously through the curtains, hoping he hadn't disturbed the neighbors. In just two hours, he would drive to the Cotswolds.

Aboard the ship, the engineering crew worked tirelessly to ready themselves for the arrival of the new fuel payload. The commander, well aware that any mistake at this critical juncture would prove fatal, ensured that every piece of equipment on the ship underwent thorough checks and double-checks. The mission required them to reach the mother ship and depart the galaxy in just a few hours.

FORTY-SIX

Kath O'Brian opened one eye and peered at her watch, which was blank, flat as a pancake. She tapped the face twice. "Feckin, fangled gadget." Then tapped it half a dozen times more.

Kerry stared at her from the other side of the room.

"Hell, Kerry, you made me jump. I didn't expect you to be awake. What's the time?"

"Time for me to get away from your snoring, Kath."

"Who, me?" she said, looking hurt.

"Yes, you."

"I don't snore. You must be dreaming."

"How the hell would you know that?"

"Patrick said."

"Patrick must be a bloody good liar or as deaf as a post. That's all I can say!"

"Well, that's true enough," she said, clutching her neck. "Come to think of it, my throat feels like I've been gargling bleach or chewing sandpaper. Perhaps you're right. I might have been snoring."

"No, might about it, Kath. Either bleach or the bottle and a half of Roger's rocket fuel last night had a lot to do with it."

"Aye, there was a bit of a kick to it. I can always tell when I've had a drop too much. I sing. Just can't help myself."

"Yep! The full nine yards last night. I now know every Irish song that's ever been sung."

Kerry unzipped the sleeping bag and draped a cardigan around her shoulders.

"Jeez, you're bleeding," said Kath

"Sorry?"

"From your ear, it's all the way down your neck, and it's soaked into your pajamas."

"Oh, yes, I had a scabby bit just inside my ear. Must have picked it off in my sleep."

"Do you want me to take a look? That looks nasty."

"Thanks, Kath, but I'll sort it out. Looks much worse than it is."

Kerry went to the ladies' room and could see quite a lot of blood had congealed on her pajama top and her neck, and her hair matted around the ear. She knew it should bother her, but for some strange reason, she didn't seem to care.

She washed the blood away in the sink and tidied herself up before tiptoeing to reception. Three bunches of keys hung inside the metal wall cabinet, but not one for the storeroom. She remembered the spare master key.

Kerry eased the small lab door open and traced her fingers along the dusty surface on top of the test kit cupboard and found the spare. The silence in the corridor required careful movement, only interrupted by the unrelenting snores echoing behind her. She looked left and right and remained still, listening. Nothing apart from the constant roars of Kath O'Brian. She eased the key into the lock, stopped, and listened again before turning the key to the left. The lock made a small click that sounded deafening in the quiet corridor. Kerry held her breath and pushed the door, which opened smoothly. Once inside, the set of steps made it easy to reach and push the ceiling tile off its aluminum frame. It clattered. She stopped and listened for a few seconds before groping around in the dark void above. Her hand brushed the side of a bag and, by standing on tiptoes, she found the bag's handle and dragged it forward a few inches, opened the parcel inside, and pulled out the flask.

A noise made her freeze. The main entrance door opening in reception. Was someone was coming in or going out? She waited, not daring to breathe. Silent. Even Kath had stopped bellowing. Pushing the cupboard door open, Kerry peered into the empty corridor before making her way to reception. The carrier bag Roger brought the booze in was still on the reception desk and, with the flask inside the bag, Kerry crept out and made her way up Church Street.

Ben watched from the graveyard of St. David's Church, peering round a row of bushes in dismay as Kerry walked past with a carrier bag. He'd been awake for some time, trying to block out Kath's snoring and when the snoring stopped, noises coming from the store cupboard had him dressed and ready. At 5:40 am it wasn't someone looking for a ream of photocopier paper. He stepped outside to see who would emerge and whoever it was, there would be no blame. How could he? The only blame was on himself, for putting his staff at risk, albeit a calculated risk, which should lead them to the alien spaceship. He watched her until she disappeared into an alleyway a few hundred yards up Church Street.

Back in the building, Ben ran to the unlocked store cupboard. The stepladder was still in place at the far end of the stationary rack. He looked up at the missing tile, now perched on the top of a shelf, which confirmed everything.

Claire wandered in, staring at the dark space caused by the missing ceiling tile.

"What's going on Ben?"

"I heard someone in here, which was strange for anyone to be looking for pens and paper at this unearthly hour, and guessed it must be someone on the hunt for something else. I realized whoever it was would leave the building, so I hid in St Davids Church to see who it was. Kerry is the latest host, and she's just taken the flask." He stood on the ladder, pulled down the bag containing the parcel, and opened it to show her. Everything was still inside except the small silver flask.

"Shit, I should have put it somewhere else," said Claire. "Shouldn't have kept it in the building."

"Too late for thinking about what we should or shouldn't have done. We need to locate that ship before it takes off again."

"Did you find her, Ben?" said Kath, who now had a full set of perfect teeth.

"Yes, and I have a good idea where she's going, so don't worry about it, Kath, and thanks for telling me about her ear."

"Ear?" said Claire.

"I'll explain in the car. Get dressed as quick as you can."

He pulled the mobile from his pocket. The aliens now had the flask in their possession and the plan devised, with a little help from Ron, had to work.

FORTY-SEVEN

Jimmy Griffiths opened the five-bar gate, drove the van into the field, parked it tight to the hedge out of sight, shut the gate, and abandoned it. A half-mile walk across three fields to reach the gravel pit would only take ten minutes. The journey from Abergavenny took under two hours with very little traffic until he reached Tewkesbury, when the morning rush hour began. The stroll across open fields was a welcome break from the monotony of driving. He didn't understand why he had stolen the van, why he had taken the route, or why they wanted him to walk across three fields.

He tried to think of Dr. Sharman talking to him in the hospital, but every time he could hear Ben's voice in his head, his mind went blank. Had he said there were aliens? Flashes of the conversation drifted in and out, but he just couldn't hang on to any thread, like catching a hint of smoke in the air and before he could say what was burning, a gust of wind blowing it away, just out of reach.

The rain on the meadow grass soaked through his training shoes, turning his feet ice cold, but he didn't feel it. The pain in his fingers and the throbbing headache had vanished. He wasn't aware of the cold nip in the air or the swaying branches of hedgerows as the wind swirled and bustled and drizzle turned into something more ominous as skies darkened a deep blackish blue of towering cumulous clouds.

Jimmy strode up the slight incline of the second field, registering a lull in the wind. Hedgerows stopped swaying, wet grass stopped rippling in the wind eddies and he could now see ahead without squinting. A still, eerie silence before a palpable change, just as the skies darkened ahead, then lit up for a second as a distant lightning bolt arced sideways across the heavens in long clawed fingers, heralding the approaching storm. His pace quickened. The last field was tricky to approach with a quagmire in the gap in the hedge between the two fields, where a small brook had turned into a thick, flowing slurry. Hanging onto an old fencepost, he tried to straddle the deep mud, but the rotten wood underneath gave way, and he jumped backward. Logic should have made him look for another route to avoid getting his shoes filthy, but the unseen force inside his head compelled him to step forward. Up to the knee on the first step into the slick mud and as he steadied to take another, the hedge next to him moved. A soldier, who had been there all the time, hidden in plain sight, stepped out.

"Jimmy Griffiths. Stop right there."

Jimmy peered down the barrel of a rifle. There was no shock or fear. Nothing other than the burning desire to keep going. He stared at the soldier, looking for any sign of intent, but found no hint in the man's eyes, no emotion, no clue.

"Come with me, now," the soldier shouted. "Don't do anything stupid, lad."

Jimmy continued to stare with a growing compulsion to run across the third field. He acted on impulse and dragged himself through the mire without hesitation, which he knew was absurd when faced with an armed, professional soldier. A second soldier lying in wait in long grass rose from his hiding place and charged, rugby tackling him into the sodden earth. Jimmy went down like a full strike on a bowling alley, landing face first with his mouth submerged in grass and squelching mud. The other soldier dropped his weapon and pulled out a syringe. They lifted Jimmy Griffiths, turned him over, and held him in position. He looked up at two soldiers' faces disappearing into blackness as the contents of the syringe did its work.

Richard Jenkins pulled into a lay-by a mile from the farm. Three police cars screeched to a halt in a planned pincer movement, hemming him in. He stepped out of his car to protest, and police officers handcuffed him and pushed him face-first onto his car's side. He didn't see the soldier getting out of the lead squad car with the syringe.

Tracy Doone got a mile outside Moreton when an unmarked van passed her and screeched to a halt in front after mounting the pavement. Three soldiers dragged her into the van and even though she broke one man's wrist, they subdued her. As she lay face down in the back of the van, screaming at them, the prick of the needle in her arm brought instant calm.

Kerry Williams drove through a series of back lanes with the screen wipers working overtime. The lane became a stone track and narrowed to a dead end, making it impossible to drive any further.

Clutching the flask, she straddled a stile into a field full of cattle that watched her pass with curiosity as torrents fell from the black clouds, plastering her hair to her head. The sky flashed and roared overhead as she scrambled up a muddy path, running up the side of a crumbling dry-stone wall, tripping and sliding through water cascading from the steep slope above. At the top of the hill, the gravel pit appeared through a section of collapsed dry stone wall. Kerry slipped and fell, sliding through a thick slurry. The flask bounced down the hill, coming to rest in a puddle of fresh rainwater.

She crouched, sliding down, gripping soaked tufts of grass to steady herself. Thunder crashed across the hill, shaking the ground. The flask was in her hand once more and after reaching level ground, Kerry, with both arms outstretched for balance, could just about walk toward the pit without falling over.

She saw light pulsing deep in the water at the base of the gravel pit and lowered herself over the edge, trying to hold on to the steep bank, but the wall of dirt, grit, and wet moss crumbled, cascading down into the pit. Her grip failed and just before she slid down, something erupted from the water, gripped around her waist and lifting her clear above the surface.

Lowered to the edge of the black pool, the thin metal snake released her and curled around the flask, but she snatched it away. It curled around her waist, lifting her up once more, and pulled her across the water's surface.

"No!" screamed Ben, in the control unit parked in the barn.

"Unit one open fire," said the commander, seated next to him.

There was a burst of rapid fire and the metal claw of the snake sheared off, dropping into the depths, sending Kerry and the flask tumbling into the water. She surfaced, still holding the flask, treading water, gasping for breath.

Ben ran four hundred yards from the barn to the pit, falling over half a dozen times, getting up, stumbling, sliding, cursing, and threw himself down the steep pit wall. He landed on the bank as the remaining portion of the metal snake emerged from the depths, wrapping around her torso and pulling Kerry under. The light, deep beneath the surface, pulsed, then faded to nothing.

"Shit, shit, shit, that wasn't supposed to happen!" He screamed, hands on knees, breathing heavily.

"Ben, stick to the plan," said Ron in his earpiece.

"But Kerry's down there."

"We saw this before. I think she'll be okay. The jammer is being turned on."

As soon as they activated the jamming device, the ship's commander plunged into a state of complete panic. The flask hauled aboard the ship revealed nothing but a tiny amount of plutonium residue that wouldn't provide enough power for the required escape velocity from the planet's gravitational pull, let alone facilitate a return to the mother ship. The humans had outwitted the commander, who seethed with anger and vowed revenge, though the present moment was not the time for it. They needed to act swiftly, with their meager remaining solar energy. Cut off from all communications, their paramount aim was to put as much distance between them and their current location as possible. The launch sequence started, and all external devices retracted.

Kerry, released from the snaking grip, rose immobile and as she broke through the water's surface, the entire pit lit up from beneath. Ben, with a determined lunge, dived headfirst to reach Kerry's motionless body. Reaching her he grasped her chin from behind and propelled himself backward toward the bank, with legs kicking vigorously. A soldier waded in and, with considerable effort, hauled them both out of the water. Kerry, still retching, was pulled to her feet as they attempted to ascend the waterlogged bank.

Halfway up, the bank collapsed, and they slid back, Ben falling back into the water.

The soldier screamed, "We need a rope to get us out of here and quick before it launches."

A winch cable lowered toward them on the side of the bank from an army personnel carrier. Ben saw it and signaled to the soldier to get ready. They gripped Kerry with one arm each and both held onto the winch hook and cable.

"Take us up," screamed Ben.

The winch hauled them upward at a snails pace. Ben looked down into the pit where huge vapor bubbles rose and burst open on the surface while the ship's light below pulsed and glowed as the launch sequence progressed. He looked up at three wide-eyed faces with arms outstretched, waiting to pull them clear.

Kerry came around and twisted sideways. The soldier tried to correct himself, losing his grip, and dropped back down to the edge of the pool. The winch pulled them upward inch by inch. Kerry clinging to Ben's neck as he struggled to keep a grip on the rising winch hook.

"Hold on tight," he shouted and released his other arm to grab the hook. With only a few feet to go, the water steamed, boiling below.

The soldier ran around the pond and managed to scramble up the far bank after several attempts.

Ben's fingers were numb. He had to hold on or the searing blast from the ship would cremate them as it launched. The roar of the ship drowned out Kerry's screams as it lifted out the water, breaking the surface, starting to revolve. Ben felt a hand on his wrist, but they were still not high enough for the soldiers to drag them clear. The ship spun faster and faster, with the noise of its engines building to an ear shattering crescendo. Another hand caught Ben's sleeve as the entire surface of the pond shuddered, soil cascaded down all sides of the pit, and rocks plummeted into the depths as the ground around the pit vibrated so much it began to lose solidity. The intensity of the ship's engines shook the sides of the steep banks, creating mudslides slewing into the pool. Ben felt himself being pulled clear. The soldiers lifted them away from the edge, lifting them upright. They ran down the steep muddy road toward the farmhouse, with Kerry being dragged by two soldiers, with the toes of her shoes scraping along the ground. The wall of the pit collapsed into the water and a blaze of light appeared above the crumbling lip, scorching the wet grass all around the opening. Clouds of boiling steam spread out in a spiraling, wide, glistening ring.

They were a hundred yards away when the deafening screech of the ship's engines moving to full power erupted. Soldiers pushed them to the ground as the ship accelerated into the sky like a white hot bullet. Ben looked up in awe as the dazzling orb streaked away, wondering when it would be back to do its worst and wipe out humanity. As it passed into the blackness, the dense clouds above lit up, and a noise louder than any clap of thunder exploded all around the farm. Then silence.

Ben stared up into the clouds above, which had returned to a dense black mass, and cursed the plan that had failed. It was his fault entirely. Too many aspects of the plan relied on assumptions. Heavy rain fell, replacing fine drizzle, just to add to his misery. He put his arm around Kerry, who was sobbing, curled up in a fetal position, then pushed her away, remembering she was the latest host. Kerry shook her head.

"Don't worry, Ben, it's gone," she said, turning her head and lifting her hair to show the trickle of blood running down her neck.

"Look!" shouted a soldier, pointing up at the clouds.

Pieces of brilliant white debris dropped from the sky, landing in dense corn two fields away.

In his earpiece, Ben heard the crew in the control unit cheering.

"What the hell was that, Ron?"

"The RAF took it out. Air to air missile, direct hit. That giant flash in the clouds wasn't lightning. They got the bastards!"

"Bloody hell, that was a close call," said Ben, smiling with relief.

"Close isn't the word. You were about five seconds from being roasted in that pit, which was the RAF's original target."

FORTY-EIGHT

"Roger, I was only joking when I said champagne," said Claire, examining the bottle. "Looks expensive, not like you to splash the cash."

"Not from me. Ben sent me out to pick it up. He wants to see us all in the lab."

"I'll bring some glasses," said Claire.

"Sorry to put a downer on it, Claire, but your mate pulled up outside," said Roger.

"Mate?"

"You know?" said Roger with a wry smile. "Your mate from Cambridge with the runny nose."

"I never thought for one minute I would say this, but I'll be pleased to see him."

Roger's eyes widened. "Hells bells, you've changed your tune."

"Yes, he's not so bad."

Roger laughed. "Are we talking about the same 'booger Logan' that you loathed with a passion?"

Claire smiled. "Yes. He is still as disgusting as ever, but apart from the trail of stinking tissues, he has done an amazing job during this investigation, and if it wasn't for him, the aliens would have got away."

The whole team, plus Ron, sat around the lab front bench, and as Ben looked at them, he smiled, grateful and proud to be surrounded by every one of them.

"Okay. The reason I dragged you all here is to thank you and to give you an apology."

Claire looking puzzled. "Apologize for what?"

Ben raised his palms up. "I'll come to that in a moment. But first a huge thank you for all working so hard on this case. It has been exhausting and not comfortable sleeping here and I would also like to pay special thanks to Ron and all our colleagues and good friends from the Cambridge Scientific team who have been a pleasure to work with, not just in this case, but in everything we've done before."

Claire grinned as Ron blushed.

"The apology is more of an explanation than an apology. Claire, I removed the plutonium before you put it in void above the store cupboard. In fact even before I sent it down from Cumbria. Far too risky for the aliens to find. I didn't want you in on that for obvious reasons. Reducing the number of people with that knowledge was essential."

"What if the aliens had used you as a host?" said Claire. "Where did you hide it?"

"Back where it came from. Even if they got to me, I didn't know exactly where it was. I sent the plutonium to Sellafield, using a courier, the day I sent the package down for you ti pick up. You put it in the store cupboard and left the flask hidden here, which had traces of the metal inside and would still show low levels of radiation. I bonded the lid of the flask to the body to make sure it would be very difficult to open and check the contents.

"The rest was set up between myself and Ron, who has been coordinating with the RAF and special forces. We identified the location of the spacecraft as soon as they tried to get past the jamming system during Jimmy Griffiths' brain operation. So desperate to infiltrate the jamming frequencies at Nevill Hall Hospital, they gave their position away."

"Why didn't the RAF blast the site once they knew its location?" asked Claire.

"The target needed to be above water to be successful. Twenty or thirty meters down, and they couldn't guarantee a clean strike. The original plan was for us to be all clear of the gravel pit. Special forces were going to take the ship out as it emerged from the water."

"Until they got me," said Kerry.

"That's right," said Ben. "I expected, wrongly, that they would take the flask and leave enough time for us to withdraw and let the special forces do their stuff. Kerry would not interest them and I thought they wouldn't waste time taking her under the surface. They did, which changed the plan."

"Good job the RAF was involved," said Claire.

"They were always going to be above the farm as a fallback, which proved critical. Full credit to the pilots flying in atrocious conditions."

"The one thing I don't understand," said Roger, "is why the victims were making their way to the gravel pit?"

"To create a human shield around the spaceship. With them in place, the aliens assumed we wouldn't attack them. Jimmy Griffiths told me that when the aliens were leaving, they would make the hosts go to them. I tipped off the military to intercept and immobilize each one they captured to prevent any further communication with the aliens.

"The other good news is that all the former hosts, including our Kerry here, have recovered and are back to normal. Now that the alien ship has been neutralised the implants used to control the hosts are dead and useless. But it is such a pity about the fatalities."

"What will happen to Helen Groves and Colin Beech?"

"That's the downside. Potentially, to be charged with murder, but after talking to Robyn, that won't be the outcome. The problem is the evidence will be so unbelievable to your average Joe. Who knows what the verdicts will be, particularly for Helen Groves, with the backstory of the illicit affair with another person involved? Don't forget the other offences committed such as Jimmy Griffiths stealing a car and Tracy Doone breaking and entering, arson and physical assault. It's all in the mix at the moment, but I hope that the judicial system will see sense when they understand what was going on. I also suspect that Home Office will pull some big strings to keep as much of this under wraps as possible. Not that I think they will succeed, as there have been too many people involved. Too many moving parts to sweep it all under the carpet."

"It isn't fair. Those poor people, including our Kerry, have done nothing wrong."

"Yes, and no doubt we will get pulled in as witnesses. As I said, Home Office is involved, so I wouldn't worry too much about Helen Groves and Colin Beech. Personally, I think nothing will end up in court, but you never can tell. Enough of me. Shall we crack open a few bottles?"

"I'll drink to that," said a voice from the back. Everyone looked round as Kath poured herself a third glass.

FORTY-NINE

The mother ship left the galaxy with over a thousand scout ships back on board. Only two did not return. One developed a fault close to the mother ship and the crew, contaminated by a severe radiation breach on board, were not welcome back. The crippled scout ship with eighty crew members on board evaporated as two lasers from the mother ship converged on their target, as the risk of bringing the irradiated crew on board did not sit right with the supreme commander.

The other scout ship, sent to a blue planet in a solar system three light years away, had not re-joined and despite attempts at contact with the ship's commander, there had been no response.

A scouting mission not returning to the mother ship automatically attracted the protocol for failure. They would abandon them, assume they are all dead, and remove all evidence. The supreme commander selected the code, uploaded it to the ship's weapons system and a track-and-destroy drone discharged from the weapons pod and hurtled toward the distant blue planet.

Satisfied with an almost perfect mission, the supreme commander ordered navigation to take them home. They would not be returning.

It took the track-and-destroy drone three weeks to reach Earth's gravitational pull. The drone circled many times until it had scanned every inch of the planet detecting only small indications of the missing ship's debris then entered the atmosphere, dropped out of the sky and detonated in a cornfield, destroying itself and the last remnants of the missing scout ship.

The windows of the nearby farmhouse rattled from the explosion. Inside, Farmer Hurley almost choked on a piece of beef and dropped his knife and fork. He got up from his half-eaten supper, opened the farmhouse door in his slippers and underpants, with his beloved Rizzini twelve-gauge shotgun under one arm, and cursed at the strands of burning corn stalks raining down from the star lit sky.

ACKNOWLEDGMENTS

I would like to thank the following people who were kind enough to help me with invaluable feedback and support:

Des Burns
Christine Williams
Caroline Noe
Ellen Waite
KT Toppin
Lawrence James
Nikki Snaith
Amanda Dooley
Jen Willey
Cheryl Meredith

I would like to apologize to the folk living in and around the beautiful Cotswold town of Morton-in-Marsh, for the liberties taken in some descriptions of the area. Most are factual, but I have added and subtracted physical features and locations, on several occasions, for the sake of dramatizing the storyline.

Why Morton-in-Marsh as the prime location? Because I know it quite well, having spent six months there, back in the early 90s when I was training at the Fire Service College. The town, location and other interesting features made it an ideal location to fit the story.

For anyone who has never been to this part of the Cotswolds, please go and visit. It's a stunning jewel in the British countryside.

ALSO BY ROB NESBITT

Beneath **- Book 1 in the Moreton Scientific Investigation Series - Available on Amazon - Kindle, Kindle Unlimited and Paperback**

Apollo Explorer - Book 1 in the U-SAM Sci-fi Series - Available for you to buy on Amazon Today

The Voke Empire - Book 2 in the U-SAM Sci-fi Series - Available for you to buy on Amazon Today

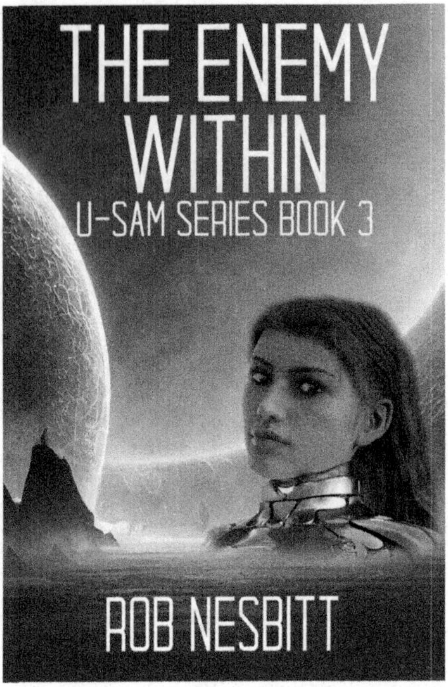

The Enemy Within - Book 3 in the U-SAM Sci-fi Series - Available for you to buy on Amazon Today

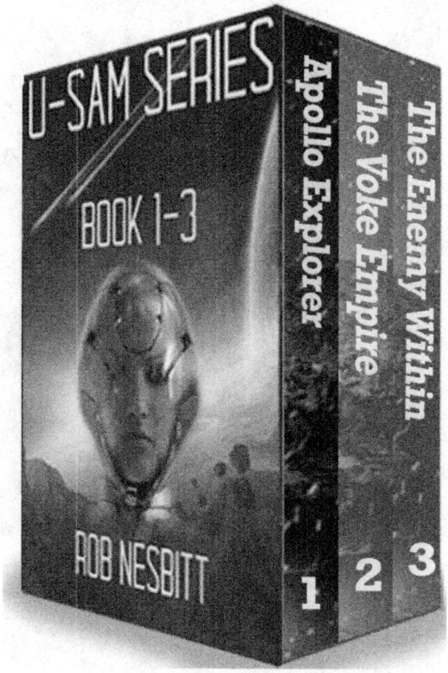

Box Set - Books 1-3 in the U-SAM Sci-fi Series - Available for you to buy on Amazon Today

Mind Sight - Book 4 in the U-SAM Sci-fi Series - Available for you to buy on Amazon Today

BEFORE YOU CLOSE THE BOOK...

If you would like to read my other books, receive free short stories and other goodies please sign up to my author mailing list here at https://rnesbitt.com

This book is a work of fiction. The characters, incidents and dialogue are drawn from the author's imagination and are not to be construed as real. Any resemblance to actual events or persons, alive or dead, is fictionalized or coincidental.

Beneath

Requests to publish work from this book should be sent to
r.m.nesbittauthor@gmail.com

Cover Design by Rob Nesbitt

Editor Melanie Underwood

Written in American English

Printed in Dunstable, United Kingdom

78161741R00181